"You can't stand the fact that you want me, can you?" Leanne asked.

"No. It's not that." Mitch put a finger to her lips to silence her when she might have called him a liar. "I'm…surprised."

"Surprised?"

"I didn't think I was going to be celibate for the rest of my life, but I never expect[ed to want] anyone quite this much. Of [course, it's been] a long time, and—"

"I know." Lea[nne...] to be with som[eone...] it's me. I'm just the [...] you right now." And the o[ne...] going to share his life and his home [for the] next year. For a year was what she'd promised. And then she was supposed to walk away.

"I don't think it's that," Mitch said, then swore softly. "It would be so much easier if it was just that."

It was more than she expected—not just that he would want her for herself, but that he would admit it.

Dear Reader,

It's no surprise that Intimate Moments is *the* place to go when you want the best mix of excitement and romance, and it's authors like Sharon Sala who have earned the line that reputation. Now, with *Ryder's Wife,* Sharon begins her first Intimate Moments miniseries, THE JUSTICE WAY. The three Justice brothers are men with a capital M—and they're about to fall in love with a capital L. This month join Ryder as he marries heiress Casey Ruban for reasons of convenience and stays around for love.

Popular Beverly Barton is writing in the miniseries vein, too, with *A Man Like Morgan Kane,* the latest in THE PROTECTORS. Beverly knows how to steam up a romance, that's for sure! In *Wife, Mother...Lover?* Sally Tyler Hayes spins a poignant tale of a father, a family and the woman who gives them all their second chance at happiness—and love. *Reilly's Return* also marks Amelia Autin's return. This is a wonderfully suspenseful tale about a hero who had to fake his own death to protect the woman he loved—and what happens when she suddenly finds out he's really still alive. In *Temporary Marriage,* Leann Harris takes us to the jungles of South America for a tale of a sham marriage that leads to a very real honeymoon. Finally, Dani Criss is back with *For Kaitlyn's Sake,* a reunion story with all the passion you could wish for.

Let all six of these terrific books keep you warm as the winter nights grow colder, and come back next month for even more of the most excitingly romantic reading around, right here in Silhouette Intimate Moments.

Yours,

Leslie J. Wainger
Senior Editor and Editorial Coordinator

Please address questions and book requests to:
Silhouette Reader Service
U.S.: 3010 Walden Ave., P.O. Box 1325, Buffalo, NY 14269
Canadian: P.O. Box 609, Fort Erie, Ont. L2A 5X3

WIFE, MOTHER...
LOVER?

SALLY
TYLER HAYES

Published by Silhouette Books

America's Publisher of Contemporary Romance

SILHOUETTE BOOKS

ISBN 0-373-07818-8

WIFE, MOTHER...LOVER?

Copyright © 1997 by Teresa Hill

Printed in U.S.A.

Books by Sally Tyler Hayes

Silhouette Intimate Moments

SALLY TYLER HAYES

lives in South Carolina with her husband, son and daughter. A former journalist for a South Carolina newspaper, she fondly remembers that her decision to write and explore the frontiers of romance came at about the same time she discovered, in junior high, that she'd never be able to join the crew of the Starship Enterprise.

Happy and proud to be a stay-home mom, she is thrilled to be living her lifelong dream of writing romances.

As a writer, I find it amazing how often the most obvious things escape me, especially things about my characters. Sometimes I can write all around the obvious for weeks before the little light bulb finally clicks on and I "get it."

Mitch McCarthy was one of those characters. From the beginning, I understood him. I genuinely liked him, even came to love him. And he seemed so familiar to me. He's one of those terrific fathers. I could see him, first thing in the morning, wrestling on his bed with his two little boys. I could hear the three of them laughing. I could see them in the backyard tossing a ball back and forth for hours, could see the boys racing for the front door and dancing with excitement just because Daddy was home.

Mitch is the kind of man whose son, when asked to write a paper in school about his best friend, would say, "My best friend is my dad."

Finally I "got it."

Mitch's character was based on my favorite man of all, my husband, whom I've come to appreciate and to love even more as I've watched the gentleness, the kindness and the love he shows our two children every day of their lives.

This book is for Bob.

Prologue

The postmark, from her suburban Chicago hometown, was enough to give Leanne Hathaway an incredible sensation of longing.

Inside her tent in the middle of a Nepali jungle, she hunkered down, trying to protect her camera equipment and the rolls of film she'd already shot from the falling rain. The ground was turning to mud, which meant traveling would be miserable and hot food was out of the question for days to come.

Right then, she would have given anything for a chocolate milk shake from that drugstore around the corner from her childhood home in Chicago. And some fries—the tiny, crinkle-cut ones that nobody seemed to serve anymore. And a thick, juicy burger off the grill. Her mouth watered at the thought.

And then it was too late to push the memories away. She pulled her legs to her chest and wrapped her arms around her knees, all her thoughts not of home—or what used to be home—but merely of any place in the States and all the familiar luxuries to be found there.

A bath with all the hot water she wanted. A steaming cup of flavored coffee from that little specialty store around the corner from her apartment in Manhattan. A copy of the Sunday *New York Times*. Her own bed. Her darkroom. A phone call from someone with a connection that was so good it sounded like the caller could be in the next room, instead of on another planet.

Tonight, she missed all those things.

She was just tired, she tried to tell herself. But the loneliness settled in around her, like the sound of the rain, coming at her from all sides now, falling around her. She couldn't escape it.

It wasn't just the States she missed, either. It was Chicago. Two sisters. A brother. A father. All things familiar. Home.

Was it the sight of her sister Kelly's handwriting on the letter that left Leanne so blue? Or knowing that Kelly was pregnant now, that soon Leanne would be an aunt for the first time? Maybe it was knowing that she would see her nephews—for that was what the doctors were predicting—as seldom as she saw her siblings or her father.

Her choice, she reminded herself. She'd left Chicago twelve years ago, and she seldom went back. Her job, photographing exotic places and animals all over the world for several prestigious travel and nature magazines, kept her on the go. And for a long time, she'd been content to live that way.

Lately, however, it had become nothing more than a way of life, one that left her weary and wondering about the choices she'd made. Feeling uncharacteristically melancholy, she ripped open her sister's letter and began to read:

Dear Leanne,
I find myself in the odd predicament of missing my

mother terribly these days, even though I am a grown woman of twenty-five and she's been dead for eighteen years. It must be that being pregnant, like getting married, is just one of those times in a woman's life when she wants her mother nearby.

There are so many new things I'm feeling and hearing, so many horror stories people have told me about their labors from hell. (Why do people do that to pregnant women?) And stories about what having children can do to your marriage, not to mention your sanity when the kids are really little. I find myself wishing Mom could be here when Mitch and I bring the twins home from the hospital, or when some little thing goes wrong at midnight and I don't know what to do or whom to call.

Mitch says I'm being silly for expecting trouble, and I tell him it's one of those rules of nature—pregnant women worry.

But that's not why I wanted to write. I wanted to take this time to tell you that the more I thought about all of us, the more I realized that it isn't Mom I'm missing now. It's you.

Most of my memories of Mom are so vague. I swear they're more your memories than mine. All those nights when you'd sit up with me because I was scared or worried, and I'd beg you to tell me another story about Mom...those are the things I remember best. The things you told me. And the things you did for me.

That's when I knew that you're the person I want with me when the boys are born.

Because you're the best mother I ever had.

There, I've said it. I should have done that long ago, and I hope it's not too late to make things right between us. I know now that Alex and Amy and I were so unfair to you once Daddy married Rena and you left for college. I know you did everything you could for all of us during the six years we were alone with you and Daddy, that it was more than anyone could have expected from someone who was still a child herself.

And I love you, for all you did, all that you sacrificed for us.

I've been thinking about what I want for my boys, and one very important thing is for you to be here for their christening, if not for their birth, because I want you to be their godmother. No one but you can do that very special job.

Mitch and I are also making out our wills. His ever practical partner swears that it's irresponsible for anyone with kids to neglect to make a will. The biggest decision is choosing someone to take custody of the children in the remote possibility that anything happens to both of us.

Leanne, there's no one else I'd trust but you. No one I know who would love my babies and take care of them and raise them as I'd want them to be raised. Please say you'll do that for me.

I know how long it takes to get mail to you at times, but I hope when you receive this you can hop on a plane and come home to us. I can't wait to see you.

All my love,
Kelly

Leanne tried in vain to blot the pale-blue paper dry. She didn't want her tears to smudge the writing.

You're the best mother I ever had.

Those were some of the sweetest words she'd ever heard, especially after all the years she felt she wasn't truly a part of her own family anymore. She held herself deliberately apart from them because that was easier than getting her feelings hurt. But now Kelly understood. And forgave her. And missed her. And loved her.

Leanne had been given a wonderful second chance to be a part of her sister's life.

She had another sister, Amy, and a brother, Alex, both of whom she missed terribly. Amy and Alex had been so little when Leanne had left, only eleven and eight to Kelly's thirteen. Her stepmother's influence was so much stronger on the little ones.

Leanne imagined going home to Chicago and being welcomed there. Suddenly, nothing mattered more to her than getting home.

Checking her watch for the date, she saw that it was already April 28.

"Darn," she muttered. Kelly's babies were due May 15, but her doctor claimed he'd never had a patient carry twins to term. He was happy with anyone who made it to her thirty-seventh week.

Counting backward, Leanne realized Kelly might have already had the twins. Or that they might arrive any day now.

There was no time to waste. Leanne had to get home.

Twenty-four grueling hours later, Leanne made it to an airport where the word *schedule* was nothing but a pipe dream. The planes arrived when they arrived, and took off when they were good and ready. Sometimes days went by before a seat was available.

She had a ticket for the first of a series of lengthy flights that would take her home, but there was no telling when she would actually arrive.

Standing in a long line for one of the few public phones, she hoped to get lucky, that her call would go through and someone would be home. By the time it was finally her turn, the noise in the terminal had reached a dull roar. To her left, three men were arguing in three different languages and a little girl was crying. To the right, a man shouted into another phone to make himself heard.

Leanne's connection was filled with static, the signal

incredibly faint. It took a minute to figure out she'd reached Amy. Then she asked about Kelly.

"Too late." Those words were all that came through at first.

"I missed it?" Leanne asked. "Kelly's already had the twins?"

"Yes."

"Both boys?" That was what the sonogram had showed.

"Yes."

"Are they home from the hospital yet? Can I talk to Kelly?"

More static followed, the voice coming from so far away.

"Too late."

"What? Too late for what?"

"Kelly."

The line cleared for a moment. Amy's blunt, rushed explanation followed.

Finally, Leanne understood. The boys were fine, but Leanne was too late to talk to Kelly.

Because Kelly was gone.

Chapter 1

Sixteen months later...

Exhausted after the series of long flights had finally
brought her back to New York from Australia, Leanne
dropped her camera bag and her single piece of luggage
on the floor.

Glancing around her apartment, she saw that her pile of
mail had grown so large it covered the big chair in the
corner and spilled over onto the floor. The plant next to
the refrigerator, which she'd meant to pawn off on someone before she'd left four weeks ago, was drooping pitifully, and she was ashamed of herself for not having made
better provisions for its well-being. Betsy, from down the
hall, threw Leanne's mail on the chair once a week or so,
but she was hopeless with plants.

"Told you I wouldn't be around," Leanne muttered to
the fernlike thing, which had been a gift from someone
who did not know her well.

Coffee was her first priority, especially after she found

some of her favorite flavored coffee beans in the freezer. While she waited for it to brew, she tackled the mail.

When she came to a small, cream-colored envelope with a Chicago postmark, her sister Amy's name written on the return address, she thought for a second that fatigue had made her delusional. But there was no mistake. The letter was from Amy, who hadn't bothered to write in years.

Ripping open the envelope, she found a rather formal request that she call home. Amy said she was worried about Mitch and the boys.

An awful sense of déjà vu came over her when she glanced at the postmark—dated three weeks ago. Unable to help herself, she thought of another letter, from her other sister, one that had arrived too late.

Sitting down on the sofa and closing her eyes tight, Leanne remembered going home then, but not to the homecoming she'd envisioned. Her relatives had gone through the motions of mourning her sister with a quiet dignity and restraint befitting the strained relationships within her family.

Turning to the answering machine on the desk in the corner, she saw the message light blinking. She walked over to the machine on shaky legs and hit the button, then waited until she heard a voice. It was Amy.

"I don't know where you are, Leanne, or when you'll be back. I don't even know if it matters to you, but Mitch is in trouble. He says he's not sure he can take care of the boys on his own anymore.

"I didn't think he meant it at first, but he's been saying it for weeks now, and I'm afraid of what he's going to do. Mitch is...he's thinking of giving up the boys.

"I honestly don't know why I'm even telling you," Amy continued, her voice breaking now and then. "I don't know if you even care or what you could do, but...dammit, Leanne, are you ever going to come back home?"

Leanne just stood there, rooted to the spot.

Mitch is thinking of giving up the boys?

The babies? Kelly's babies?

Leanne remembered the night she'd first seen those beautiful babies. So tiny, so peaceful, they'd been wrapped up in their blue-and-white sleepers, snoozing quietly in a single crib in their sunny yellow room. She was glad they were so little, because they couldn't realize they'd just lost their mother.

Of course, one day they would, and they would mourn her.

Those precious, little boys were all that was left of Kelly. Mitch wouldn't give them up.

Something must have happened, Leanne decided, though she couldn't imagine what might have pushed Mitch to this point.

She'd been in Chicago for three days after her sister's funeral, had talked to Mitch and offered to do anything she could for the boys. But he'd turned down her offer of help.

Feeling like more of an outsider than ever within her own family, and telling herself it was probably too late ever to mend fences with them, Leanne had taken off again, working in a pure frenzy. Sporadic reports over the phone from various relatives told her the boys were growing quickly and that Mitch was a rock.

Apparently, the rock was showing signs of cracking.

Quickly, efficiently, Leanne dumped the contents of her suitcase on the floor beside her bed, then opened the drawers and the closet doors so she could pack her suitcase once again.

Mitch couldn't give up the boys. She wouldn't let him.

Mitch McCarthy, one of Chicago's finest, was busy tailing a suspect, though his mind was on something other than ridding the city of crime.

He was anxious to get home to make sure the boys were all right. This morning, he'd left them with a virtual stranger, a nineteen-year-old college dropout, the daughter of a friend of a friend, someone the boys had never seen before.

Of course Mitch didn't have much of a choice. He'd missed so many days of work already, either because the boys were sick or because yet another sitter had quit, that he couldn't miss any more. He had some family in the area and a few good friends, but he'd taken advantage of every one of them in the past sixteen months as he struggled to raise the boys alone.

This morning, there simply hadn't been anyone else available to watch the twins. He didn't know who was going to take care of them tomorrow. Or the next day. Or the next week. Hopefully, one of the agencies he'd called would come up with someone. Or his network of friends and family would come through again, either with a temporary replacement or a permanent one.

It wasn't the life Mitch wanted for his boys. And he knew they were suffering because of it. It was getting harder and harder for him to make it out the door without feeling as if he were abandoning them every day.

His partner's wife, Ginny, who had two small children of her own, assured him that all children went through a phase when they clung to their parents and either wept or pitched a fit when left with anyone else. Despite the fact that it could darn near break a parent's heart, it was perfectly normal.

Mitch wouldn't know about that. Normal didn't quite apply in this situation. His boys didn't have a mother. Their father worked too much, so he could feed them and clothe them and keep a roof over their heads, and the room in his house where the live-in nanny slept might as well have a revolving door on it.

Something had to give, Mitch told himself yet again. He'd given up on telling himself everything was going to get better.

Picking up the radio, he had the dispatcher patch through a call to his house. He wanted to make sure everything was okay. When the call finally went through, Mitch could hear one of the boys crying in the background. He had to shout to be heard.

"Erin?" Was it his imagination, or was the baby-sitter crying, as well? "This is Mr. McCarthy. What's wrong?"

"One of the boys..." Breathlessly, the girl explained that she simply couldn't tell them apart. "He fell. Just a minute ago. I turned my back for a second. I swear, that was it. And they're so fast—"

"Erin—" he cut her off and willed himself to be calm, to keep driving the car and to think "—is he hurt?"

"He had a cut. On his head. And a split lip. He was bleeding. I was so scared. And both the boys were crying."

"What did you do?"

"Your mother came—"

"My mother? She lives in Ohio, Erin." Four hours away. She didn't show up unannounced.

"Mother-in-law," she corrected herself. "She got here right after the accident, and she thought your son needed to see a doctor, so she took him to the hospital. And I'm here. With the other one."

The other one? Dammit.

"What hospital?" he asked.

"Uh...St. Something."

"St. Luke's?"

"Yes." She hesitated. "I think so."

Mitch groaned. Kelly had died at St. Luke's. Mitch hadn't set foot inside the place since.

"I'm really sorry," the girl said to him.

"How long ago?" he asked.

"Maybe twenty minutes."

Surely if the problem was serious, someone would have gotten word to him by now.

"What should I do now?" the girl asked.

He barely managed to be civil. "Take good care of *the other one* until I can find someone to come and get him."

"Yes, sir."

Mitch broke the connection, then waited for another police car to continue the tail. All the while, he told himself that one of his sons couldn't be seriously hurt. Surely it was enough that the boys had lost their mother two days after they were born. If there was any justice in the universe, they were due smooth sailing from there on out.

Of course, being a cop for all these years, he had grave doubts about the amount of justice left in the universe.

And he was scared. Being a parent, seeing how incredibly helpless and vulnerable his sons were, had given him a new appreciation for the concept of fear.

The boys were only sixteen months old. They could barely walk without falling over their own feet. Teddy said very little. Timmy could say about two dozen words that were barely comprehensible to someone who knew him, and Mitch had left them with a teenager he'd never met before.

Mitch swore aloud in the empty car, a luxury he wouldn't have in the crowded hospital.

At that moment, he missed his wife so much.

Kelly would have known what to do, what to say, just how to soothe her injured child. And she would have been here every day to keep his boys safe and healthy and happy—something Mitch didn't seem able to do himself.

Finally, he was free to swing his car down the nearest freeway exit and head for the hospital. The drive seemed to take forever. He spent the time talking to his dead wife, hoping she was listening. Maybe she had the answers he didn't. Maybe she would tell him what to do. Or show him. Because he just didn't know anymore.

I love 'em, Kelly. You know that. I love 'em so much.

But the boys needed so much more than love.

At the hospital, calling on every bit of crisis-management training he'd ever received, he managed to speak clearly and calmly, his tone dead even, when he asked about his son. He managed to stand there for a full thirty seconds and say nothing else when the clerk shuffled through some papers before directing him to treatment room five.

Rounding the corner, he found the room. It was empty.

For a second, Mitch leaned against the wall and had to work hard to breathe.

"Mr. McCarthy?"

He turned to see a no-nonsense-looking woman in the pinkish garb the nurses at the hospital wore. "Yes. Where's my little boy?"

"He's been taken upstairs for a CT scan—a precautionary measure, the doctor believes. Try not to worry too much. I can show you where he is, but you have to promise to get your butt back down here soon and fill out some paperwork for me, okay?"

Mitch quickly cut a deal with the nurse. He must have looked as bad as he felt, because she took him by the arm and led him down the hall, showing him where to go.

"Timmy's a cutie," she said, chatting to him as they went. "Going to have a real shiner for a couple of days."

Twenty minutes later, Timmy was back downstairs in a treatment room, waiting for the doctor.

Mitch held the little boy, who was exhausted from all the commotion and excitement. Timmy had fallen asleep while struggling in vain to find a way to get his right thumb into his mouth so he could suck on it, despite the fact that he had a swollen and cut lip as well as a cut above his eye.

Rena, his mother-in-law, had been banished to the waiting room after subjecting Mitch to an earful about the unsuitable conditions she'd found at his house today. It was a mess, the boys obviously weren't being supervised properly and God only knows what the sitter had been doing when Timmy got hurt, Rena told him.

She'd never come at him full steam like that before. Instead, she'd been quietly concerned, had merely made suggestions about the right thing to do for the boys.

Mitch would do the right thing, if only he knew what it was.

Squeezing his son a little more tightly, he tried to reassure himself with the doctor's words. Timmy was going to look battered and bruised, but his injuries were not serious.

But whatever had happened today was very serious to Mitch. And to his mother-in-law, who felt the boys should be with her and her husband.

Mitch hadn't thought he'd ever be the kind of man to give up his kids, but he'd begun to consider it. Today's accident forced him to think even harder about what was best for his sons.

Certainly, they deserved a better life than they'd had with him these past few months. They deserved better than to have lost their mother, too, he thought bitterly, but there was no righting that particular wrong.

Mitch closed his eyes and savored the sensation of having his son this close, and thought about the finality of what he was considering.

Giving up the boys.

He couldn't even say the words aloud. But there were nights when he thought of nothing else, and it made him absolutely sick inside.

Still, all he had to do was glance down at Timmy's bruised face and remember how hysterical the sitter had sounded and the way Teddy had been crying, and he knew something had to change. Because he and his sons couldn't continue to live this way.

Chapter 2

Leanne boarded another plane leaving New York three hours later. From the airport in Chicago, she tried calling her father and Amy, before finally finding someone home at Mitch's house.

"Hi. Is Mitch in?" she asked.

"No, he's not. Who is this?"

"His sister-in-law, Leanne Hathaway," she replied, not recognizing the woman's voice.

"Oh, sorry. You startled me. For a minute... You sound so much like Kelly."

Leanne closed her eyes and swore she wasn't going to cry. She hadn't been back to Chicago since Kelly had died. Now that she was here, she had to be prepared. There would be places where she'd expect her sister to walk around the corner any minute. She would meet people who knew Kelly, who thought Leanne looked like her and sounded like her. It was going to be difficult, in a totally different way than mourning her sister all alone had been.

The woman on the phone said, "Mitch is at the hospital

with Timmy right now. He had a little accident this afternoon, but I don't think it was serious.''

Trying to calm herself, Leanne remembered three different times she'd ended up calling a neighbor to take her and one of her siblings to the emergency room. Her father had worked second shift, she'd been on her own with her brothers and sisters from after school until her father came home around midnight. She'd seen them through Amy's broken arm when Amy was eight and fell off her bike, a cut on Kelly's chin that needed six stitches, a high fever that had made Alex delirious one evening.

Kids had accidents all the time, she reminded herself.

She managed to ask what hospital Timmy was at, then remembered to inquire about her other nephew.

''He's fine. He and my little boy are playing right now.''

Which meant the children were still living in Mitch's house. She wasn't too late this time.

''Thank you,'' she told the woman, then found a taxi to the hospital. In the emergency room, someone directed her to Timmy's room. Then she stood outside, trying to calm herself anew.

Peering through the glass treatment-room doors, she saw Mitch. His back to the wall, he was watching Timmy, who was curled up asleep in a big, metal crib. Mitch's chest was heaving. Leanne saw those big shoulders of his rise and fall with each labored breath. He almost seemed to be suffocating.

Raking a hand through his hair, he gazed down at the floor, up at the ceiling, then back at the crib. When he finally turned slightly, she saw a single tear on his cheek, before he hastily wiped it away, all the while looking even grimmer than before.

And then Leanne couldn't go inside. It hurt too much to see him this way, to imagine what it must have been like months ago when Kelly had died.

She couldn't help but think of that day she'd finally made it home, too late for the funeral. Standing by the grave site, she'd thought she was alone, when she turned and saw a tall, lean, utterly dejected-looking man. *Mitch.*

Heedless of the dark-blue suit he wore, he'd been leaning against the wide trunk of a tree with his hands shoved into his pockets, his eyes downcast. Leanne saw dark circles under those bloodshot eyes, saw an ashen tint to his complexion, a look of disgust on his face.

"You're late," he announced bitterly.

She'd flinched, then closed her eyes to block out the sight of her sister's husband in utter misery. "Mitch..."

He waved off her words with an impatient hand. He had hair the color of a field of wheat, a deep brown shot through with gold. Normally, his eyes were green, not tinted red, and his lips wore just a hint of a smile.

"She wanted you with her when the twins came, because she was scared," he accused. "She hadn't asked you for anything in so long. Couldn't you have given her that at least?"

"I didn't get the letter," Leanne cried. "Not until it was too late. I would have come back, but it was too late."

"It's too late now," he said, his gaze as sharp and as cutting as a razor blade.

"What happened?" She'd gotten only the sketchiest of details as she'd struggled to get back to Chicago.

"A blood clot," he said, puzzled even now by the explanation. "Some out-of-the-blue kind of thing that isn't supposed to happen." He shoved his hands back into his pockets and stared off into the sky. "Women aren't supposed to die having babies anymore. They aren't supposed to die when they're twenty-five years old."

Leanne had no answer, suspected no one did. "And the boys?"

"They're fine." He stopped to take a labored breath and shake his head, as if he still couldn't believe it. "Except they just lost their mother."

Leanne had wanted to weep, even though she would have sworn she had no tears left. And she'd wanted to go to Mitch, to tell him how sorry she was and to offer to do something. But she couldn't imagine what that would be.

"What about the boys?" she asked. "How are you going to manage?"

"I don't know. I haven't thought that far ahead." He raked a hand through his hair and looked as if his world had ended. "We'll manage, I guess. What choice do we have?"

"In the letter...Kelly asked me to help with the boys."

He stared down at her, measuring her, assessing. "Leanne, you've been back...what? A half a dozen times in the past ten years?"

"Yes." Maybe that many times.

"What kind of help could you possibly be with the boys?"

She flinched as if he'd struck her. What had there been to come back to? she wanted to shout at him. No one had wanted her here.

Except Kelly. Kelly had wanted her. Five weeks earlier. And Leanne had been too late.

She'd understood her brother-in-law's anger, hadn't even tried to defend herself.

If she'd ever felt needed or wanted, she would have come. Maybe she still could. "If you need anything, anything at all, for the boys..."

He gave her a look that felt like a blast of wind coming across the polar ice caps. He wouldn't need anything from her.

"I'm sorry, Mitch," she said, then turned and walked away.

And that's where they'd left it.

Until now. Until she couldn't run away anymore. After all, she'd made a promise to Kelly to do what she could for the boys, and that was one promise she intended to keep.

Looking into the treatment room, Leanne vowed not to let anything Mitch McCarthy said convince her to leave this time. Taking a deep breath, she pushed the door open. Mitch turned at the sound, and she felt his gaze rake over her, felt the chill that found its way into the air.

He didn't want her here. His look said so all too clearly.

Well, that was no great surprise. Leanne straightened her shoulders and forced her chin up. "Hello, Mitch."

"Leanne."

"How's Timmy?" She stared down at the sleeping child. His lip was all swollen, the area around his eye swollen, as well, and there was a bandage over his right eyebrow.

"He'll be fine." Mitch's voice was rough and low and chilling. "What are you doing here?"

She thought of her options. *I was in the neighborhood?* He'd know better. As he'd so succinctly pointed out to her at the cemetery that day, she was hardly ever home.

"Amy called me," she said finally.

"Oh? I didn't know you and Amy were speaking to each other."

"Mitch, don't." Leanne couldn't help but flinch as the words cut into her. She'd never known this man to be cruel. Fiercely protective of his wife and no doubt now his sons, but not cruel.

She and Mitch were the same age, both thirty-two, and Leanne had known him for a long time before he'd married her sister. And what she'd known about him, she'd liked.

Unable to help herself now, Leanne studied his features. He'd folded his arms in front of him, a move that had the fabric of his shirt straining across the muscles of his shoulders and arms. He was pale under the tan, with shadows under his eyes and hollows to his cheeks that hadn't been there before. Of course he was still an incredibly handsome man, an appealing one, too, as long as he wasn't looking at her. So often when he did look at her, his mouth had settled into a grim, straight line, as it did now. There was a wariness in his eyes, and something that had her feeling all his defenses were on alert when she was around.

"What did Amy tell you?" he asked.

"That you were thinking of giving up the boys."

Mitch turned away and swore. But he didn't deny it.

"It's true? Would you really do that?"

"I don't see that it's any of your business, Leanne. Now, why don't you hop on a plane and go somewhere. Take some pictures with that fancy camera of yours, before you lose the light."

Leanne was trembling in the wake of his attack, but she refused to let him see it. Years of practice had made her adept at hiding most any emotion, particularly from her family.

"I can't let you give them up," she insisted.

He raised an eyebrow at that, then settled for staring her down once again. Leanne didn't let herself fidget under his gaze, or turn away, or lash out at him in return.

He'd loved her sister very much, she reminded herself. Surely he loved the boys, as well. Leanne couldn't imagine anything happening that could make him give up his boys. And she found herself wishing she had been here in the past sixteen months. She felt guilty now that she hadn't.

"I don't see that it's any of your business what I do with my sons," he said.

Leanne refused to be intimidated by the sheer size of him and by the fury within him. "Look, we don't have to fight about this." She decided to throw out her bottom line. "If you don't want them, I do."

"You want them?" Mitch laughed sarcastically. "Why? So you can tote them onto an airplane every few weeks and drag them around the world with you? That would be a great life for two little boys who desperately need some stability."

"I don't have to travel." Leanne thought it through as she went. "I don't even have to work. I've earned a lot of money over the years, and I've hardly spent any of it."

"You can't be serious."

"About the money? Do you want to see my bank balance?"

"No, the boys. You can't be serious about wanting them."

"Why not?"

"I never knew you had such maternal instincts."

Surely he couldn't have forgotten, Leanne thought. Just in case, she reminded him. "I raised my brother and sisters for six years after our mother died."

"And then turned your back on them and walked away."

God, this man could wound with his words. Until the day of Kelly's funeral, she hadn't known just how good he was at it.

"Not by my choice," she said simply, then closed her mouth. She wasn't sure she could maintain her composure long enough to give him a much more detailed explanation.

"What? Richard kicked you out once he married Rena?" Mitch taunted. "That's not what Kelly remembered. She said she begged you to stay. That Amy and Alex did, too, that they felt as abandoned by you as they did when they lost their mother."

Leanne bit down hard on her lip for a moment. She refused to cry in front of him.

"Kelly understood," she whispered, her pride hanging by a shred. "She told me so. In the letter. Surely she told you about the letter she sent me."

He nodded. "She told me she wanted you with her when the boys were born, and I told her not to get her hopes up."

"Kelly understood," Leanne insisted. "She also told me that the two of you were making out wills and picking a guardian for the boys, in case anything ever happened to both of you."

"Yes," he admitted.

"Who did you pick?"

"We hadn't come to an agreement on that," he said warily.

"Who did she want to have the boys? I'm sure she told you that if she couldn't raise them herself she wanted them to be with me."

"You can't be serious about wanting the boys," Mitch said. His hands clenched at his side, a muscle twitching in his cheek, he stood there looking like a man who'd been to hell and back.

Leanne asked herself whether she was serious, even as she argued with him. She thought back to her sister's letter; she'd memorized every word on that long trip home to Kelly's funeral. She thought about standing over her sister's grave, about the promise she'd made there. This was the last thing she could do for her sister.

"I mean it," she said. "If you don't want the boys, I do."

He said nothing for the longest time. Leanne held her breath, waiting for some response from him.

"It's not that I don't want them," he said, his expression guarded. "It's never been that."

"I'm sorry." Relieved, Leanne nearly started to cry then, for him and for the boys. And for her sister, who'd been cheated out of the life she deserved with this man and their children.

Before she could say anything else, the door behind her opened with a swish and a pretty, young woman in a long, white coat, with a stethoscope around her neck, walked in.

"Hi, I'm Dr. Weston. I hear someone in this room needs stitches," she said to Leanne. "You're the mother?"

"No." Leanne stumbled over the explanation, then Mitch jumped in.

"I'm the father." He stuck out his hand. "Mitch McCarthy."

"Hi." The doctor shook his hand, then leaned over the crib. "And this must be Timmy. Poor baby. We'll have him fixed up in no time, but we're going to have to keep him still while I stitch that cut. Can you hold him down for me?''

Mitch paled.

''We can strap him to a backboard, if that's what you want.''

''Are you going to hurt him?'' Mitch struggled with the words.

''Not on purpose.'' Dr. Weston smiled reassuringly and let one of her hands rest on Mitch's shoulder for a second. ''The injection to numb the area will hurt a little. The stitching itself won't be painful, but he'll feel a tugging sensation as the needle goes in and out. Usually, more than anything, it's being strapped to the board that scares the little ones.''

Mitch nodded grimly. ''I'll hold him.''

''Okay. Let me get my supplies, and I'll be right back.''

The doctor walked out, leaving Mitch and Leanne alone with the sleeping child. Leanne had seen the way Mitch looked when the doctor talked about stitches and needles.

''Do you want me to stay with Timmy while they stitch the cut?'' she offered.

''Do you think you can handle this any better than I can?''

''I've done it before,'' she said, gently now. ''For Kelly, when she was ten.''

Mitch's anger seemed to drain out of him as quickly as it had come. Obviously, he was remembering his wife.

''That cut on her chin?'' He touched his finger to the spot on his own face.

Leanne nodded. ''She fell out of a tree one night.''

''Where was your father?''

''At work, where he always was.''

Mitch considered that. She thought he might apologize for the way he'd talked to her earlier. Instead, he turned all wary on her again.

''I can do this,'' he said.

''Okay.'' She turned to go. ''I'll wait outside.''

"Leanne?" She faced him again. "If you want to help, you could go to the house and stay with Teddy. My partner's wife is there now, but she has kids of her own, and it's getting late."

Leanne saw that it was hard for him to ask that of her. She wondered if it was his pride or the fact that he still wanted to somehow punish her for hurting Kelly.

I loved her, too, she wanted to tell Mitch. *I loved her so much. And I miss her.*

Instead, she said, "I'll be at the house with Teddy."

"Thank you." He turned, his attention back on his son.

Leanne headed for the door. Just before she opened it, she glanced into the room across the hall and saw her stepmother and her father sitting in the waiting area.

"Oh." All the breath rushed out of her body. She took one step back, then another. She hadn't seen Rena since that last, awful duty visit she'd paid her father after Kelly had died.

It was silly of her, but it always took her a little by surprise that Rena looked like an absolutely ordinary woman. Because in Leanne's mind, Rena was something of a monster—the kind that had her wanting to hide in the closet in the dark when she was a child. Somehow, Leanne had never gotten over being irrational where Rena was concerned.

Her stepmother was of medium height, medium build, had light-brown hair, ice-blue eyes. She was a totally nondescript woman. And she was but forty-two years old now, only ten years older than Leanne. How could she still be so afraid of her?

Beside Rena sat her father, who appeared older than his fifty-six years. Whereas it frightened Leanne to look at Rena, it hurt to look at her father, who'd always taken his second wife's side over his daughter's.

"Leanne?"

Mitch's voice came from beside her. She turned, realizing she'd forgotten for a moment where she was. From the expression on his face, she had to wonder just what he'd noticed in the time she'd forgotten to try to hide her reaction at seeing her father and stepmother.

Amazingly, Mitch seemed almost concerned. What would it take, Leanne wondered, for Mitch ever to be concerned about her?

"What's wrong?" he asked.

She had to work to make her voice function properly. "Rena's here. In the waiting room."

"I know."

He studied her as if trying to look inside her and figure out what she was doing such a poor job of hiding. When he spoke again, his tone was softer, though still wary.

"If you don't want to see them, there's another door." He nodded to the right. "It leads to the nurses' station. You can get out that way without having to walk down the main hall."

"Thank you," she said before she turned and rushed away, escaping from what would surely have been an unbearable scene with her stepmother and father.

"Mitch?"

A few minutes later, Mitch turned and found Marc Dalton, his partner and a good friend, standing in the doorway.

Timmy was once again resting in the big, metal crib, having cried himself to sleep.

Marc knelt on the floor to get a better look at him, then whistled. "Poor little guy. Looks like he went ten rounds with somebody and lost." He ruffled Timmy's hair.

"Four stitches," Mitch said, then had another flash of a needle working its way in and out of that soft, smooth flesh of his son's forehead. *Dammit. Four stitches.*

"I tried to phone and tell you, but I had trouble getting the hospital to put a call through to you in here. Ginny was headed for your house an hour and a half ago, with Hannah and Will, to take care of Teddy."

That was good. Teddy loved to play with Marc and Ginny's children. Maybe he wouldn't be so afraid with them.

"Thanks," Mitch said. "I appreciate it. I don't know what I would have done without Ginny's help. And yours."

More than once, Ginny had saved him by taking care of the boys when something came up. And then he remembered Leanne.

"My sister-in-law showed up today."

"Missy?" That was Mitch's brother's wife. They lived about forty-five minutes away.

"No, Kelly's older sister, Leanne. I wasn't sure if you'd gotten ahold of Ginny or not, so I asked Leanne if she would go to the house and stay with Teddy."

"I'll call Ginny and let her know," Marc said. "One more thing—I thought you should be warned. Rena's in the waiting room, running her mouth. You can imagine what she's saying."

"I've already heard it. Straight from her."

Marc swore. "The perfect addition to an otherwise rotten day. Do you want me to try to get rid of her?"

"Nothing short of arresting her would work this time."

"Hey, don't let her get to you."

"What if she's right, Marc? What if the boys would be better off with her?" Or maybe someone else. Anyone but him.

"I've said it before—she's done a number on your head. Rena wasn't exactly one of Kelly's favorite people, remember?"

"No, she wasn't. And I know it was hard on Kelly having a new stepmother when she just turned thirteen. But Rena was there for her every day," Mitch said, though right then all he seemed to think about was Leanne's reaction earlier at merely catching a glimpse of her stepmother.

Mitch was a cop; he knew what fear looked like. And this afternoon, his sister-in-law had been so afraid. He didn't think he'd ever seen her show that much emotion so clearly on her face.

He'd thought she was a coldhearted woman, one who always held herself a little apart from everyone and everything around her. Of course, he had always seen her around her family, and the relationship between them had been strained almost to the breaking point for years. Mitch supposed that could explain the carefully composed expression his sister-in-law normally wore.

Still, he was surprised by the strength of her reaction to seeing Rena. And now that he was actually considering giving the boys to Rena, Leanne's reaction left him decidedly uneasy.

"Mitch," Marc began, "you're not going to make any decisions about the boys right away, are you? You've got to give this some time. You don't know if Rena is the answer."

Mitch wasn't sure of anything today, except that he'd left his sons with someone he barely knew, someone who had allowed Timmy to be hurt. "Rena isn't perfect. I know that. But it wouldn't be like leaving the boys with someone new every week or every month. She wouldn't be someone who was hired to do a job or who turned out to be so damned irresponsible she let something like this happen."

"Wait a minute." Marc put a hand on Mitch's shoulder. "Hannah's had stitches twice already, and you know it's not because Ginny and I aren't taking good care of her. Little kids have accidents, no matter how closely someone's watching over them. So don't think you'd be saving Timmy from ever ending up in the hospital again just because you gave him to Rena."

"I don't think that, but..." Mitch swore, using words he never would have uttered if his son had been awake. "They deserve better. They deserve someone who's always going to be there for them."

"Maybe a father?"

"No, someone who can be home with them every day.

Someone who won't leave because another employer offers her more money or because her husband gets transferred out of town." He could go on and on, but he knew what the bottom line was. "They deserve someone who loves them, not someone I pay to take care of them."

"You mean you want them to have a mother," Marc said. "Think about it, Mitch. You don't need to find yourself another sitter. You need to find a wife."

Mitch closed his eyes and saw his wife's beautiful face, saw her smile, saw the excitement in her eyes as she turned sideways to show him how big her tummy was getting and made jokes about not fitting through the front door any longer.

He could see the worn photograph of her that he carried in his wallet. He could see the videotape of their wedding reception, the one he'd watched dozens of dozens of times late into the night because it was practically the only video he had of her.

And he remembered that nightmarish day at this very same hospital when he'd lost her, remembered the day he'd buried her.

"I love my wife," he said. Present tense. *Love,* not loved.

"And you love the boys, too," Marc said.

Mitch couldn't argue with that. And it did make him stop and think.

"You'd do anything for them," Marc said.

"I would."

"Then don't give up on them yet. I know it's been awful, and it's more than any single person should have to cope with. But just because the three of you are all alone in this right now, it doesn't mean you'll always be alone."

"Marc..."

"Once you give up the boys, that's it. It's over. Think about that."

Chapter 3

It was nearly dusk when Leanne pulled to a stop in front of the modest brick house in the suburbs where her sister had lived. She saw a bright-red ball on the front lawn, a toy bulldozer on the steps that led to the porch, a stuffed animal in one chair.

Obviously, the boys were growing up.

Leanne closed her eyes and waited a minute before she got out of the car. Coming home just never got any easier. Rushing all over the world for her job hadn't solved that problem.

And now, she simply couldn't run away anymore. Leanne wanted her family back. She decided to start here, with her nephew. Wearily, she walked to the front door and rang the bell.

A beautiful little girl with long, golden curls and incredible blue eyes opened the door. She grinned and said, "Hi."

Leanne was enchanted. She thought the girl might be four, and she looked like a princess. She even dressed like one. She had on what Leanne guessed was her mother's nightgown, complete with embroidered flowers, long, flowing sleeves and a plunging neckline. When the girl lifted the dress to curtsy quite formally to her, Leanne saw pink, plastic high heels on her feet.

"I'm Hannah," she said. "I live ov'r'dare."

"Over there? Across the street?"

Hannah beamed. "I'm a pwincess."

"I can tell." Leanne remembered Kelly's princess phase, with feather boas, baby-pink nail polish and pilfered lipstick. "You make a lovely princess."

"Who are you?"

"Leanne. I'm a friend of Mr. McCarthy's."

"Hannah?" A woman's voice called out from inside. "Who's there?"

The princess turned and ran, as fast as her plastic high heels could carry her, into the living room and stood at the end of the hallway. "It's Wee-Ann, and she's wooking for Mr. Carthy."

"Be right there."

Leanne glanced around the living room and saw toys strewn everywhere, a newspaper on the floor, a plate from someone's lunch, a cup and a soda can. The house was a mess.

When Leanne looked up, a little boy came careering around the corner on shaky legs. He was headed for the open door, obviously thinking of escape, but Leanne blocked his way.

The boy's eyes were as dark as the wisps of hair on his head. He smiled, showing off two baby teeth on top and none on the bottom, as he skidded to a stop in front of Leanne.

"Da!" He looked confused for a minute, then demanded, "Da!"

"Sorry, darling. I'm not your daddy." Leanne looked to the blond-haired princess. "This isn't Teddy, is it?"

"No, dat's my bwudder." She rolled her eyes in disgust.

"Will. He's so much trouble. He gets into ev'rythin'. We just chase him and chase him. Mommy says that's all we can do, 'cause he don't know nothin'. He's just a baby.''

"Oh, I see. He does look like he could cause an awful lot of trouble.''

Will seemed to be considering charging the door, to see if he could get around Leanne and make it outside. Princess Hannah, a little mother herself, took him by the hand and tried to turn him around.

"C'm'on, Will. We can't go out now.''

He gave a grunt that sounded like an indignant "Out!'' but Hannah held on tight.

From around the corner came an attractive blond-haired woman, in her late twenties perhaps. She had another little boy in her arms. This one had a sandy blond head pressed against the woman's chest, and he appeared to be a little older than Will.

"Oh.'' Leanne felt the air rush out of her lungs at the sight of that little, turned-up nose, the impossibly long lashes, the curve of those lips. This, Leanne knew, was Teddy.

Leanne offered her hand to the woman, who had a cloth diaper draped over her shoulder and was carrying a baby bottle in one hand, the little boy in the other.

"Hi, I'm Leanne Hathaway,'' she said.

"Of course. Kelly's world-traveling sister.'' The woman juggled the bottle and put out a hand. "I should have introduced myself to you earlier on the phone. I'm Ginny. My husband, Marc, is Mitch's partner, and we live across the street.''

"Oh, of course. Kelly...'' Leanne stumbled over the words. Kelly had mentioned becoming good friends with Mitch's partner's wife. "My sister said you were very kind.''

"So was she. I miss her very much. We all do.'' Ginny had tears in her eyes, which she quickly blinked away. "Hannah and Will are mine. And this—'' she turned sideways, bringing into full view the face of the sleeping boy snuggled so tightly against her ''—is Teddy.''

''Oh.'' Leanne had to catch her breath all over again. ''He looks so much like Kelly.''

''I know. And Timmy is Mitch all over again, yet the boys still resemble each other so much.'' Ginny shifted the boy in her arms. ''Do you want to hold him?''

''Yes, please.'' Leanne closed her eyes as the sleeping toddler snuggled against her. He was warm and soft, his body seemingly boneless as he draped himself against her. She put her face against his head and breathed in his clean scent.

Ginny laughed. ''It's wonderful, isn't it?''

''Yes.''

''Have you been to the hospital?'' she asked.

Leanne nodded again. ''Timmy's going to be fine, but he's getting a few stitches. I told Mitch I'd stay here with Teddy until he and Timmy get home.''

''Good. You can hold Teddy while I clean up a bit. The last thing Mitch needs is to come home to a mess tonight.''

Leanne watched the chaos of the house give way to some semblance of order, watched Princess Hannah try her best to boss her brother around, watched Will career from one near disaster to the next as he ran from one end of the house to the other with more energy than any ten children should have. Ginny, smiling and laughing through it all, seemed to be in her element.

Leanne sat there holding Teddy close and kept thinking that it should have been Kelly who was sitting on this couch, talking to her friend, seeing her children grow up. This was everything her sister was missing, everything she'd been denied.

Finally, when the worst of the mess was gone, Ginny sat down and said, ''So where have you been this time?''

''Australia. The outback.''

''It must be fascinating to travel like that.''

''At times,'' Leanne said noncommittally.

Leanne's first impression of this woman was that she was indeed very kind and caring, that she missed Kelly and knew Mitch and the boys well. She must know what Mitch was considering.

"I was wondering about something," Leanne said, choosing to confide in this woman.

"Yes?"

"About Mitch?" God, this was so awkward. "He's upset, I know. But at the hospital he said he was thinking of—"

"Hannah?" Ginny cut her off and turned to her daughter. "Would you take Will into the kitchen? The cookies we brought over are on a plate on the table. You can have one each."

Hannah dutifully took her brother by the arm, and he perked up as she repeated the word "cookie" to him.

"Sorry." Ginny turned back to Leanne. "I didn't want Hannah to hear what I was afraid you were going to say."

"Mitch is thinking about giving them up." Leanne looked down at Teddy, sleeping quietly against her shoulder, as the words slipped out. "I don't understand how he could do that."

Ginny sat down on the sofa, but kept one eye on the kitchen and her children. "I'd like to believe that Mitch couldn't actually do it. But I worry that he's reached the point where he believes that might be best for the boys."

"But they're his children. They're all he has left of Kelly."

"I know, but he's been under so much pressure ever since Kelly died. You don't have children, do you?"

"No." But once it had felt as if Kelly, Amy and Alex were her own.

"Raising one baby is hard enough, but twins... Mitch is raising twins by himself, with a full-time job that's incredibly stressful and comes with long, irregular hours. He's exhausted. And worried. And still trying to deal with

Kelly's death. Now that Rena's been—'' Ginny broke off. "Sorry. I know she's your mother."

"Stepmother," Leanne corrected her.

Understanding, Ginny nodded. "That woman has really done a number on Mitch."

"Rena's specialty," Leanne said, remembering when she'd been the target of her stepmother's manipulations. "She's trying to convince Mitch to give up the boys?"

"Yes. Rena wants to raise them herself."

"Oh, no." Leanne cried. "Mitch can't let her have them. I won't let him do that."

"Then it's a good thing you're here."

It was after nine when Mitch arrived at home with Timmy in his arms. As he reached for the doorknob, the door swung inward.

"How is he?" Leanne asked as she stood in the doorway.

"Tired. He slept all the way home." Mitch walked inside and found his house was neat and tidy for a change. Despite his best efforts these days, the place was usually cluttered at best. Some wonderful smell coming from the kitchen reminded him that he hadn't eaten dinner and that he was hungry. "How's Teddy?"

"Worried about Timmy, I think. Does he call Timmy 'Tee'?"

"They call each other 'Tee.'" Mitch managed to smile at that particular quirk. "It takes some getting used to."

"Well, I promised Teddy that Timmy would be here when he woke up. I gave him a bath, dressed him in his Batman pajamas and read him three stories. By then he was so tired he went right to sleep."

"Thank you," Mitch said.

It grated on his pride that he needed help, but losing Kelly and trying to raise two little boys alone had taught him to grit his teeth and take what help was offered.

He watched his sister-in-law. No doubt, she expected an

explanation of why he would ever consider giving up his children.

If Leanne had been there the past sixteen months, struggling as he had to do what was best for the twins, what would she think was in the boys' best interests? Mitch wondered. Maybe later, he would ask her.

"I'm going to put Timmy down," he said, turning and heading for the stairs. "Then we can talk."

"I made a casserole," she said. "If you're hungry."

He paused on the landing where the stairway curved at a ninety-degree angle, and looked down at this woman he'd never quite understood. They'd gone to the same high school, graduated in the same class, though he barely remembered her from then.

Later, he'd watched as Kelly had cried herself to sleep more than once after one of those rare visits from her sister, when the distance between them had seemed unbreachable.

In many respects, Leanne had been a mother to Kelly, until Leanne had turned her back on her whole family for a scholarship to a fancy Boston college and a job that took her all over the world. Mitch couldn't fault her for wanting an education or a job. But she could have made time for Kelly and her siblings.

In the end, Kelly might have come to forgive her sister for hurting her that way, but Mitch hadn't.

"Mitch?" Leanne said.

"Sorry." He'd been lost in thought. "I am hungry."

"I'll set the table."

And then he forgot about his sister-in-law as he slipped up the stairs and into a room at the end of the hall. It boasted two cribs, but the boys used only one. Although they were big enough now that they were crowded in the one crib, they still didn't like sleeping apart. In the morning, Mitch usually found them snuggled against each other, usually Timmy pressed against Teddy, who was often scrunched in the corner against the padded rails.

It looked uncomfortable, but the boys didn't seem to mind. Every time he tried to separate them for the night, no one got any sleep. Mitch didn't, either. The boys would stand in their respective cribs, hang on to the railing and jump in protest. They'd hold their arms through the rails, reaching for each other and fussing until he gave in and put them both in the same crib. It was a moot point now that they'd learned to climb out of their cribs.

Tonight, Teddy was already snuggled into his corner. Deciding they could both use the comfort of each other, Mitch put Timmy down right beside his brother. Timmy barely stirred, and Teddy just sighed and rolled over, toward his brother.

In sleep, they were incredibly peaceful, looking like angels. Awake, they were like two small tornadoes, incredibly fast, totally unpredictable, wreaking havoc wherever they went.

And he loved them so much it hurt.

He would do anything for them.

Tired to the bone, Mitch walked into his bathroom, stripped and stepped into the shower while the water was still running cold. It helped to wake him up, to clear is head.

He had no idea what he was going to say to Kelly's sister. As he hurriedly dressed in sweats and a T-shirt, he thought again about what she'd said—that she would take the boys.

He couldn't believe for a minute that she meant it. After all, Leanne didn't know how to stay in one place. He knew because Kelly had subscribed to the magazines Leanne contributed to on a regular basis; he'd watched while Kelly studied them for her sister's photo credit and told him of the places Leanne had been.

Had Kelly been wondering what her sister found in those far-off places that she couldn't find at home? Or had Kelly envied her sister for getting to travel all over the world? Mitch had promised to take Kelly to some of those places someday. Of course, someday hadn't come soon enough for her.

"Damn." Mitch sat down on the side of the bed, leaned forward and put his head in his hands for a minute.

Missing his wife was like being ravenously hungry when there was nothing to satisfy his appetite. There was a hole inside him, and nothing could fill it. He feared nothing ever would.

The suggestion Marc had made at the hospital was ludicrous.

He needed a *wife?*

As far as Mitch was concerned, he still had a wife. He just couldn't see her, except when he closed his eyes. He couldn't touch her, smell her or taste her, unless he was caught somewhere deep in sleep. Then she was gloriously real, if only for a few moments. He couldn't feel her close to him except in these brief snatches of time when he thought he was either losing his mind or being given some incredible gift.

Still, Mitch didn't want any other woman.

When the shower shut off, Leanne pulled the casserole out of the oven, then sat down at the small table in the corner to wait.

Finally, Mitch, wearing faded gray sweatpants and a snug-fitting T-shirt, his hair still wet from the shower, appeared in the doorway. Leanne looked away, thinking there was something much too intimate about being here this late at night with a man still wet and clean-smelling from the shower. Especially a man as attractive to her as this one had always been.

She thought it was the height of injustice that she'd always found Mitch McCarthy attractive, that from the time she'd been a shy, introverted girl of fifteen and she'd first seen him in the hallways at school, he'd left her absolutely breathless.

He looked over the meal set out on the table. "You didn't have to do this," he said.

It was almost as if he hated the fact that she had, she thought. "It was no trouble, really." She couldn't figure out exactly what she'd done wrong, except that maybe he didn't want to be put in the position of sharing a meal with her. And he couldn't very well kick her out after she'd made dinner. He was stuck with her, at least for the next twenty minutes or so.

Mitch sat down opposite Leanne at the table, which seemed to shrink in size now that he was sitting there. She dished out a helping of the steaming chicken casserole to him, then herself, and Mitch passed her a basket of rolls.

The two of them ate in near silence, Mitch taking three servings of the dish before he finished. In response to her questions, he told her quite succinctly that her brilliant brother, at twenty-two, was close to finishing his Ph.D. in Chemistry, that Amy seemed very happy with her fiancé, that the boys had been walking for only two months and were still quite wobbly on their feet.

When they finished eating, Mitch helped her clear the table and load the dishwasher—something that had her working hard to avoid brushing up against him in the small, narrow kitchen. Then there was nothing left to do but talk.

"I'm going to have a beer," he said. "Would you like one?"

"No, thank you."

"There's probably some wine around here somewhere…."

"No, really. One drink is probably all it would take to put me to sleep."

He glanced at the clock on the stove and Leanne did the same. It was shortly after nine here.

"I was in Australia yesterday," she said. "Or was it today? I always get confused when I cross that many time zones. And my body has no idea what time it really is."

"Oh."

"I came as soon as I got Amy's message." She pulled a business card out of her pocket with all sorts of phone numbers, then underlined one. "Mitch, if you ever really need me, call my agent. He always knows where to find me. It may take a few days to get word to me and a few more days for me to get back, but I will come."

He took the card, but looked wary of her offer. He would never use that number, she decided. Nevertheless, she told him, "I wish you had called me."

Mitch popped the top of his beer and motioned for her to follow him into the living room. "I've called just about everybody I know for help with the boys from time to time. Between the family I have in town and yours, there's almost always someone who's willing to take them for a day or two."

"Then what is the problem?"

"They need someone who's going to be here every day. Not for a few weeks or a few months." Mitch took the chair in the corner and left her with the couch. "As soon as they get used to one person, she leaves and we have to start all over again."

Leanne said, "So you just haven't found the right person."

"I don't know that I'm ever going to find the right person. I don't know if that person exists. There aren't a lot of people willing or able to take care of two energetic little boys all day, especially not for what I can afford to pay."

"I have money, if that's what you need." She watched as color flooded his face, and knew that she'd offended him. "For the boys. You'd take it for them."

"Maybe." His gaze, challenging and questioning, locked on hers. "If I thought money was the answer. But even that won't solve the problem. Just look at what happened today."

Leanne had wondered about that.

"Our sixth sitter—"

"Sixth?"

"Yes, sixth."

That was an average of one new person every two and a half months. Leanne could imagine how the boys had reacted to that.

"She took off Friday to go to Iowa," Mitch explained. "Her daughter, who's pregnant, just found out she needs to spend the next six weeks in bed if she's going to carry her baby to term. And this daughter already has a two-year-old.

"I was scrambling all weekend to find someone. I ended up with this nineteen-year-old, the daughter of a friend of a friend, who obviously couldn't handle the boys. I planned to replace her as soon as I found someone else, but before I could do that, my son ended up with four stitches in his forehead."

"Mitch, kids get hurt. It happens."

"If the cut had been a little lower, Timmy might have lost his eye," he said grimly.

"Oh." She hadn't realized that.

"The whole time I was sitting in the hospital, I was asking myself what could happen the next time I brought in someone at the last minute to watch them." Mitch pushed a hand through his hair impatiently and glanced at the clock. "Look at the time. I have to be at work in less than ten hours, and I have no idea who's going to take care of the boys tomorrow."

"I will," she offered.

He was surprised. "You think you can handle them?"

"Alex was two when our mother died, Mitch. I know what it's like to take care of a child that age."

"You don't have to," he said, instead.

"I know. I want to. It's time I got to know my nephews."

"Okay, that solves tomorrow. It doesn't fix the real problem. They need stability, Leanne. I don't work a nine-to-five job. I get called out in the middle of the night.

Sometimes I don't come home until the middle of the night. Day care is out.''

"All right. So you need live-in help."

"I've had a couple of live-ins. It was nice while it lasted."

"But that's not the real issue, is it?" Leanne knew it had to be something more than that. "Tell me, Mitch."

He looked uncomfortable, then he looked downright mad. Finally, Mitch explained.

"I got into a tight spot at work last month. I was tired. Or maybe just worried about the boys. My head just wasn't in the right place, and in my job I can't afford to have my head in the wrong place."

"What happened?"

"Damned if I know, even now. I pulled over this kid in a fancy sports car. He was mouthing off, saying all sorts of crazy things. Next thing I knew, I was staring down the barrel of my own revolver, in the hands of this seventeen-year-old who was high as a kite and talking about blowing my brains out."

"Oh, my God." Leanne started to tremble.

"And I kept thinking that if I didn't get myself out alive, there was no telling what would happen to the boys. That they didn't have anyone else but me, and I was doing a lousy job of raising them anyway."

Leanne felt a little queasy just imagining what might have happened. And she couldn't look at Mitch, couldn't imagine the boys being without him as well as their mother. "Cutting yourself out of their lives isn't the answer."

"Tell me what is," he demanded. "If you've got the answers, tell me. Because I don't know what to do anymore."

He was wearing that bleak, worn-down look she remembered so well from Kelly's funeral. She folded her arms across her stomach, because she hurt for him and the boys and her sister, and she didn't know how to make that ache go away. She didn't know how to help or what to say, but she was afraid it was up to her to make things right.

She decided to get the obvious points out of the way. "You think Rena's the right person to raise them?"

"She wants them," he said.

"Because she's selfish?" Leanne tried not to let her own hostilities toward her stepmother come through, but suspected she hadn't succeeded in that. "Because Rena regrets not having children of her own and it's too late for her to do that now?"

"I don't know why she wants them," Mitch admitted.

"Maybe because she thought she was going to get four children when she married my father. But I never saw her as a mother. Kelly did for a while, but she's gone now. Even Alex and Amy aren't that close to her anymore. You know that, don't you?"

"I know there's some tension there."

"Tension?" Leanne almost choked on the word. "Rena nearly drove them crazy. She's incredibly manipulative and opinionated and downright selfish."

"Opinionated," Mitch said. "I'll give you that one. And she can be a little pushy at times. But I think her heart's in the right place. I think she loves the boys."

"For as long as they do what she wants."

"She's only forty-two," Mitch argued. "She's in good health, so she could reasonably be expected to live until they're adults. She could be home with them every day. She and your father are financially secure now. They have so much time and energy they could devote to the boys."

But that wasn't the real issue, Leanne wanted to shout at him. Instead, she settled for asking, "Do you want Rena to raise those boys? Do you think that's what Kelly would have wanted?"

"Kelly wanted to raise them herself. I wanted to raise them with her, but that's not one of our options."

"Neither is giving them to Rena." Leanne had to make him see that. "Mitch, you don't know her the way I do, and I think if you'd just take some time to think this through, you'd see that I'm right. It must have been incredibly difficult in these past months, but things are going to get better. If you'll just give it some time.''

Mitch started to object, but Leanne cut in. ''You don't have to decide anything right now. I'm here. I can stay a few days and give you some time to think and to find someone to take care of the boys.''

There was nothing to keep her from staying. She certainly didn't need the money, and she was overdue for a break. ''Please, Mitch. Let me do this. If not for you, for Kelly.''

He thought about it long enough to make her nervous, to make her wonder what her next argument would be. Finally, he answered.

''All right. Stay for a few days.''

''Good.'' She relaxed a little, then considered the practicalities. ''Is there a hotel nearby?''

''Not close.'' He hesitated again, then said, ''Look, you might as well stay here. I need to leave early in the morning, and it's probably going to be after six before I'm done tomorrow night.''

It made sense, yet it still made her uncomfortable. She would have liked some distance between herself and this brokenhearted, yet altogether disturbing man.

''Why don't you take the room next to the boys','' he said.

''All right.''

''And, Leanne?''

''Hmm?'' She worried for a minute he'd already changed his mind about having her here.

''Thank you for coming. Thank you for staying.''

Chapter 4

Soon after dinner, Mitch retired upstairs, while Leanne sat in the living room with a book on her lap. Tired, but reluctant to go to bed, she looked around the room.

On the table beside the sofa was a small, silver-framed photograph of her sister. Leanne tried but failed to judge it objectively, as if it were something related to her work, not a terribly intimate portrait of a young, beautiful woman she had loved very much.

Kelly wore a dress in a deep blue that brought out the color of her eyes. She was sitting on the ground, which was covered with autumn-colored leaves. The light was filtering through the branches of a massive tree, leaving patches of shadows and light all over Kelly's face and her body—something that Leanne would never have allowed if she'd been the one photographing her sister that day.

Leanne saw a woman whose seemingly perfect life was about to be shattered. Kelly was smiling brightly with her face lifted toward the camera, a patch of sunlight caught in her hair, turning it to spun gold. From the look on her face, Leanne knew Mitch had been behind the camera that day, and the love so obviously between them was like a tangible thing caught within the mix of chemicals on the film.

Leanne had envied them that love. She had envied everything about her sister's life—her husband, this house, the fact that Kelly saw Alex and Amy, even their father, at times. They were a family, one she hadn't felt a part of in a long time.

The rift reminded Leanne of one of those feuds, the kind where the fighting had gone on so long no one remembered exactly why it had started. It simply existed, with a life all its own.

There was an awkwardness that settled around her family whenever they came together. Nothing felt right or natural. The complications just piled up on top of one another, until there were walls so high they might have protected a fortress.

Or two fortresses. Her family in one, Leanne alone in the other.

Leanne picked up the photograph of Kelly and held it to her. Closing her eyes, she remembered how it had felt to hold Teddy this afternoon, and she yearned to hold her sister just like that.

One more time, Leanne thought. If they could talk one more time... There were so many things Leanne wished she could say.

Why she had never managed to say them when Kelly was alive she simply didn't understand. Why Kelly's letter had come so late? Why she hadn't gotten home in time...why?

A choking sound that Leanne hardly recognized rose up in her throat and into her mouth. A sob tried to escape her next, but she managed to smother it by clamping her lips together and sucking in a ragged breath. Tears overflowed and ran down her cheeks.

Then she had the feeling that she was no longer alone.

Standing and turning around at the same time, she felt the photograph slide from her grasp. It bounced off the sofa cushion, then hit the floor with a thud.

Leanne held her breath, but the glass didn't shatter.

She looked up and saw Mitch standing on the landing, a glass of water in his hand. He was still wearing his sweatpants, but he'd taken off his shoes and his shirt. Leanne had a quick impression of long, sleek expanses of muscle and warm, brown skin before she turned away.

"Sorry," he said. "I couldn't sleep. Didn't mean to startle you."

As Leanne picked up the photograph, she swiped at the tears on her cheeks and wondered what he'd heard, what he'd seen.

The next thing she knew, Mitch was beside her, and she tried not to look at him. Not his face. Not the broad expanse of bare skin. Not anywhere.

His hand was coming toward her, and she tensed before she figured out that he only wanted the photograph.

"It's fine," she said, flustered to the core and still reeling from the emotions brought on by being in Kelly's house, holding one of Kelly's babies close, seeing the look in Mitch's eyes when he talked about his wife, even now when more than a year had gone by since he'd lost her.

"I'll take it upstairs with me." He handled the photograph as though it were made of pure gold. "It's one of my favorites."

Mitch turned to go, then paused. She saw the rise and fall of his shoulders, saw the tension in the set of his jaw, before he faced her once again, as if it were the last thing in the world he wanted to do.

"Are you all right?" he asked.

She nodded, despite everything she was feeling and all she wished she could say.

She wanted to know about Kelly, about those moments before her sister had died.

When Leanne finally made it home after the funeral, her

family had closed ranks. It was as if they didn't think she deserved to grieve for her sister. So she'd never really gotten any details, yet she had so many questions.

Mitch was not the one to ask, she told herself. Clearly, he'd suffered most of all, was suffering still. She would ask anyone but him.

Leanne turned and dared a glance at the stern-looking almost-stranger who was her brother-in-law. He hadn't left, hadn't moved from her side. And he seemed to be fighting battles of his own right now.

Did he hate her for everything that was wrong between her and Kelly? Did he want to lash out at her again for not being there when Kelly needed her? Leanne suspected he did, and she stood and walked to the opposite end of the room. Putting her back to him, she wiped away another stray tear.

"Do you need anything?" Mitch inquired.

Leanne laughed sadly, the sound alone enough to scare her. She needed so very many things, and he would never be the person to give them to her.

Still, when she heard footsteps behind her, coming near, she was so afraid that Mitch had found an ounce of compassion inside himself for her and that he was going to make the mistake of being kind to her. If he did, she would simply shatter into a million pieces.

When Mitch was close enough to reach out and touch her, she turned slightly and put out a hand. "Don't," she said, with more force than she intended.

"My mistake." His voice was clipped and even harsher than hers. "I should have known better."

Leanne waited and listened. His footsteps sounded on the living-room rug, then on the wooden steps. Finally, when she heard nothing else from anywhere in the house, she dropped her hand to her side and hung her head.

Loneliness, as powerful and as overwhelming as any she'd ever known, came over her like a tidal wave. It chilled her and threatened to sweep her away, the force of it so strong she could scarcely fight it.

She couldn't let Mitch help her now, couldn't let anyone. Because for fourteen years, there had been no one. And before that, there had been only her brother and sisters. But she had been the one to take care of them. She'd nursed them all through their grief and their loneliness after their mother's death.

It had been draining and exhausting and had eaten up so much time that Leanne didn't think she'd ever had time to mourn herself. And with Kelly? Well…she hadn't given herself time. She'd jetted off around the world, working in a frenzy so there would be no time to stop, no time to think. There wasn't supposed to be time to hurt, either.

But in this house, surrounded by everyone Kelly loved, Leanne couldn't escape. Not from her memories or her grief.

Swallowing hard, Leanne sank onto the sofa. She wrapped her arms around her waist and rocked back and forth because she simply couldn't be still. Hot, heavy tears burned as they streaked down her face. Alone, she mourned for the sister she would never see again, for all the things left unsaid between them.

Mitch stalked back up the steps and into his bedroom.

Carefully, he placed the photograph of his wife on the nightstand by his bed, then thought better of it. It would be one of the first sights he saw when he opened his eyes every morning, and he wasn't sure if that was wise.

The days were too long and too difficult for him to start out missing Kelly, although inevitably, every day, that happened. Something always reminded him that she was gone, that nothing would ever be the same again. Mitch tried to stay busy every second of the day, and that had worked for a while. If he was exhausted, he simply didn't have time to think that much.

Well, he was certainly exhausted tonight. He should

have been well into that wondrous oblivion that was asleep, maybe lucky enough to be dreaming of his wife. But he wasn't, because Leanne was downstairs, hurting, and she didn't want him anywhere near her.

He supposed she must regret having let Kelly down by not being there when the boys were born, and a part of Mitch was still so angry over that he wanted her to suffer because of it.

But tonight…he actually felt sorry for her.

He took a deep breath and tried to calm down. A glance at the clock told him it was after midnight. He had to sleep.

But he'd left her downstairs, her shoulders shaking from the effort to make her tears stop.

He didn't even close his eyes or so much as glance toward the photograph he'd brought upstairs, but Kelly's face came to him then, so close it seemed he could almost reach out and touch her. He felt oddly comforted, felt a peacefulness inside her that he hoped was real.

She smiled, one of those knowing smiles that told him she was about to talk him into doing something he didn't want to do.

And then he thought of Leanne.

Much as he hated to admit it, Mitch knew Kelly would never have left her sister alone like that. His wife had found good in everyone and everything. She'd been forgiving and compassionate, whereas he was more likely to want to lay blame.

What would Kelly have done? Mitch asked himself. Forgiven Leanne? For everything? Had Kelly done that already before she died? Mitch had been here. He'd seen Kelly's nervousness before each and every one of her sister's visits, seen the despair when those visits hadn't turned out the way Kelly had hoped.

Kelly hadn't known how to fix things. And she'd grieved for her sister. For some reason, being pregnant with the boys had made Kelly feel those old hurts even more strongly than before.

Mitch remembered when Kelly had written that letter to her sister, a letter he'd never seen. He remembered how hopeful she'd been, how doubtful he'd been that things would work out. And he'd gotten angry at his sister-in-law all over again.

Today had brought it all back to the surface. Mitch didn't want Leanne to be nice to his boys or helpful. He certainly didn't want to need her, but he did.

So what do I do now? he asked his wife softly.

She didn't come to him like some ghostly apparition, like an image with no substance floating through the air. Mitch wasn't so far gone that he expected anything like that.

Still, he talked to Kelly sometimes because it made him feel closer to her and because he believed in God and in some sort of life after this one.

Kelly, the essence of her, still existed somewhere, he thought. Maybe she was watching over them all. Maybe she was listening to him now. Maybe she would find a way to show him the right thing to do.

Mitch figured he could use all the help he could get—something he'd told Kelly often enough in these late-night talks he had with her.

And then, when he closed his eyes, he saw Leanne's face. He thought of her showing up out of the blue and offering to help him when he needed it most.

Why? Mitch wondered, still seeing her face as plain as day.

And then he thought, what if...

Oh, no, he said aloud. *Kelly? No. Not her.*

His only answer was a sudden whish of the wind cutting through the trees and swirling around the house, then dying down as suddenly as it had begun.

Mitch fought the feeling that he had to do something for Leanne. But at some point, he came to understand that was what Kelly expected from him. And he would have done anything in the world for his wife. So shortly after one o'clock in the morning, he put on his shirt and went back downstairs.

At first he thought the room was empty, then he spotted Leanne curled up on the sofa, asleep. He grabbed the afghan that was draped over a chair and covered Leanne with it. He thought of leaving her there, then remembered how terrible he always felt when he slept on the thing. He always woke up with his neck stiff and sore, his head pounding; Leanne would, too.

She would have the boys by herself tomorrow, and that was difficult enough without a headache and a stiff neck.

Mitch decided he had no choice but to wake her.

Sitting on the edge of the sofa, he put a hand on her shoulder and shook her gently. She groaned, then turned so that he could see her face, still wet with tears.

Obviously, she'd cried herself to sleep.

Mitch felt like a heel for having left her there, no matter what she'd said to him. Kelly had told him once that Leanne always found it difficult to accept help from anyone, that she thought it came from the way Leanne had grown up. Leanne was the one who'd taken care of everyone else, Kelly had explained.

Mitch wondered if that was true, if what he'd perceived as out-and-out rejection of him was nothing more than an instinctive reaction from Leanne. Maybe she truly never let anyone help her.

Maybe there was no one to help her.

Mitch heard the words so clearly in his head, as if someone had inserted them directly into his mind. He was certain they hadn't been spoken aloud. Still, he turned and looked all around the room. But he saw nothing, heard nothing more.

"Great," he mumbled. "Now I'm going nuts."

Leanne sighed and shifted on the uncomfortable sofa once again. This time her hand landed on Mitch's thigh. Mitch froze at the contact and stared at her hand. He felt a sudden rush of heat, an uncomfortable stirring in his body in places that hadn't stirred in a long, long time.

"Dammit," he muttered, pushing her hand aside and feeling as if his own body had betrayed him.

He didn't want any other woman's hands on him, didn't want to kiss anyone, to hold anyone, definitely didn't want to share his bed with anyone. For reasons he could not understand, some people had felt the need to tell him about certain aspects of being widowed. Eventually, they claimed, his sex drive would return. They said it wasn't anything he should be concerned about or feel guilty about, no matter what happened.

How in the hell was he supposed to keep from feeling guilty about having sex with another woman? He wanted to scream at anyone who dared broach the subject with him. But at the same time, he didn't want to have such a conversation. He wished people would just leave him alone with his grief.

His sex life, or lack of a sex life, was no one else's business but his, and he knew what he wanted.

No one. No one but his wife.

And she was gone. Forever.

Impatient now, Mitch put a hand on Leanne's shoulder and shook her harder than he had at first. Her eyes came open, and she blinked and turned her head away from the light from the stairway. Then she looked at him as if she didn't quite see him, rubbed at her eyes and finally sat up.

"What is it?" she asked. "Is it morning? Already?"

"No. It's a little after one, and you need to get to bed. This sofa is the most uncomfortable place in the house to sleep."

"Oh. Sorry."

She rubbed a hand against one eye, then paused in the midst of doing that. Her hand came away from her face, and she stared at her own fingers, wet with her tears. Then she seemed embarrassed by the idea that she'd been downstairs crying and that Mitch knew it.

"I'll be up in just a minute."

"Leanne." Mitch knew he sounded frustrated and impatient, which was the last thing she needed right now. He tried to remind himself that Kelly would want him to help her, but he just didn't know what to do.

What did Leanne want? he wondered. What did she need? What did he possibly have to give?

He watched as she sat up and scooted to the end of the sofa with her legs drawn up to her chest, her arms wrapped around her legs, so she was barely touching him now. And she kept her face turned away so he couldn't see her expression at all.

Mitch knew he would find no peace tonight until this was settled.

"Earlier," he said, "when you were looking at Kelly's picture, what were you thinking? What was wrong?"

Leanne stared at him as if he'd lost his mind even asking her such a question.

Searching deep inside himself, he found an inkling of patience and drew on it. "Tell me," he said softly. "Maybe I can help."

"Why would you want to help me?"

"You're helping me—with the boys," he said. It wasn't an answer, but he hoped it would suffice.

"Mitch," she said lightly, "you don't have to be nice to me to get me to help you with the boys. I'm doing it because I want to, and I'm doing it for Kelly."

"I know that." Mitch decided to switch subjects, to see if he could make it through those barriers of hers with some combination of bluntness and honesty. "Kelly said you never let anyone help you with anything."

"She did?" Leanne looked surprised and wary.

Mitch nodded. "If she was here now, she would try to help you."

And then Leanne started to cry. He watched her eyes fill with tears, watched her fight an impossible battle to stop them.

For Kelly, he reached for her, pushing aside all resistance she offered, and pulled her into his arms. It was awkward at first, and her resistance was strong. She would not let herself relax, would not stop fighting for control over her emotions.

But soon she was crying too hard to fight him. Mitch held her against him, urged her head down to his shoulder and hung on tight, telling himself he would do the same for a stranger he encountered on the job who'd experienced some tragedy. Surely he could do the same for Kelly's sister.

He closed his eyes, then felt the chill in her body and the way she was trembling. The only thing he could think to do was hold her closer, and somehow, she ended up sitting in his lap. Because she was still cold, he ran his hand up and down her back. Because she was shaking and crying so hard, he bent his head down to hers, put his lips next to her ear and whispered to her, trying to calm her as best he could.

"I miss her so much," Leanne said brokenly.

"I know," Mitch said. "I do, too."

"And I need her. I need to talk to her and to explain...."

"What?" he asked, thinking she needed to get this out. "If she was here, what would you tell her?"

"That I loved her. Mitch, I always loved her, and I missed her so much all those years I was gone."

"She missed you, too," Mitch said, thinking that might help. But it seemed to make her cry even harder.

"I would give anything now if I'd just come home while she was still alive, so I could have told her all these things, so we could have had some time together without fighting and without all the misunderstandings between us."

And then Mitch knew exactly what she was feeling. He had yearned for the same thing, had begged for it.

One more chance, one more hour, one more minute, to tell Kelly how much he loved her and needed her, that she was everything good and beautiful in his life. To beg her not to leave him. To ask her to stay close to him and guide him as best she could. To give him some sign that wherever she was, she was all right.

Mitch felt strangely comforted that the woman he now held in his arms understood the myriad of emotions he'd felt upon losing his wife.

Maybe he could help Leanne through this, he thought. Maybe she could help him with the boys, and he could help her. And together, they would all get past this. And Kelly would be happy.

Leanne shifted in his arms, lifted her head from his shoulder and inched away just enough that he could see her face. She looked absolutely miserable and utterly lost and sad.

He wondered if he'd been wrong about her all these years—that she wasn't at all cold or remote or somehow oblivious to all the pain her leaving had caused her brother and sisters. Or maybe she'd changed, maybe Kelly's death had changed her.

It had changed Mitch in ways he was still trying to understand. He wanted to move more slowly through life, to take the time to enjoy the special little moments, to not get so upset when things didn't go his way. He wanted to be kinder, and maybe this was some sort of test for him. Maybe Leanne was here for a lot of different reasons, some of them having to do with him and the lessons he needed to learn about life.

Reluctantly, he put his hand to her face and wiped away her tears. Leanne froze and sucked in a breath. He decided he couldn't have surprised her more if he'd slapped her in the face.

Did she think he was such an ogre? Yet she'd still come back to Chicago, determined to stop him from giving up the boys.

Mitch found himself wondering what was going on inside her head. At once, he became aware of the fact that she was closer to him than any other woman had been in years, that she was warm now, that her shaking had given way to a fine trembling he could still feel because she was so near.

He looked over her face, taking in the flush of her cheeks, the wetness clinging to her lashes, the moisture still on her cheeks, the soft, fullness of her lips.

It felt good to be this close to her, to warm her with his body and comfort her. And now that they were this close, it would be so easy to dip his head and press his lips to hers.

Her lips were already slightly parted, and he wanted to taste her. What would it be like to have a taste of her?

Blood moved in a dizzying rush to his groin, and he felt his body harden, felt a stab of desire so strong it staggered him. And embarrassed him. And shocked him.

Whatever the hell had happened, it must have frightened Leanne, because she shifted on his lap, probably trying to get away from him, and for an instant, he felt her bottom pressed firmly against him.

He wanted to sink into the floor right then and there. Leanne, her face flaming, a look of utter disbelief on her face, jumped to her feet and ran upstairs.

Mitch stood, too. He thought about going after her. There had to be something he could say to defend himself and to explain. But what?

"Dammit!" he swore. What had just taken place here?

He felt as if the world had shifted on its axis, throwing everything off balance and changing all the rules on him yet again. And he didn't want that to happen. He wanted to go back to the way things had been before, just as, after Kelly had died, he'd longed to go back to the days when she was still with him.

He turned and looked to the mantel, which held a photograph of her taken two winters ago, when she was pregnant with the boys, and then closed his eyes and tried to feel her presence in the room with him. He tried to remember as clearly as he had the day before and the day before that how it had felt to have her in his arms, how she tasted and the little sounds she made when he kissed her, how it was to sink deep inside her.

Aw, Kelly, he said to her, hoping she would hear. *Don't leave me. Not now. Not this way.*

But he already felt the loss. The memories were still there, but they were fading on him. Already, it seemed as if it had been forever since he'd touched her.

Obviously, his body was going to make certain physical demands on him, even if emotionally, he simply wasn't ready.

Well, to hell with his body and anything it might want, Mitch decided. He still loved his wife.

Wearily, he climbed the stairs, passed the closed door of Leanne's room and quickly checked on the boys. Then he climbed into his bed, knowing he wouldn't sleep now.

Punching his pillow, which felt all out of sorts when he put his head down on it, he tried to get comfortable by shifting this way and that. Finally, he rolled over. The moon was nearly full, and its light was shining in the window through the open blinds. The light fell across the photograph in the silver frame that he'd brought upstairs not an hour ago. It seemed to bring almost a glow to the face of his wife.

For a second, he thought she was alive inside that photograph and smiling just for him, as she had that day at the lake when he'd snapped the picture. And he would like to think that she had something to be happy about now, though for the life of him, he couldn't figure out what that would be.

Tell me, sweetheart. Tell me, and maybe I can be happy, too.

But she didn't. Her image just smiled back at him from the photograph. Mitch felt strangely comforted by that, before he drifted into a deep, dreamless sleep.

Leanne did not sleep. She lay in her bed, listening as Mitch came up the stairs, as he walked past her closed door, then went into the boys' room, then into his own bedroom. She heard the bed give beneath his weight as he lay down, heard the slight creaking of the bedsprings a few minutes later as he rolled over once. And then she heard nothing at all.

How could he sleep? she wondered. After what had happened downstairs....

Her face flamed at the memory. She'd fallen apart, sobbed out her loneliness and her deepest regrets to him, let him hold her while she cried. And honest to God, all that had been on her mind was the fact that she hated letting anyone, especially him, see her that way.

But then other little thoughts started creeping in—that it was nice to have someone hold her. To have a man hold her. To have *him* hold her.

There, she'd admitted it to herself. It had felt so good to have Mitch hold her tight.

For so very long, no one had. She hadn't allowed anyone to get that close to her, hadn't allowed herself to depend upon anyone that way. She told herself she didn't need anyone, but her loneliness made a mockery of that idea.

Still, she couldn't need Mitch.

She couldn't want him, either.

And if he, for some sliver of time in the darkness downstairs, thought he might want her? Well, it couldn't have been her that he wanted. He didn't even like her.

He must be lonely.

Men got lonely, just as women did. And Kelly had been gone nearly a year and a half now. How long could any man be expected to be faithful to a wife who was nothing more than a memory?

Leanne wasn't a prude and she wasn't easily shocked. She told herself she wouldn't have been offended by the idea of Mitch becoming involved with another woman this long after Kelly's death.

But what had happened downstairs—that had shocked her.

Nothing had happened, she told herself. He hadn't even kissed her. But she'd imagined what it would be like if he had kissed her.

It had been as though they were caught in some invisible web, with his mouth so close to hers. She hadn't been able to move or even to look away, hadn't been able to see anything but him, hadn't felt anything but his body against hers. She'd nearly tasted his lips on hers. And then she'd moved ever so slightly on his lap and realized he was fully aroused.

And then he'd looked at her as if she were the devil come to life in his own living room.

Did Mitch blame her for what had happened? Did she blame herself?

Leanne couldn't say for sure. She was still too surprised by the whole thing. Glancing at the clock, she saw that it was nearly two now. Adjusting her pillow and burrowing deeper into the bed, she tried to close her eyes and to relax, but it didn't work. She couldn't think of anything but Mitch.

Soon she would have to face him again. Maybe they would both pretend that nothing had happened and leave it at that. She hoped she could manage the feat, that Mitch would let her.

Otherwise, staying at Mitch's would be nearly impossible. She had enough guilt inside her. She couldn't handle any more—especially not the guilt of wanting her sister's husband.

Chapter 5

The boys rose indecently early, sleeping until six-thirty on the best of days. And they were disgustingly cheerful upon waking. They giggled and chattered and bounced around with enough energy to power a small city, all before the sun rose.

The next morning was no exception. Mitch lifted one eyelid and found himself almost nose to nose with a near-matched set of grinning toddlers who were laughing and shouting, "Papa, Papa, Papa," as they held out their arms to be lifted into his bed.

"You climbed out again!" He tried to sound stern, because it scared him that they could get out of their cribs while he slept and because if a baby gate had been invented that they couldn't outsmart or outclimb, he hadn't yet found it.

The gate at the door to their bedroom stumped them some days, but not all. The one at the top of the stairs—they hadn't gone through yet. But Mitch suspected it wasn't from lack of trying, merely that they came to find him as soon as they awoke.

He lifted Teddy into his bed, then a bruised and battered-looking Timmy. Teddy grinned and nearly stuck his finger in Timmy's bruised eye, then chattered on excitedly.

"Boo-boo! Tee! Boo-boo!"

Timmy pushed his brother's hand away, and the next thing Mitch knew the boys were rolling around on his bed and giggling.

Mitch closed his eyes and tried to soak up the happiness radiating from them. They were his strength—the only reason he managed to get out of bed every day and do all the things a normal, sane man was expected to do.

After Kelly had died, Ginny Dalton, his partner's wife, had told him to concentrate on taking care of the boys, on simply meeting their physical needs at first. A mother of two herself, she'd known how draining and how all-absorbing that task would be. Once their basic needs were met, it was time to concentrate on making them happy, on showering them with love. Because he *would* love them, even if he could have sworn after Kelly died that he'd never love another living thing for fear of losing it.

Ginny, he'd found, was a very wise woman.

When all else failed him, he focused on doing what had to be done for Timmy and Teddy, which left little time for feeling sorry for himself or worrying about how he would manage to go on living.

He simply *went* on.

Somewhere along the way, when he wasn't thinking about getting on with his life or about getting through his wife's death, he'd made it past the worst of it.

Sixteen months, he thought. Obviously, he was going to live.

At the moment, with the boys laughing and climbing all over him, life wasn't bad.

Doing their best baby lion impressions, the boys growled at each other as they rolled across Mitch's bed.

Deciding to get in on the game, he snagged one of them by the ankle and pulled. Timmy, now ready to defend his captured brother, leaped across the bed and landed hard on Mitch's chest.

Mitch decided an early-morning play session was in order. He flipped them both onto their backs and started tickling them. Before too long, he was on his back and the twins were on top of him.

"Gotcha, Papa! Gotcha!" they chorused.

Mitch growled at them. They shrieked in response. He tickled Timmy's belly and tried to protect himself as best he could when Teddy started bouncing on his stomach. Lord, they would be able to hurt him before too long when they played this way.

Then Teddy stopped moving, stopped howling. He just stood there in the middle of the bed, staring. Mitch snagged Timmy a whole two seconds before he would have plowed into his distracted brother and probably knocked him off the bed.

"Dat?" Timmy said, pointing toward the doorway.

It was a generic expression the twins used to ask, "Who's that?" Or "What's that?"

Mitch saw Leanne standing in the doorway. Plainly, they'd woken her up, maybe even frightened her, because she seemed to have been in a hurry to get there.

He watched as she impatiently pushed a hand through her hair, which was loose now and hung just past her shoulders. She was wearing what he suspected were a pair of men's pajamas, the cuffs of the oversize, long-sleeved shirt rolled up to accommodate the length of her arms. Briefly, Mitch wondered whose pajamas they were, before he told himself it was none of his business anyway.

Her cheeks were flushed. Embarrassment, he decided. He was certainly embarrassed himself at having to face her this morning. The boys had been enough of a distraction that he hadn't even begun to figure out how he felt about what had happened last night or how he might explain himself to her.

So he took a minute to study her, instead. Her eyes had dark circles under them, maybe of hint of redness in them, too. Had she been crying again? Not this morning, he concluded.

"Sorry we woke you," he said, watching her as she stifled a yawn. "The boys have seen the *Lion King* a few times too many. Their favorite game is pretending they're lion cubs wrestling in the jungle."

"Oh." She looked relieved. "What's the *Lion King?*"

The boys heard the name of their favorite movie and started chanting their own mangled version of the title and marching around in a circle on Mitch's bed. Leanne looked so perplexed Mitch wanted to laugh, and he was grateful for the distraction of his sons this morning.

"You'll find out soon enough," Mitch said. Hard as it was to believe, a few years ago he would have been as clueless as she was about the title of a popular kids' movie. He'd seen this one so many times he could practically recite the dialogue line for line.

"I should warn you," Mitch added, "the boys can get the VCR cabinet open all by themselves now. If the TV's already on, all they have to do is put the tape in the VCR and the machine turns itself on and automatically starts to play."

"You have toddlers who can operate a VCR?"

Mitch nodded. "Scary, isn't it?"

"Yes," she said, watching the boys and not him.

Mitch couldn't blame her, not after what had happened downstairs the night before. Time enough to talk about that tonight, when the boys were in bed, he decided. It wasn't a conversation he cared to have with the boys present.

"The twins get up at the crack of dawn," he warned her. "Sometimes even before that."

"I thought I'd woken up in the middle of a war zone."

Mitch found himself wondering if she'd actually done

that and thought he might ask her sometime. He was probably going to need all the neutral topics of conversation he could find. Then he turned to the boys and asked them to hold the noise down.

That brought the boys' attention back to Leanne once again.

"Dat?" Timmy said again, pointing at her this time.

Mitch caught them close, hoping to keep them still long enough to make introductions. "Timmy, this is your aunt Leanne. Can you say hello?"

"Wee-Ann?" Timmy said.

"Wee-Ann, Wee-Ann, Wee-Ann," Teddy chanted as he bounced.

"Close enough," Mitch said. "They always mangle their L sounds, but I'm told that's normal at their age."

Leaning against the doorway, Leanne nodded and tried to smile, but it was obviously a struggle for her. She looked so serious and so hesitant, as if she had to tell him something, but didn't want to.

Mitch didn't know what she was thinking, but something warned him he probably wasn't going to like it. "You're not having second thoughts about staying, are you?"

"No," she said quickly. "I was just watching the boys. They're talking and walking and playing as if they were baby lions. I guess I've been gone longer than I realized."

Mitch felt sorry for her then, because she'd missed so much.

"They look so happy now," she continued.

He hugged the boys closer and felt the need to defend himself and the job he'd done with them. "They are happy. Quite often, at least."

He realized it was true. Despite the fact that they didn't have a mother, despite all the problems he had raising them on his own, the boys were surprisingly happy.

Maybe they were just that way by nature. Maybe most kids were. But it didn't take much to please them. Bouncing on their father's bed as if it were a trampoline. Splashing in a puddle of water a half-inch deep. Sinking their fingers and toes into the mud hole that after each rain formed in that corner of the backyard where grass refused to grow.

They *were* happy here.

And he was thinking of giving them up.

Once again, tension settled like a ball of fire deep in his stomach when he thought about living without the boys.

He'd never been certain he could do it.

Then he glanced at Timmy's poor, bruised face, the bandage covering the cut on his eyebrow—the result of leaving his sons too many times with someone who shouldn't be taking care of them.

He thought about leaving them today with Leanne and not knowing whom he might leave them with next week or next month, thought about what kind of position they'd be in if anything ever happened to him and they had only him to depend on. They would be left with no one then.

Just imagining it had Mitch mad all over again.

He glanced up and saw Leanne still standing in the doorway. She looked as if she expected him to lay into her at any moment.

"Hey, I'm sorry I snapped at you," he said. "It hasn't been the best of weeks."

"I know," she said softly as she stood huddled against the door.

Mitch remembered how often Kelly had asked him to cut her sister some slack, and resolved to do just that. "I'll try not to take out my bad days on you."

"It's all right," she insisted.

But Mitch knew it wasn't.

"I didn't mean to imply that they were miserable here or that you weren't taking care of them," she added. "I just worried that they might be sad about losing Kelly."

"They never knew her," Mitch said, wondering once again if that was a blessing or a curse. Was it easier for them because they'd never had a mother and therefore didn't know what they'd lost? Or had they simply been cheated out of any memory of Kelly?

He tried to reason it out sometimes, using himself as his guide. Would he have been happier if he'd never known Kelly?

A few people he knew who had lost a spouse had told him that eventually he'd be grateful for the time he'd had with Kelly, that his happy memories would far outweigh the pain of losing her, and he'd be grateful that she'd given him the boys.

Mitch was grateful for his sons. Teddy, curled up against him, looked as if the morning's wrestling session had made him tired again. And Timmy tugged on his brother, trying to get Teddy to come play again before they got kicked off Mitch's bed.

They were so sweet, so precious, such an incredible gift.

For a minute, he could barely breathe just thinking about living without them.

What had he been thinking these past few months ever to imagine he could give them up?

He couldn't, he realized. They were everything that was good in his life, the only thing he had left of his wife.

There was no way he was giving up his boys.

The boys were perfectly happy until they figured out their father was leaving. Timmy was angry, and he yelled and stomped his feet. Teddy just cried and clung to his father. Leanne felt like the worst kind of monster when Mitch literally pried his sons' hands off him so he could get out the door.

Once he was gone, nothing Leanne said seemed to make anything better. Timmy remained defiant. He wouldn't let Leanne near him. And Teddy laid his head against her shoulder and sobbed as if the entire world were coming to an end. And then Timmy started babbling in something that didn't sound like any language Leanne had ever heard, and she'd heard a great number of languages. When Teddy stopped crying long enough to answer his brother, Timmy nodded in understanding, then started talking again in the same gibberish. Leanne knew she was in trouble.

They'd made up their own language. She'd heard of twins doing that, but seeing it and hearing it was an incredibly unnerving experience.

"Hey," she said to Teddy, because she suspected he'd be more sympathetic to her than Timmy. "What about me? Talk to me?"

Teddy merely ignored her and resumed his cryptic conversation with his brother.

Finally, Leanne said, "Anyone want to watch the *Lion King?*"

"WioKee?" Timmy said, his interest clearly piqued.

Leanne nodded, because she thought that was what Timmy had said. Then she whispered excitedly, "It has baby lions in it."

"I know dat," Timmy boasted.

She smiled and turned to Teddy, whose sobs had been reduced to hiccups and shakily drawn breaths. "Teddy, want to watch the *Lion King?* We can pretend to be baby lions."

Teddy's lower lip was trembling. His face was still wet with tears, but he was clearly interested, too.

"Maybe you could help me with the VCR. To make the movie play. I don't know if I can make it work by myself."

"Me do dat," Timmy said.

"Me!" Teddy shouted.

And then the race was on to get to the TV. Leanne saw that the boys could indeed operate the VCR. She spread a blanket across the living-room floor in front of the TV and fed them breakfast cereal there. They had little cups with the weighted bottoms to keep the containers upright, and plastic tops to keep their juice from spilling. Leanne spooned their cereal into their mouths. So the mess was minimal.

After breakfast, the boys wrestled with and growled at each other along with the cubs on the screen. Leanne sat back and watched them, then got caught up in the movie herself.

An hour later, the phone rang. Leanne answered it. Wanting their turn to talk, the boys gathered around her.

"Shh," she told them, then tried to keep her voice even and calm as she spoke into the receiver. "McCarthy residence."

"Hi."

A deep, familiar voice greeted her, and for some strange reason, it sent shivers down her spine.

"It's Mitch. I wanted to make sure the boys calmed down after I left."

"They're fine now," she said, her voice breaking only a little. "They're right here. Do you want to talk to them?"

"I'd better not. They might get upset again."

"Oh, of course." She cleared her throat. "You didn't tell me they speak their own language."

"Only when they're mad or when they don't get their way. Leanne, are you crying?"

"No," she lied.

"What is it?"

Obviously, Mitch was ready for the worst. She felt silly, but she couldn't let him worry for nothing. "We watched the movie. You didn't tell me the daddy lion died."

Mitch laughed, damn him.

Leanne had been devastated. She hadn't been expecting that little plot twist at all.

"It was so sad," she told Mitch. "And I was worried that it would upset the boys, but it went right over their heads."

"But not yours?"

She must have been mistaken in what she thought she'd heard. Mitch McCarthy never teased her. He antagonized her and criticized her and tried his best to protect his family from her—as if she'd ever do anything to harm anyone in his family. They were, after all, her family, too.

"Why do you find this so amusing?" she asked, glad that they were capable of having a civilized conversation.

"Because Kelly had exactly the same reaction."

"Oh." And he must have teased his wife about being too sentimental, as well, Leanne decided.

"Hannah was watching that movie one day at our house when Kelly was baby-sitting, and Kelly just bawled. Then she lit into Marc for not warning her. But the boys have always loved the movie," Mitch reassured her.

"I could tell. It was the only thing I could think of to get them to stop crying this morning."

"I'm glad you thought of it," he said. "Leanne, I'm going to have to go now."

"Okay. Don't worry about the boys. They're fine."

Leanne hung up the phone before she realized that was the most pleasant conversation she'd ever had with her brother-in-law. And maybe, with luck, he'd never bring up what had happened the night before, and they would never have to talk about it.

That afternoon the day turned warm and sunny. Leanne and the boys went with Ginny and her children to a nearby park. The twins and Will Dalton ran for the big sandbox in the corner. And Hannah, pouting because she hadn't been allowed to wear her high heels to the park, sat on the swings, looking absolutely dejected and waiting on her mother to take pity on her and indulge her in some other way.

"Oh, her little heart is broken," Leanne said.

Ginny smiled easily. "It happens a half-dozen times a day, and she just can't accept the fact that I'm immune to her pouting. I'm afraid she's just rotten. Has been from the day she was born. And if you think she's bad with me, you should see her with Marc. He just can't say no to her, and she knows it.''

Leanne smiled, too, thinking that Ginny Dalton had just about everything. The stab of envy Leanne felt ran deep, and she wasn't very proud of herself for feeling this way. But from what little Leanne had seen of this woman's life, it looked perfect.

Leanne watched Hannah pout. "How long will this last?"

"For hours sometimes. Hannah's quite stubborn." Ginny put her hand on Leanne's arm. "Do you mind if we talk about Mitch?"

Before last night, Leanne would have given an unequivocal yes. But now she wasn't so sure it was a good idea. "What about Mitch?" she asked, instead.

"I don't want you to think I'm prying. Honestly, I think of Mitch as practically family." Ginny led her to a park bench and motioned for Leanne to sit down, then sat herself. "Marc told me you're staying for a few days to give Mitch some breathing room."

"That's right."

"I'm glad. I can't bear the idea of him giving the boys up, and I'm not sure Mitch would survive it. He's been through so much already."

"I saw him playing with the twins this morning." Saw him in his bed without his shirt, actually, but Leanne didn't feel the need to mention that. "He's wonderful with them."

"I think so."

Ginny obviously cared about Mitch and was worried about him and the boys. Leanne told Ginny what she knew.

"Mitch said he doesn't want to give them up, and I believe him. But he thinks they need stability in their lives, and he doesn't think he can give them that. He's also worried that if anything happened to him, the boys wouldn't have anyone."

"Oh," Ginny said. "Marc told me about the incident with the gun last month. He said it really spooked Mitch."

"It did." Leanne thought of what that incident had led Mitch to consider. "I won't stand by and watch the boys go to Rena. I'll fight Mitch on that."

"Maybe it won't come down to a fight," Ginny suggested. "Maybe the two of you can work together."

Leanne wasn't sure if she and Mitch could cooperate on anything. "Mitch doesn't like me very much," she confessed.

"Mitch likes everyone."

Leanne laughed nervously. "Not me. He thinks that over the years I did some unforgivable things to Kelly."

Ginny looked quite serious. "That's the other thing I wanted to tell you that really isn't any of my business. But Kelly's gone, and I may be the only one left to say it. She missed you terribly."

"I know." Leanne braced herself, not sure if she wanted to hear anything else Ginny had to say.

"Do you know what she wanted more than anything for her whole family?" Ginny smiled, as if to soften the words. "Kelly told me she wanted you to find a way to start over again with her and Alex and Amy. Maybe even with your father."

Instantly, Leanne was fighting back tears, and Ginny put her hand on Leanne's shoulder before she continued.

"The last year she was alive, we spent New Year's Eve together. It's a tradition that just before midnight, we all gather in the same room and take turns making some public resolutions for the coming year. Kelly didn't say anything about it then, but she was in the kitchen with me later, and she seemed so sad. I asked her what was wrong, and she told me she wished you were comfortable enough to spend time here. She wanted her family back together."

When Leanne looked up, Ginny had tears in her eyes, too. "I thought you'd want to know," she said. "I thought it would be important to you, that you might find a way to do what Kelly wanted.''

''I don't know how to do that,'' Leanne confessed, choking on her own words. ''Maybe if Kelly were still here, she could show me how. But she's not, and I don't think I can do it on my own.''

''Maybe you could stay awhile. Maybe if you were here, you'd find a way. Maybe Alex and Amy would help you,'' Ginny suggested.

''Maybe.''

''Kelly's death could be the catalyst to bring you all back together. Maybe your brother and sister want the same thing, but they don't know how to make it happen, either.''

''I wish they wanted that,'' Leanne said wistfully.

''Have you told them how you feel?'' Ginny inquired gently.

''No.''

The mere thought filled Leanne with dread. Emotional confrontations weren't her strong point. Who was she kidding? Emotions in general had never been her forte. As she'd found over the years, it was so much easier to run than to stay and fight.

''So,'' Ginny said, ''how do you know what Alex and Amy are thinking if you haven't asked them? Or told them how you feel?''

It was a sobering thought. Someone had to make the first move. This whole stalemate took hold because her family tended to follow the path of least resistance. Making peace meant shaking things up, talking things out, maybe everyone give a little when it came to long-held grudges.

Could Leanne do that?

If she wanted her family back, she had to. Waiting for someone else to make the first move certainly hadn't worked.

''There's one more thing I didn't mention earlier,

Leanne. Kelly didn't just want this for herself and for you. She wanted it for the boys, too. She wanted them to grow up surrounded by their family, their happy family.''

"Oh, God, I hadn't even thought of putting them into the middle of all our old fights. I don't want to do that to them. They've lost their mother already. They're going to need the rest of us close by to help them. Maybe if I approached Amy and Alex about doing this for the boys' sakes…''

Leanne thought about it, a knot of tension growing ever tighter in her stomach. She wanted her family reunited so badly. It seemed she had wanted it forever, and she was ashamed of herself for waiting until it was too late for her and Kelly. But it wasn't too late for her and the rest of her family. It wasn't too late to do this for the boys.

"I want to," Leanne began.

"Then take some time and think about it." Ginny settled her hand over Leanne's and gave it a little squeeze. "Think about staying."

Leanne was tempted. She honestly hadn't thought much beyond the day and how she was going to get through it. But as she turned and looked at the boys, who had their dump trucks roaring through the sandbox, she knew she didn't want to leave them. As exhausting and bewildering as her day with the boys had been, she wouldn't have traded it for anything in this world.

Now she was asking herself how she was going to tear herself away from this place one more time. She was asking herself why she couldn't simply stay.

"There's no place I have to be, not for weeks," Leanne said, realizing it for the first time herself. She'd finished her last job well ahead of schedule, thanks to some incredibly good luck and perfect weather. And she'd left her calendar blank for a few weeks after the scheduled completion date for her last job because she'd intended to take a vacation.

Leanne thought of all the reasons to go. Mitch didn't

like her. He made her uncomfortable. Rena didn't like her and seemed to live in fear that Leanne would somehow steal her family away. Except it had been Leanne's family first, and Leanne wanted her family back. And she wasn't eighteen years old now or absolutely bewildered by her stepmother's selfishness and her greed. Leanne could fight for herself and for what she wanted this time.

Maybe she could even win.

Chapter 6

Walking into his house that night, Mitch found it was fairly quiet and neat. He was certainly grateful for that. Following the sound of voices, he headed into the kitchen, where Leanne was standing at the stove, stirring something that smelled wonderful.

His sons were sitting on a thick towel laid across the floor. They had six plastic bowls between them and were working earnestly to transfer something—water, he hoped—from one bowl to the next. Totally absorbed in their task, they didn't even notice him at first.

Smiling, Leanne turned to say something to the boys, but her smile dimmed when she saw him.

Did she dislike him that much?

Honestly, he had never cared how she felt about him. But things were different now. He was coming to know her, to see that the front she presented was simply that—nothing more than a self-defense facade.

He wanted to know what was behind the smile she pasted on her face, behind the stiff set of her shoulders.

Last night, he supposed. They'd danced around it this morning and while they'd talked on the phone, but they couldn't avoid it forever.

"Something smells good," he said, hoping his own smile didn't appear as forced as it felt.

Leanne looked as if a compliment were the last thing she expected from him. Then the boys figured out he was home and came running at him. Two bowls of water were spilled in their haste to get to him, but the towels soaked it up. Leanne cleared the kitchen floor while he pulled his sons into his arms and stood. Two pairs of short, skinny arms came around his neck, and he twirled the twins in a circle until they cackled.

"Papa, Papa, Papa," they chimed. And then they ranted on in their jibber-jabber description of their day, both of them talking at once, the words a total jumble accompanied by broad, sweeping hand gestures.

"The park," Leanne translated. "With Hannah and Will. The swings. The sandbox. A cat. Ice cream."

"Did you have fun?" Mitch asked, turning to the boys. They were positively beaming. An immense sense of relief came over him, because he'd worried about them today and because it was so nice to come home and find them happy.

The smile he gave Leanne then was a genuine one. Curiously, she didn't relax one bit. If anything, she looked even more tense than before.

Mitch sighed, realizing this was going to be more difficult than he'd thought.

Leanne, feeling the need to get out of the house alone and to clear her head, donned a T-shirt and a pair of workout shorts, then set off for a run. When she came back forty-five minutes later, she was surprised to find two place settings at the table. Obviously, Mitch hadn't eaten yet.

"You didn't have to wait for me," she said.

"I got busy with the boys," he explained. "And it was

already so late I thought we might as well eat without them at the table—if you could call what goes on with the two of them at the table 'eating.'"

"They're not the best dinner companions," Leanne agreed, thinking it had been much easier to be in the same room with him when she had the boys as a buffer. Looking down at her clothes, she found a reason to escape, to buy herself some time before she had to tell Mitch what she'd decided. "I should shower and change."

"We don't worry about the little niceties like dressing for dinner in this house. The way I see it, we're doing well to be sitting down at the table to something that didn't come from a cardboard container and wasn't warmed up in the microwave."

"Oh. Okay."

"Have a seat," he said. "You cooked. The least I can do is bring it to the table."

Leanne sat and started doctoring her tea. Mitch pulled the salad she'd prepared from the refrigerator along with two kinds of salad dressing. She'd left a loaf of bread warming in the oven, and he brought that to the table, too. The spaghetti sauce she'd prepared was warming in a pot on the table, and it smelled good, even if she did say so herself.

"I haven't boiled the noodles yet," she said, remembering.

"I know," he acknowledged as he brought those to the table, as well. "I did."

"Oh."

Exasperated, Mitch asked, "Was it so awful to have dinner with me last night?"

"No." She was flustered enough that she almost spilled her tea.

"You're sure?"

Her cheeks flushed, Leanne nodded and barely glanced his way.

"Leanne, I'm sometimes blunt to the point of being

rude. I guess it comes from being a cop, because when I want to know something on the job, I ask."

"Should I take that as fair warning you're going to be blunt?"

He nodded. "Do you dislike me that much?"

Leanne had to think about it. What was the right answer here? She could find none.

Into the silence came the sound of Mitch swearing, and she rushed to fill the void that followed. "I don't think it's nearly as simple as liking or disliking you."

And it was as complicated as knowing he disliked her and knowing how much her sister loved him. That didn't even take into consideration the fact that she'd known him in high school and that she would have given her right arm for a chance to go out with him. It didn't help matters at all that he was even more attractive now than he had been seventeen years ago, and that she hadn't so much as had a date in the past two years.

Or that, unless she was sadly mistaken, he'd nearly kissed her last night.

"It's...complicated," she said, trying to explain again, totally unwilling to share any of the thoughts running through her head.

Mitch nodded as if he could happily chew nails at the moment.

"Can we just have dinner first?" she asked.

"Of course," he said.

Leanne put some noodles onto her plate, then reached for the bread, wondering if she was going to choke on it. Or if he would.

They both managed to eat without incident. Mitch insisted on cleaning up, and Leanne prowled around the living room as she thought about pleading her case before him. He had to let her stay.

Glancing at the mantel that held another photo of her sister, she offered up a silent prayer.

Help me, Kelly. Tell me what to say to him to make him understand.

And then Leanne headed into the kitchen, where Mitch had just finished loading the dishwasher.

"Would you like a beer?" he asked.

"No, thank you."

Mitch popped the top on a light beer, then leaned back against the cabinet. With one leg crossed in front of the other, he watched her. He couldn't possibly be that relaxed, she told herself, unless there really was no justice in the world.

"So, tell me about how much you dislike me," he said, throwing the first jab.

"Do you want to tell me why you dislike me so much?" she shot back.

"I'm not sure how productive that would be," he admitted, and just maybe, he admired the way she'd stood up to him then.

Leanne wondered if cops were just used to getting their way and tried to remember if Kelly had ever mentioned that being one of Mitch's more annoying habits. The man could be truly maddening.

"Instead, why don't you tell me why you're so nervous?" Mitch suggested as he took a drink of his beer.

"Because of what I want to say to you," she answered quickly. "Well, to be perfectly honest, what I don't want to say."

"Which is?"

"Did you find someone else to watch the boys?"

"No."

"Good. I looked at my calendar today, and I talked with my agent. Mitch, I don't have to be anywhere for the next month, and I'd like to spend it here with the boys, if you'll let me."

Mitch couldn't have been more surprised. He'd expected her to say she was jetting off to one of the far corners of the world within the hour. "You want to stay for a month? And take care of the boys?"

"Yes," she said immediately. "Today was wonderful. It was hectic and a little frightening because they can move so fast and go in two different directions at once. But I had fun. I hadn't realized how much I would enjoy being around little children again. And these are my nephews. I want to get to know them."

Mitch considered her offer for a minute. It would be a godsend—if Leanne was serious.

"This way you wouldn't have to rush to find someone new to take care of the boys," she said.

"I know." But he believed there was more to her offer than that. "What's the catch?"

"Just that you take this time to think long and hard about giving them to Rena. You have to promise me that."

"Leanne, it's not something I'd do lightly," he said, maybe just a little too defensively. "I don't know what Amy told you, but I love them more than anything in this world."

"I know. I didn't meant to imply that you didn't. Or that you wouldn't think this through. I just don't want you to be under any sort of pressure to make a decision quickly. Please let me do this, for the boys and for Kelly."

Mitch watched her as though he might watch a suspect while trying to assess the person's guilt or innocence. Was she acting out of guilt? He didn't want her to stay because she was seeking some sort of absolution. On the other hand, he and the boys desperately needed her right now. And a whole month? God, what he could do in a month's time.

"Look, if you say you're going to be here for a month..." You damned well better be here, Mitch wanted to add.

"I will. I swear it."

Still, Mitch was wary. "You'd stay here? In the house?"

"If that's what you think would be best..." she offered.

Mitch thought of the intimacy that came from sharing living quarters with someone, thought maybe it wasn't such a good idea, given what had happened the night before. Still, he decided he had little choice.

"What with the hours the boys and I keep, you might as well stay here," he said. "Are you sure this is what you want?"

"Yes."

"Anything else?"

"Rena. You can't give the boys to her, Mitch. And if you'll just think about it, you'll understand what she's offering isn't for their benefit. It's for hers. If she truly wanted to help you with the boys, she could do that without taking them away from you. She lives ten minutes from here. If she wanted to help, she could watch the boys whenever you needed her to. If she wanted to spend even more time with them, she could be their full-time babysitter. But you'd still be their father.

"She hasn't offered because that's not what she wants. She wants things on her terms or not at all. Please," she urged. "Think about it."

"I have thought about it," he admitted. "I don't know how everything got so crazy these past few months, but it's been as bad or worse as the first few months after Kelly died. It's like sinking into a hole and not being able to get a foothold anywhere so I can climb out. But I think I am coming out of it now."

Especially now that he had some time because she was here.

He owed her a debt he would never be able to repay. The least he could do was put her mind at ease on this issue.

"I'm not going to let Rena have the boys," he said, feeling so much better himself, now that he'd said the words.

"Really?"

"I don't know how I ever thought I could. They're..." He searched for the right phrasing. "They're everything good in my life."

She smiled at him then, and the expression absolutely transformed her face. What he'd always taken for plain and somewhat subdued became something else entirely. She was pretty, he realized, in that girl-next-door sort of way. She'd gotten some sun on her face today while playing with his sons. That, coupled with the smile, and she was absolutely glowing.

Leanne put her hand on his—a gesture that he would swear was purely impulsive. He didn't think she'd ever touched him before of her own volition.

"You'll let me stay? For a month?"

"I'd be grateful if you could. It would be such a relief to know that the boys are safe. And happy," he added. They'd seemed so happy with her earlier, so eager to tell him about their big day.

Leanne took a deep breath. "Good. I'm glad that's settled."

When she would have pulled her hand away from his, he stopped her by capturing it between the two of his. Much as he dreaded what he had to say, he didn't think they could ignore it altogether.

"We have to talk about last night." They were both adults, Mitch rationalized. They could talk about this.

"No," she said.

He saw she was immediately flustered. And embarrassed, if the color flooding her face was a reliable indication. He let go of her hand, then turned and put his back to her as he walked across the kitchen. Maybe this would be easier for both of them if he didn't have to look at her. His own embarrassment threatened to silence him. How could he explain?

"I don't want you to get the wrong impression," he began. "I don't want you to think Kelly meant so little to me that..." That he was out lusting after other women so soon after her death. "I haven't so much as kissed another woman since she died, Leanne. I swear to you, I haven't. I haven't wanted to. And last night...I don't think if I talked all night long I could explain what happened then."

"You don't have to explain anything to me, Mitch."

"I made you uncomfortable, and I'm sorry for that, especially because I invited you into my home and you're going to be taking care of the boys. I didn't want you to worry that anything like that would happen again."

"Oh, no. I wasn't thinking that at all."

She answered so quickly he was instantly relieved. "Good. I'm glad you're going to be staying."

With that, she murmured an excuse about being tired and fled up the stairs.

Glad to have that little jewel of a conversation over, Mitch sat downstairs in the dark for a long time, thinking about the day he'd had. Work had been fine. His head was where it needed to be because he trusted Leanne to take good care of the boys.

Coming home, seeing the boys so happy and excited, listening to them chatter on about their day, finding dinner cooking on the stove, having time to spend with them—it had been...nice, he realized.

He could get used to all this, he decided. Everything except the fact that it felt nice to have his hands on a woman again.

Leanne awoke the next morning to the sound of groans and shrieks of laughter, coming, she suspected, from Mitch's room. Squinting at the clock, she saw that it was a quarter after six. The boys must be up.

Leaning back against the pillows for a second, she took stock of all that had happened the day before. She was enchanted with the boys, had found her sister's dearest wish was for Leanne to come to terms with her family, and decided there was no place she could be right now other than Chicago.

And she'd convinced Mitch to let her stay.

It was the right thing to do. Leanne was sure of it. And she felt good waking up in this house to the sound of the boys' laughter, knowing that they had the entire day—no, a month of days—to play and explore and learn about one another.

Leanne wouldn't leave until Mitch had made whatever arrangements he needed to ensure that the boys would be safe and well taken care of. And maybe in that time, she would find her way back to her family.

Pulling in a deep breath and turning to see sunshine flowing through the window blinds, she realized she felt better this morning than she had in a long, long time. She was glad she wouldn't be spending this day alone with her camera and a pack of film, maybe with some wild animals and a few people who spoke only the most rudimentary English.

Grabbing her robe, she headed for the bathroom for a quick shower, then couldn't resist glancing into Mitch's room, where he and the boys were wrestling on the bed again. She saw a tangle of arms and legs and smiles. It took a few moments before any of them noticed her. Finally, Teddy did. He gave her one of his most precious and shy smiles, then muttered something she took to mean that he was wresting with "Tee" and his papa.

"I know." She smiled brightly at him. "It looks like fun."

Timmy saw her then and said something that sounded like "Oooh wettle?"

"What?" Leanne had a long way to go before she spoke their language.

"I think he wants to know if you'd like to wrestle with us this morning," Mitch said as he hauled his sons to his sides and held them still for a minute.

Leanne had been trying not to look at him, but he'd left her with no choice. She should have been better prepared this morning for what she'd find, but maybe there were no adequate preparations for the sight of Mitch McCarthy, his hair mussed, his jaw dark and rough looking, his torso shirtless so that every muscle in his chest and his arms was on display, as he sat in the middle of a rumpled bed.

Leanne felt as if she owed her sister an apology just for looking.

With a mumbled excuse, she left the doorway and went into the bathroom. She rushed into the shower, then dressed and went downstairs. There she found coffee waiting for her.

She hadn't expected the boys to pitch a fit when Mitch left for work. After all, they'd spent the entire day before with her, and they'd been quite happy. But still, they fussed and clung to their father as he made his way out the door.

Mitch swore that it was normal, that it took them time to get used to new people. He predicted they had another three or four days of this before the boys settled down.

Leanne wanted to cry with Timmy and Teddy, who sobbed as though their father were abandoning them to the worst of fates. "I thought you liked me," she said to them as she dried their tears. "I thought we had fun together yesterday."

Timmy looked sullen and said nothing. Teddy, his bottom lip sticking out and his eyes swimming in tears, looked more receptive to what she had to say.

"It looks like it's going to be a beautiful day. We could go to the park again, maybe with Hannah and Will," she suggested as she took them by the hand and led them into the kitchen so she could make them some breakfast. "You'd like that, wouldn't you?"

Teddy gave her his lost-puppy look. Timmy put on a big frown, one that seemed to say he was no pushover and he would not be comforted or bribed.

Leanne had an idea. "Hey, you know what? I need a camera." She'd been itching for one ever since she'd first seen the two of them together, and as unbelievable as it was, she'd been so upset when she'd left New York she hadn't packed a single camera. "Maybe we could go buy a camera, and you two could be my models. What do you think, Teddy? Want to be in my pictures?"

Teddy wasn't certain, but he had stopped crying so pitifully. Leanne thought she was making progress.

She chatted all through the breakfast preparations, handing them sip cups filled with juice, which they managed to sprinkle across the floor despite the tops specially made to prevent spills. Every time she turned her back, they turned the cups upside down and shook them until something came out. They thought they were fooling her, too. Giggling and smiling at each other, they delighted in their mischief making. Leanne let them have their fun because she realized she would do just about anything to see them happy.

They'd finished their breakfast of juice, toast and oatmeal and were just heading upstairs so she could dress them, when the doorbell rang. Odd, Leanne thought as she checked her watch. It was barely eight o'clock.

Bracing herself, afraid she was going to come face-to-face with Rena, she went to the door, with the boys trailing after her. There she found a middle-aged, no-nonsense-looking woman in a severely cut tweed suit.

"Is Mr. McCarthy in?" she inquired.

"No. He's already left for work," Leanne replied, feeling uneasy all of a sudden and gathering the boys closer to her. "Who are you?"

"Margaret Adams." She pulled some sort of identification from her purse and showed it to Leanne. "Children and Family Services. I'll need to come inside."

"What?" Leanne didn't remember stepping aside, but the next thing she knew Ms. Adams was standing on the threshold, taking stock of the room.

Children and Family Services? That sounded like some sort of social services agency, and the ID had been issued by the state of Illinois.

"Are you the new sitter?" Ms. Adams asked, eyeing the three of them, concentrating on Timmy's battered-looking face.

"No, I'm Leanne Hathaway, Mr. McCarthy's sister-in-law. What are you doing here?"

"I'm here on behalf of the state to evaluate the boys' living conditions."

With the boys huddled against her legs, Leanne managed to ask, "Why?"

"We've had a report that there may be some problems with the care the boys are receiving."

Leanne felt a chill envelop her entire body.

She knew what this woman was saying—she had come to see if this was a fit home for the boys. There was only one person who could have made this complaint about the boys' care.

"Rena sent you, didn't she?"

"I'm not at liberty to say who made the complaint, Ms. Hathaway."

"I know it was her. It's just like something she would do."

Ms. Adams stood her ground. "If you'd like to call Mr. McCarthy, I'll explain things to him."

This couldn't be happening, Leanne thought. This woman couldn't seriously imagine the boys were in any danger that necessitated the state stepping in.

But Rena lied so well. And she was so convincing. And ruthless. Rena could do it. Leanne was afraid her stepmother could do just about anything. She felt sick inside at the realization that Rena must want the boys desperately for her to sink to this level.

"Wee-Ann?" Teddy said as he tugged on her pant leg.

He looked a little weepy again and a little afraid. Leanne scooped him up into her arms because she wanted to hold him close right then. "It's all right, Teddy." She tried to soothe him, then reached for Timmy's hand. "Let's go into the kitchen."

She had to let go of Timmy's hand to pick up the phone. After consulting the list of numbers posted by the phone, Leanne dialed Mitch's number at work and waited for what seemed like forever for him to come on the line. The man who answered didn't want to put her through right away, but Leanne insisted, telling him it was an emergency.

She tried hard not to let her panic come through in her voice because she didn't want to frighten the boys any more than she already had. But when she heard Mitch's voice, she wanted to weep.

"It's Leanne," she said. "I think you'd better come home."

Chapter 7

Mitch made it to the house in fifteen minutes flat and barely managed not to take the steps at an all-out run and plow through the front door like a madman.

That kind of performance wouldn't win him any points with social services. Neither would flying off the handle, though he was sorely tempted.

Who in the hell did this woman think she was to imply that he wasn't fit to take care of his own sons?

Leanne was sure Rena was behind this, but Mitch found that difficult to believe. Of course, he found it hard to believe that anyone would sic social services on him.

He opened the door, trying hard not to slam it behind him. Leanne was on the rug in the corner, with the boys sitting solemnly beside her. Toys from the box beside them were scattered over the rug, but the boys weren't playing. They must have picked up on the tension in the room, because they looked a little scared.

Damn them, Mitch thought. These people had scared his sons.

"Hi, guys." He forced a big smile, then went down on his knees as the boys ran into his arms.

"Papa!" they shouted, their anxiety forgotten for a moment.

Mitch hugged them tight, but he was watching Leanne as she got to her feet and went to sit on the sofa. Mitch stood up, the boys in his arms, and went to sit beside her.

"Tell me again. Slowly this time," he said, seeing the strain of the morning showing in her paper-white face. She was wearing that look he'd always taken as a signal of a coldness that ran to the core of her. He wasn't fooled by it anymore.

"She just appeared up at the house, showed me some ID and said she'd come to evaluate the boys' living conditions, that there'd been some sort of complaint about the care they were receiving. And she wouldn't tell me any more. Then she started snooping around the house and asking questions."

"It's all right." He put his hand over hers for a second and found that she was cold to the touch. "You called me. That was the important thing."

"Can she do this? Just barge into the house and start snooping around?"

"I don't know, but I'm going to find out," Mitch said. He'd been working homicide for years, and the few times he'd had to call in social services it was usually to take children away because their parents had either been killed or arrested. He wasn't sure what the agency could do when the children's parents were very much alive.

"I was so upset and so shocked I didn't even try to stop her. Mitch, do you think I should have stopped her?"

"No. We'll let her look. After all, there's nothing for her to find."

Mitch hoped he was right about that.

Surely there was nothing for social services to be concerned about here. Surely they wouldn't try to take his sons away from him.

* * *

Ms. Adams was there for hours, taking all sorts of notes, asking Mitch all sorts of questions. She seemed particularly interested in the six nannies they'd gone through, in Timmy's injury and in Mitch's lack of a regular sitter for the boys.

He figured out right away that she was there to ask the questions, not to answer his. And with difficulty, he held his temper and answered them.

The worst of it was when Ms. Adams used his own words against him. He'd talked about being unable to properly care for the boys, hadn't he? He'd mentioned giving them up? Did he truly want them at all?

Once, on the job, Mitch had been stabbed with a switchblade. It hadn't hurt as much as hearing his own words come back to him this way.

After he finally showed Ms. Adams the door, he walked around the house and into the backyard. The boys were digging in that mud hole in the corner with their plastic shovels and rakes. They were giggling and covered from head to toe in mud, and Mitch thought they were the very picture of happiness.

Then Timmy turned his head, and Mitch caught sight of the bruised eye and the bandage, stark white against his son's little face. Had the accident truly been serious? Mitch told himself no, that nothing was going to come of this. But inside, he was shaking.

He had no idea what his rights were, but he had to find out. And then he had to find out who had done this to him. And why.

Mitch sat down on one of the patio chairs next to Leanne. "The woman's gone," he said.

"What did she say?"

"That she had a lot of people to speak to, and she'd be in touch."

"Mitch, what are you going to do?"

He glanced at his watch, saw that it was almost twelve-thirty. He had to be calm, he told himself. He could handle this if he kept his head. "I'm going to put the boys down for their nap and then I'm going to find a lawyer, someone who knows the social services system inside and out."

"Do you know someone like that?"

"No, but I'm sure I know someone who does."

It was one of the longest days of Mitch's life. And one of the worst. He waited for what seemed like forever to see a woman named Jane Gray, someone three different cops had said performed miracles in dealing with social services. A children's advocate and a crusader, she more often than not worked to get children removed from dangerous circumstances involving their parents or guardians. But she knew the system, and she was reputed to be a real barracuda when it came to fighting for what she believed was in the best interest of the child.

She had to believe it was in the best interests of his boys to remain with him before she'd agree to take on his case. That meant she wanted to talk to the social worker, read the report from the physician who had treated Timmy and speak with three or four of Mitch's friends and colleagues. Mitch admired her thoroughness and her ethics, but was impatient to get her on the case.

She did offer him a basic rundown of what social services could and couldn't do, and said that on the face of it, he shouldn't have anything to worry about.

So why was he so worried?

Heading home that night, he felt as if he'd been beaten to a pulp. Whatever was left in his stomach was churning around, and he was as weary as he'd been during those first mind-numbing weeks following Kelly's death.

"Mitch?" Leanne called as he closed and locked the front door behind him.

"It's me," he said, turning to find her standing on the landing of the steps. "The boys all right?"

She nodded. Walking down the remaining steps, she paused a good five feet away from him. "They were so cranky and out of sorts I put them down to sleep early. I just checked on them, and they're both out. Sorry. I knew you'd probably want to see them before they went to sleep, but I wasn't sure how long you'd be."

"That's fine. I'll catch them in the morning."

Mitch decided she looked as bewildered and as worried as he was, and he had a sudden urge to pour out all his troubles to her. It would be nice to have someone to talk to, someone who understood his problems, someone who loved the boys, as well.

Mitch didn't think he'd realized until this moment just how much he missed simply having someone to talk to after the boys went to bed at night.

"Did anything else happen here today?" he asked, bracing himself.

"Amy called. Rena told her about Timmy's accident, and she wanted to see how he was doing. She didn't mention anything about social services, and I didn't tell her. That was it. Will you tell me what you found out?"

"Sure," he said, wondering what she would do if he revealed how scared he was, if he asked if he could hold her for just a minute because sometimes he felt so alone he ached. He settled for saying, "Come and sit down."

She took the chair in the corner, and Mitch sat on the sofa. "I found a lawyer," he said. "A real tiger, I'm told. And she says if everything I told her about the situation is true, I shouldn't have anything to worry about. Social services barely has the time or the resources to go after the kids who are in serious danger, much less come after someone like me."

"But they did," Leanne said.

Mitch shook his head. "They're just checking out a complaint, which they're required by law to do. The whole thing should be dropped within a month. It's probably going to take that long to process the paperwork. At least, that's what my lawyer thinks."

"Do you believe her?"

Mitch took a deep breath and tried to figure out why nothing Jane had said made him feel any better. "I believe Jane told me the truth—that she doesn't think anything will come of this. But in my gut...I think there has to be something else going on here."

"It's Rena. Mitch, I know it is."

Mitch couldn't imagine that it had been anyone else. "Why would she do it, Leanne? If there's no way social services is going to take the boys away from me, what does she have to gain? Except to antagonize me."

"I don't know. I've never understood why she does the things she does."

Mitch looked at his sister-in-law, at the frightened expression in her eyes and the tense set of her shoulders. He remembered how she'd appeared her first day back, when she'd stared through the emergency room doors at Rena. Even though they hadn't been in the same room, Leanne had been so scared.

He wondered if that was the problem now, or if it was something else.

"You feel it, too?" Mitch asked.

"Feel what?"

Mitch let the words come tumbling out of him, hating to say them but needing to know whether it was just him, whether he was letting his imagination run away with him. "Sick inside?" he asked. "And scared? As if this is just the beginning of something terrible."

"Yes," she whispered, her eyes growing big and round with fear. "That's exactly how I feel."

Mitch caught her hand in his and held on tight to it. Surprised by his need to reach out and touch her, yet comforted by the contact, he just sat there and tried not to imagine his life without the boys.

It occurred to him that he was even more dependent upon Leanne now than before, that she had to stay until he found the right person to take care of the boys. And it scared him to be that dependent upon her, because she hadn't stayed in town for more than a few days in years.

"Leanne," he began, "with this threat, it's more important than ever that you remain here."

"I told you I would, and I will."

To be fair, Mitch felt he had to add, "I'll pay you for your time."

"No, you won't. I won't let you," she shot back, offended that he'd even offered. "Mitch, I'm family. Why is it that you always want to treat me as if I'm not?"

"Do I do that?"

"Yes."

"Look," Mitch said, "I know we've had our differences in the past…"

"Differences?" She stared him right in the eye. Clearly, she could think of other explanations that fit much better than his.

"Okay, more than differences," he allowed, backtracking, wondering why it was so very easy for him to argue with her. "I hated seeing how upset and how hurt Kelly was every time she talked about you. Every time you made one of those duty visits of yours."

"Duty visits?"

She uttered the words with great precision, appearing even more remote than before, and he decided she must have been either desperately angry or desperately hurt.

"What would you call them?" he asked. "You always looked as if you could hardly stand to be here."

She recoiled as if he'd slapped her, and Mitch felt like a heel. He honestly hadn't meant to hurt her. But he'd managed to cut through the facade. This awful expression of pain spread across her face.

"It wasn't that I didn't want to be here," she whispered.

"Then what was it?"

"I didn't feel comfortable here. I didn't feel I belonged."

Her voice broke on the last word. What could he say to

that? He was one of the people who'd helped her to feel that way. He hadn't wanted her in his house or anywhere near his wife.

Honestly, he hadn't given any thought to Leanne's feelings. He'd preferred to pretend she didn't have any. Of course, he couldn't do that anymore, not after what he'd seen from her in the past forty-eight hours.

"I don't know what to say," Mitch began, "except that I'm sorry. Obviously, I made it even more difficult for you to be here. And the only excuse I have is that I didn't want to see Kelly hurt."

"I never wanted to hurt her," Leanne said shakily.

"I know that now." Mitch thought about reaching for her, then remembered the trouble he'd gotten himself into the night before last, trying to comfort her. He couldn't do that again.

She blinked back tears and looked away. "I never wanted to hurt anyone."

"Leanne, how did your whole family end up in this shape? Do you want to tell me your side of the story?"

"It was Rena. Everything started with her. Do you think I wanted to leave my sisters and my brother like that? Do you think I honestly had a choice?"

"Everyone has choices," he insisted.

"I was eighteen years old, Mitch. Eighteen. And she didn't want me around anymore. My father could have stood up for me if he'd wanted to, but he was more concerned with Rena's happiness than mine."

"Why would she want you gone?"

"Because she saw me as a threat to her. She wanted Alex more than anyone else—I think because he was so young and she had a better chance of truly becoming a mother to him. But I believe she wanted Amy and Kelly, too."

"But not you."

"Rena wanted my place in Alex's, Amy's and Kelly's lives. With me gone, they had no choice but to turn to her.

Don't you see? Rena always gets what she wants. I couldn't compete with her, not when I was eighteen. And I shouldn't have been put in a position to have to compete for my own place in my family.

"They were my family, Mitch. They were everything I had, and she took them all away from me."

"What do you mean—she took them from you?"

"She told me Alex, Amy and Kelly didn't need me anymore, that they had her. And then she said that because I was almost eighteen, I couldn't expect my father to continue to support me much longer." Leanne was crying now. "Mitch, she told me there was no place for me any longer in my own house."

Mitch didn't say anything at first. He honestly didn't know what to say. Kelly's version of events had been quite different, although over the years she'd had her own conflicts with her stepmother.

Rena was no saint; all of them could agree on that. Kelly had trouble getting out from under her thumb, so Mitch agreed with Leanne that Rena had a tendency to want to control everyone and everything around her.

Kelly had said Rena was a serious, sometimes stern parent, that she made rules and expected her children to follow them, that she always had an opinion and never held back on expressing it.

But she'd taken on the responsibility of raising three children when she'd married Kelly's father, and Kelly had always believed Rena had done the best she could for them.

Of course, there was a fourth child—Leanne.

Mitch had never given Leanne a chance, never really gotten to know her as a grown woman. He'd known her before, from high school. If he tried very hard, he could almost remember seeing her in the hallways one day and noticing her watching him. He'd asked one of the guys he'd hung out with who she was and found out her name. And later someone told him about what had happened to her mom—a quick downward spiral with cancer. Someone else must have told Mitch Leanne had a younger brother and two sisters, that she didn't get out of the house much because she had to help take care of them.

He'd found it hard to believe that anyone his age had such responsibilities. It was one of the reasons that, when he got to know Kelly and she told him about her strained relationship with her elder sister, Mitch was so ready to believe Leanne had left because she'd wanted to.

Looking at her now, as she sat there seemingly broken-hearted and so lonely it made him ache for her, Mitch wasn't so sure.

"Kelly thought you wanted to leave," he said softly. "She thought you wanted to finally have a life of your own."

"That's what Rena told them," Leanne argued. "She couldn't very well say she was practically kicking me out of the house, especially not if she wanted to win them over."

"Leanne, I don't want to fight with you." He let himself put his hand over hers again, hoping to soften the words. "And I want to understand. Honestly, I do. Explain it to me so I can understand. Kelly said you always wanted to study photography, that getting into college was a dream come true."

"It was. I did want to go to school. I did want to have a life of my own. But I didn't want to give up my family. Rena didn't give me a choice. I could have gone to college here in Chicago and lived at home. But she didn't want me here."

"Kelly always felt that you'd abandoned her."

"I know." Leanne nodded. "I tried to come back at first. Strangest thing, there was money to pay some of my expenses and my dorm fees, but never enough to fly me home to visit. If I earned my own money for the ticket, it just wasn't the right time for a visit. Rena made me a stranger in my own home."

"I'm sorry," Mitch said. "We've had our differences with Rena, but I never thought she was evil."

"What she did to me was evil. And I think what she did today to you and the boys was evil. You need to understand that if you're going to be prepared to fight her."

"Fight her?"

"For the boys," she said. "Mitch, she wants them. And Rena gets what she wants."

He watched his sister-in-law, saw her fear, her sincerity. However outlandish this sounded, Leanne believed it with all her heart.

"She can't take them from me," Mitch insisted.

"I hope not," she said.

Leanne tried to stay calm the next morning, and when that didn't work she settled for staying busy. While the boys watched a movie on the VCR, she phoned her agent in New York to tell him she would definitely be taking the next four to five weeks off.

"Five weeks?" Marty roared. "Are you nuts?"

Leanne laughed, because he bellowed at everyone. "I'm not sure, Marty. Maybe you should send someone over to check on me."

"You never take time off," he reminded her.

"I know." Maybe that was why she needed it so desperately right now. "And I guess I should prepare you now, just in case."

"In case what?"

Closing her eyes, Leanne braced herself to say the words. "I'm not sure if I can go back to it."

"Back to what?"

"My life."

"Leanne, you're scaring me now."

She must have been, because Marty had stopped yelling. And she found herself pouring out her heart to him. "The idea of getting on a plane and taking off for some place I've never been, where I don't know anybody, staying there a couple of weeks and then heading out again...I don't want to do it anymore.''

"Look," he said, ready to indulge her now. "You're tired. That's all. You said it yourself—you never take any time off. So you just...rest. Put your feet up. Relax—"

The boys charged into the kitchen then, stomping their feet and chattering in the foreign language that was all their own. They were tugging at her jeans and demanding something.

"What was that?" Marty asked.

"My nephews," Leanne said, practically yelling at him now to be heard over the noise. "This is their idea of relaxing."

Marty swore. "They sound like a pack of wolves."

Leanne laughed again. "I know, but I love them. And they need me, Marty."

No one had needed her in a long time, and she found she missed that.

"I'll be in touch as soon as I know anything for certain," she said, then hung up before he could argue with her more.

She bent down on one knee so that she was at eye level with the boys, calmed them down, figured out that their movie had ended, that they wanted to go outside and they wanted something to eat. After putting them off on the trip outside to play, she fed them, instead, then made one more phone call. She would need clothes, now that she was staying a month or so, but she could buy those here. Her cameras were another matter altogether. Leanne called her friend Betsy in New York, who wasn't home. Betsy had a key to Leanne's apartment, and when she called back, Leanne would ask Betsy to pack her favorite cameras and ship them to Chicago.

Just because Leanne wasn't going to accept any assignments didn't mean she would stop taking pictures. It soothed her in a way nothing else did to view the world through a lens and calculate factors on light and film speed rather than face reality. It was her insulation from the real world, her way of looking at life instead of living it.

But that wasn't the issue now. She was simply itching to photograph the boys.

She wouldn't let herself think of taking their pictures because there would come a time when she wouldn't see them every day, when she had to remember them by the shots she took.

She couldn't imagine having to say goodbye to them, knowing she wouldn't see them again for months, couldn't imagine being content with the life she'd once led after having this time with the boys.

Two weeks later, if she had any doubts about her feelings for the boys, they were gone. She was hopelessly in love with Teddy and Timmy. Each day they did something new and totally endearing. She grew used to this demanding, hectic, wondrous life, and she didn't want to give it up.

Mitch was more relaxed than she'd ever seen him. And he was a wonderful father. The boys couldn't get enough of him. They climbed all over him from the minute he walked in the door at night until he put them down to bed.

Evenings were brief, but peaceful once the boys were asleep. Leanne usually managed to get out for a run then. She tried to have something on the stove and ready before she left. Mitch would bathe the boys and put them to bed, then the two of them would have a quiet dinner together.

They'd found a half-dozen or so noncontroversial topics of conversation, which usually carried them straight through dinner. And then Leanne would hide in her room and read. Or she could curl up on the sofa and listen to some music or rediscover American television, which she was never home to see.

They'd heard nothing from social services, and Mitch was starting to believe nothing would come of it. But Leanne was still uneasy.

She continued to worry about her family. She wanted to see her father, but couldn't seem to make the first move. Secretly, she hoped he might come see her, but so far, that hadn't happened.

She knew Amy had talked to Mitch on the phone, but she hadn't tried to talk to Leanne since that first call after Timmy's accident. Leanne was going to have to do something soon. She'd promised herself and Kelly that she would try.

Rena had been to the house once, thankfully while Leanne had been out shopping for some clothes to supplement the meager supply she'd brought with her. Mitch said she'd denied saying anything to Social Services, but he knew she was lying. She'd simply run through her usual arguments about why the boys should be with her. But Mitch had stood firm. He had no intention of giving them up now.

He was advertising for a full-time nanny, and Leanne felt sure he would find someone. Her agent called once a week and couldn't believe she was so happy living in suburbia, impersonating a housewife and mother. But she was.

She had to keep reminding herself that this wasn't her life. It was her sister's. From time to time, Leanne thought that maybe she might find a man, settle down and have children with him—as farfetched as that seemed, given the life she'd led.

More often than not, she simply fantasized about being able to go on living her sister's life. With her sister's husband and children.

Leanne couldn't have been more surprised when the doorbell rang one day and she found her baby brother on the doorstep.

"Alex." She froze, hanging on to the door as though it were her anchor. Then she wished she'd pulled him close for a big hug right away, because that's what she'd really wanted to do, and now it was too late for that impulsive gesture.

"Leanne," he said.

He looked as if he felt as surprised and every bit as awkward as she did. She just stared at him, trying to convince herself that this giant truly was her baby brother. He was well over six feet tall now. For years, he'd been all arms and legs, as awkward as a newborn colt, but at twenty-two he had finally filled out in all the right places. With his dark hair, dark eyes and beautiful smile, he was a very handsome young man.

Of course, she still saw him as he had been as a baby, or at the boys' age. It seemed like a lifetime ago, but he had been only a few months older than the boys when their mother had died.

Because he'd been so little and so lost, because he'd needed so much at that age, taking care of Alex had been the hardest thing Leanne had ever had to do. Because for years Leanne had been everything to him, leaving Alex had been the hardest of all.

She wondered now exactly what he remembered of her. After all, he'd been only eight years old when Leanne had left. She wanted to ask, wondered what in the world she might say to explain things to him.

Finally, Alex broke the silence between them. Tentatively, he inquired, "Can I come in?"

"Oh." She laughed nervously, then stepped back to let him pass. "Of course. I was just so surprised to see you."

"I had a long weekend off from school." At twenty-two, he was close to finishing his Ph.D. in Chemistry. "And I thought I might see Mitch and the boys."

"Of course," she said, turning away—she hoped in time that he didn't see the hurt on her face.

He hadn't come here to see her, even though she was certain Amy would have told him Leanne was in town.

"Mitch is at work," she told him. "And the boys are napping, but they should be up soon. Can you wait?"

He hesitated just a moment, then said, "Sure."

Leanne relaxed just a little. It was a start. "Have a seat.
I just made some coffee. Would you like some?"

"Sure."

When she came back from the kitchen, carrying two
steaming mugs, Alex was sitting in the chair in the corner.
Leanne handed him a mug, then took a seat on the sofa.

"How's school?" she asked, thinking she'd stick to safe
topics for a while.

"Almost over," he answered with a boyish smile.

And that topic of conversation seemed to have been exhausted. Leanne sipped her coffee and found her emotions
were threatening to choke her. If she explained herself to
him, would he listen? Did he care about her at all anymore? Had he missed her when she was gone?

"How's Timmy?" he inquired. "Rena said he took a
nasty spill."

"He bumped his head two weeks ago. Four stitches and
a black eye, but he's fine now."

"Really?"

"I'm sure Rena made it sound much worse."

Alex paused in the midst of taking a sip. Quietly, he put
down his mug. A dull flush crept into his cheeks—anger,
she suspected. Then he got to his feet.

"You know, I think it would be best if I came back
tonight to see the boys," he said.

Leanne got to her feet, as well. Wondering how she'd
totally destroyed this chance inside of two minutes, wondering how she'd lost so many opportunities like this over
the years, she grabbed him by the arm and said, "Alex,
please don't go. It's been so long since I've even talked
to you."

"And whose fault is that?" he asked.

"I don't know. Does it matter? Do we really have to
lay blame here? Or can we forget about that and try to talk
about what's important?"

He stiffened, standing even taller and more imposing
than before. He wouldn't meet her eyes.

"What do you think's important, Leanne? Why are you even here?"

"Amy called me. She said Mitch needed help."

"Mitch needed help months ago. He's needed help ever since Kelly died."

"I didn't know," she said defensively.

"Because you weren't here. You're never here, and you won't be here for long this time, either. So I really don't see the point in going into this."

"I'm here now. Alex, anytime you need me, I'll be here."

He gave a short, cynical laugh. "And I suppose, all these years you've been gone, that all we had to do was call and you'd have come running?"

"Yes, I would have."

"You've got to be kidding," he said, his eyes blazing with anger. "You couldn't even make it to your own sister's funeral."

His words cut like a knife, the wound deep and wide. Leanne recoiled from the pain and the anger behind the words.

This was how it was when she was home, she reminded herself. If she and her siblings ever had a conversation that went beyond the polite or the superficial issues, they ended up arguing.

And this was their trump card against her—that she wasn't there for them. Unsaid was the belief that she simply didn't care.

Normally, Leanne let it go unchallenged, because she didn't hold out much hope of changing anyone's mind about herself and her feelings. But she couldn't afford to do that anymore.

Kelly was gone, and Leanne would never have the chance to say these things to her sister. So she couldn't afford to pass up this chance to say what was in her heart to her brother.

"It wasn't that I didn't want to be here," she began,

hoping that this time she would find the right words to make him understand.

Later, once the boys had woken up, Alex had taken them to play in the backyard. After trying unsuccessfully to talk with her brother, Leanne had almost pulled herself back together again, when she heard the front door open, then close so hard it shook the whole house.

"Mitch?" she said, as she headed for the door and wondered what he was doing home so early. It wasn't even three-thirty yet.

When she walked into the living room, he was still standing by the door. Something in the way he held himself warned her before she ever saw that dazed look on his face. It reminded her of the day of Kelly's funeral, when she'd found him in the cemetery all alone after the service had ended. He'd looked so lost, so utterly hopeless and bitterly angry.

"What is it?" she asked. "What's wrong now?"

He stared at her as if he hadn't even seen her at first, as if he didn't believe anything his eyes told him. "Where are the boys?" he wanted to know, his voice rough and raw.

"Alex is here. He has them in the backyard." Wishing she had the right to touch him, to comfort him, she took two steps closer, then paused right in front of him. "Mitch? You're scaring me."

"I don't want the boys to see me right now, all right? I don't want to scare *them.*"

"Of course not," she said, reaching out to him, because she was the only one there and someone had to. She settled for putting a hand on his upper arm, then realized he was trembling.

"Rena..." He said the name like a curse, nearly choking on it.

Of course, Leanne thought. It had to be her stepmother. "What? What has she done now?"

"She wants the boys," Mitch said, as if the very words left a foul taste in his mouth.

"I know she wants them, but what has she done? Mitch?"

"This." He pulled a thick stack of folded papers from his jacket pocket and held the papers up for her to see. "This is what she's done, damn her. She's going to try to take them from me."

Chapter 8

Leanne remembered the room spinning drunkenly in a circle, remembered that suddenly it hurt to breathe.

And then she was in Mitch's arms.

He was so angry and so hurt. If she wasn't mistaken, he was also very scared, and seeing him that way seemed to shake something loose inside her. She was scared, too, maybe in the very same way she'd been years ago when she had realized the coldhearted woman her father was dating was going to be her stepmother, and that nothing would ever be the same again.

She remembered Alex at eight, defiant, angry and frightened as he refused to say goodbye to her. One day he'd clung to Leanne and begged her never to leave him, and the next he'd bottled everything inside and sworn to anyone who'd listen that he didn't care if she did leave, because he didn't need anyone.

Leanne had told herself that same thing for years. Of course it had been a lie, one for which she'd paid dearly because for so long she'd believed she could make it come true.

And now that she knew the lie for what it was, it might simply be too late for her. But not for the boys. She wouldn't let Rena rip the boys' family apart, just as she'd torn Leanne's in two.

"You can't let her do that," Leanne said again and again, the words muffled because her head was pressed against Mitch's shoulder. "You can't."

"I know," he said, holding her tightly.

"You have to stop her."

"I will. There has to be a way, and I'll find it."

"Oh, Mitch." Leanne hadn't felt this miserable since those awful days after Kelly had died.

She felt him shudder as he took a deep, slow breath, and she clung to him. He could fight Rena, she told herself. He was so strong and so sure of himself, and he was the boys' father. He had rights. This wasn't anything like what Leanne had faced.

So why did it feel just the same? Why was she every bit as terrified for Mitch and the boys as she had been for herself and her brother and sisters fourteen years ago?

Why did she feel like that frightened teenage girl again?

Pressing herself closer to the blessed warmth and solidness of the man who held her in his arms, Leanne told herself that everything was different now. She was older and stronger, more powerful, not wealthy but not without financial resources, either.

And Mitch would fight like the devil himself for his sons. Closing her eyes, she clung to him, hoping that some of his strength would seep into her, wishing she could stay right there until some of the fear left her, as well.

From behind her, a door slammed shut, and then she heard Alex's booming voice.

"What the hell is going on here?"

It was only when she realized how long it took to disentangle herself from Mitch that she understood how wrapped up in each other they must have been. She drew away slowly, lifting her head from his shoulder and finding his face so near hers. She blinked, as if she were in some sort of stupor and couldn't trust her vision. Mitch's arms, which had been wrapped snugly around her, withdrew, and judging from his expression, he was as bewildered by the embrace as she was.

All she knew was that for a minute, when she was scared half to death, he'd been the only solid thing in the world.

"Well?" Alex said, when neither of them answered his original question. "Is someone going to tell me what's going on?"

Mitch stepped back and leaned against the door. Leanne watched as his shoulders heaved with the effort he was making to breathe and perhaps to calm himself. Still looking right at her, he told Alex, "Your stepmother is suing me for custody of the boys."

"What?" Alex walked into the room, then into the hallway, where Mitch and Leanne stood. "You're kidding?"

"Do I look like I'm kidding?" Mitch said, his tone dead even now.

"No, but...I can't believe she'd do that," Alex said, defending her.

"You don't have to take my word for it." Mitch slapped the papers against Alex's chest, and Alex grabbed them. "Read this. And then tell me again what your stepmother would and wouldn't do."

Mitch turned to Leanne, then touched his hand to her elbow. "You okay?"

She wasn't. She was scared, and she wished he would hold her again for just a minute. But Leanne didn't think there was much chance of that, especially not with Alex looking on. He'd been shocked enough by what he'd already seen.

However, Leanne couldn't afford to be concerned about that right now. She turned to Mitch. "I'm all right."

"I want to see the boys," he said, then headed for the back door.

Alex stood in the living room, leafing through the legal papers. He waited until Mitch was out the door before he turned to Leanne. "How could she do this?" he asked. "How could she say Mitch is unfit to raise his own children?"

"That's what she's like, Alex. That's what I've been trying to tell you for so long, and you've never believed me. Rena will do anything and say anything to get what she wants. And she wants Teddy and Timmy, just as she wanted you so badly fourteen years ago."

"No. She's not perfect—I'll admit that. She's pushy and nosy and thinks she always knows what's best for everyone. But this..." He held up the papers. "Rena couldn't do this."

Leanne shook her head, wondering how he could be so blind to Rena's faults. "Alex, she's already done it."

Two hours later, Mitch was sitting in his attorney's office, waiting for her to read through the legal papers he'd been served with that afternoon. The instant Jane put down the papers, Mitch started firing off questions.

"Can she do this?"

"Can she sue you for custody? Yes." Jane held up a hand to silence him when he would have fired off another question. "Can she win? If everything you've told me about the situation is true, then I seriously doubt anyone's going to take your children away from you. You're their father."

"You *doubt* anyone could take them away?" Mitch repeated, feeling sick inside. "But you can't be sure?"

"Mitch, no one can ever say for certain what's going to happen in a courtroom, and any lawyer who promises you that he can is lying."

"If you're trying to reassure me, this isn't the way to do it."

"Mitch, I'm trying to be honest with you. And my honest opinion, the one based on all my years in the family court system, is that once this matter is resolved, your children will be with you."

"Your opinion..."

"That's all I can give you," she said more gently than before. "Now, you have some work to do. Who's taking care of your sons currently?"

"My sister-in-law."

"And how long will she be doing that?"

"She's been here for two weeks, and she's agreed to stay for two more, to give me time to find someone on a permanent basis."

"You have to do that—the sooner the better. You have to show that you can provide the boys with a stable home life."

Mitch wanted to ask how he was supposed to find this wondrous woman who was eager to take care of his boys, would work for what he could afford to pay, would never get sick, never move to another town, never have family responsibilities of her own that would take her away.

"This bit about the six nannies in..." Jane consulted her papers. "Sixteen months? Is that true?"

"Yes."

"That's not going to help us." She held up a hand to silence him when he would have jumped in. "It's by no means a fatal flaw in our case, but it's not good. Find someone to take care of your kids, someone who's mature and dependable and trustworthy. Keep in mind that if this thing actually goes to court, we'll more than likely put her on the stand."

"Okay."

"I looked over the report from the doctor who treated Timmy's cut, and no doubt your mother-in-law will use this to try to bolster her case. But the injury wasn't serious. We have that on our side. She'll argue that it wouldn't have happened if you'd had a proper caregiver for the boys. We've talked about that, and you're going to resolve it. One more thing,'' Jane put down the papers and looked him in the eye. "Did you really say that you didn't think you could take care of them on your own?''

"Yes,'' Mitch admitted.

"Did you say that you thought they might be better off with your in-laws?''

"Yes.''

"What about now? Do you believe that now?''

Mitch made a desperate grab for air, and it was all he could do to fill his lungs. His chest was so tight, the pressure staggering. How could he have done this? How could he have said those things?

"Everything was so crazy for a while,'' he began. "I was so upset about losing my wife, and I was angry. And I was scared. The boys...taking care of them is an overwhelming job.''

"I'm sure it is. Are you certain you want to do it?''

"Yes.'' With every ounce of strength he possessed, every bit of stubborn resolve, he would fight to keep them. With every speck of love left in his body, he would cherish them and protect them.

"Are you certain you *can* do it? It's an awfully big job for one person.''

"How can I *not?*'' he asked. "They're my children, and I love them more than anything in this world.''

"I'm glad to hear it, but it takes a lot more than love to raise a child. It's hard work, day after day, year after year. It's more of a commitment than some people can make.''

"I'm committed,'' he said.

"All right. Then you need to promise me something.''

"Anything.''

"Don't ever tell anyone again that you think your sons might be better off with someone else. Because I can assure you, those words are going to come back to haunt you in court.''

Mitch felt the pressure sinking onto his chest once again. His own words? He closed his eyes, silently cursing himself and thinking that he'd failed his wife and his sons. And he didn't know how to make this better.

"There has to be something we can do," he began. "Something to guarantee that Rena won't get the boys."

Jane shook her head. "I'm sorry. No guarantees. Not in court."

"There's nothing I can do now?"

She shrugged, then shook her head once again. "You're a single father with a dangerous and demanding job and two little boys. They're almost still babies. That's tough, and as unfair as it is to you, there are still people in this world who think that more than anything else, babies need to be with their mothers."

"Their mother is dead," Mitch said.

"And now your mother-in-law wants to be the boys' mother."

"You mean if I could give them a mother, I'd win."

Jane sat back and cocked one eyebrow at him, clearly interested now. "You're thinking about getting married again?"

Mitch wasn't quite sure how they'd reached this particular point in the conversation, but he wanted to know her answer, so he nodded.

"Oh."

She looked pleased and relieved.

"That would be as close to a guarantee as I could give you. I can't imagine a judge in these circumstances taking two little boys away from their biological father and his wife."

Wife?

That word kept running through Mitch's head as he drove home from the lawyer's office. At least, he'd intended to drive home. The car seemed to have a mind of its own, and it headed for the cemetery.

After cutting the engine, he walked through the falling leaves to a spot under a huge oak tree. His wife's grave.

Wife.

To him, that meant Kelly. He'd never imagined allowing another woman to take the place in his life that she held. Except, she wasn't alive anymore. That place in his heart was horribly empty. Like an old injury, it ached and ached, sometimes pulsating with the pain. And other times, the pain sneaked up on him, catching him totally unaware. It was like walking into a wall. Like flying into one. He just crashed and burned.

Standing there, staring at his wife's name etched into the stone, he cried out to her silently, but she didn't answer. He had been in a panic all day because she wouldn't answer him the way she used to. She was slipping away from him.

Because the time was passing? Or because his own memories were dimming? Maybe because she'd done all she could to help him through this.

Eventually, Mitch knew he would have to make it on his own, without her voice inside his head or that subtle hint of her perfume or the smile on the photograph that for an instant had seemed so real.

Kelly, please. One last time, tell me what to do. For the boys.

He closed his eyes, ready to shake his fists at the clear, blue sky, to scream in a rage, anything to get some sort of a response. He simply couldn't believe his wife was gone so completely from him, especially not now when he needed her the most.

In his head, Mitch heard the lawyer's words again. *As close to a guarantee as I can give you.*

Wife.

Not that, he begged. *Kelly, How can I do that?*

For the boys. She threw his own words back at him, in his own voice, inside his head, until he thought that maybe he was crazy. *For the boys.*

Mitch felt the wind pick up abruptly and turned his face into the breeze, which was unseasonably warm. The leaves skidded and scraped along the road to his right and rattled in the trees.

Opening his eyes, he saw a woman walking toward him from the shadow of the big tree to his right. Her hair was loose and flying around her face, which he couldn't see at first. But the way she moved, that slow, loose sway of her hips, and the way she held her head—all that was familiar to him. And he thought for a moment there had been some horrible mistake sixteen months ago, that maybe his wife wasn't buried in the cold ground.

And then the woman came out of the shadows. He saw that she was taller than his wife, thinner, a few years older, and looking sadder than Kelly ever had.

"Mitch?" Leanne said, pausing a good five feet away and staring at him.

He thought he would feel devastated, that he'd feel Kelly's loss all over again. But he felt curiously at peace, as if someone had taken that empty ache inside him and simply drained it of the pain and the anger.

Could it be this simple? he wondered. Could he beg his wife for help and have it delivered in an instant, have the answer left standing in front of him?

Or was this nothing but one of those strange coincidences latched onto by the people who were too scared to accept the idea that we were on this earth all alone, that there was no one anywhere else who could help us?

Mitch used to believe that—that it was every man for himself. If he couldn't help himself, he was out of luck.

He didn't anymore. He'd sat up on dozens of lonely nights talking to his wife. He'd asked her for a lot of things, and somehow he'd always gotten what he'd needed after those one-sided conversations. And they hadn't always felt like one-sided exchanges.

But this...he'd never seen his answer so clearly, so quickly.

"Mitch," Leanne said again. "What is it?"

"You surprised me," he said, unable to stop staring at her, then found himself telling her, "you know, in all these years, I've never seen that much of a resemblance between you and Kelly."

"And you did just now?"

He nodded, wondering how he was ever going to convince her to go along with his plan.

"I can leave if you want to be alone. I can walk around the cemetery and come back in a few minutes."

"No, it's all right. I've been here awhile." He had one nagging question for her before they got down to business. "What are you doing here now?"

"Ginny's with the boys," she said quickly. "So you don't have to worry about them."

"I don't. Not when I leave them with you." Mitch took a step closer, because he felt drawn to her in some way he didn't understand. And he remembered coming home this afternoon, how scared he'd been, how the two of them had ended up clinging to each other, sharing their shock and their fear.

It had felt so natural to haul her into his arms that way, felt so much better to have someone beside him who was feeling the same thing he was. Even if it was stark terror, he wasn't alone in it.

"Why did you come here?" he repeated, although he suspected he already knew.

Leanne shrugged and smiled a little. "You'll think I'm crazy, because it was the oddest thing."

"No," he reassured her. "I won't."

"I'd been avoiding this place ever since I got back. And then this afternoon, this feeling came over me...." She shook her head and looked every bit as bewildered as he felt. "I just knew it was time, that it was okay to be here now, that I could handle it without falling apart. In fact, it felt like I had to be here now. And then out of the blue,

Ginny showed up and offered to take the boys. So I came.''

And then Mitch knew with a certainty that this was one of those life-altering moments, that nothing would ever be the same again after today.

He was certain that he'd felt his wife's presence for the last time, that she truly had done all she could. He had feared this day, had somehow known it was coming. But he didn't feel the devastation he'd expected as she slipped away from him for the last time.

There was sadness, of course. But he knew it was time to let her go.

Life seemed to have tangled him up inside itself again, and there were things he had to do. He had two little boys to take care of. For the first time in a long time, Mitch felt he knew how to do that, knew that he hadn't been given some impossible job.

He could do anything for his sons. He wondered what Leanne was willing to do for the sake of his boys.

"I know I shouldn't ask you this," Leanne began. "You're the last person I want to ask, but I need to know."

"You can ask me anything," he said. After all, *he* was getting ready to ask a monumental favor of *her*.

"Even about Kelly's death?"

"I can talk about it," he said, realizing now that he could. "What do you want to know?"

"It sounds so silly, but...I want to know that it didn't hurt her. That she wasn't scared. Or alone." Tears filled her eyes and she looked away. "I'm sorry, Mitch. They're terrible questions, I know."

"No, they're not."

"When Amy told me, I was so shocked I hardly said a word. And it was only later that I kept wondering what the end was like for her. It was so sudden, so unexpected...."

"No. She knew it was coming. I don't know how she knew. But I believe she did, because of the things she said.

The letter she wrote you, for one thing. The time she spent pestering me about making a will and naming a guardian for the boys. Those last few weeks of her pregnancy she spent hours putting together memory books for the boys. A family history, she called it. Photographs of the two of us, of you and Alex and Amy. Your parents. My parents. The houses where we lived. Everything. And she wrote pages and pages in her dairy, all things she imagined the boys would need to know someday, as if she knew she wouldn't be around to tell them. She talked a lot about your mother, too. How she wished she'd had something like this so she could remember her more clearly.''

"I didn't know,'' Leanne said.

"And I should have told you. Leanne, she was happy. So many times those last few weeks, she made a point of telling me. She was happier than she'd ever been. She thought she was the luckiest woman alive. And after the boys were born, she just sat in her room and held on to them. The nurses kidded her about not wanting to give them up for a moment.''

Mitch could see her so clearly, glowing with happiness and pride as she cradled a baby in each of her arms. "I camped out in a chair by her bed at the hospital, and we talked about so many things. When she was gone I was so angry, because, like you, I had so many things I wish I'd said to her. But she got to say all those things, and she was happy.''

He took a breath and told himself to go on, to finish it. "It happened on the second day, when we were waiting to see if she and the boys were ready to go home. The nurse came and took the boys so the pediatrician could check them. Kelly kissed them goodbye and then she pulled me over to the bed so I could sit beside her. And I held her in my arms and said I loved her. She told me it was the best day she'd ever had. Then she fell asleep in my arms. I held her for a long time, and then I sat down in that chair and held on to her hand. I fell asleep, too, and when I woke up, she was gone. Just like that."

Mitch swiped at the single tear rolling down his cheek. "Why?"

"It was a blood clot. The doctor said sometimes a bit of the placenta can get into a woman's blood stream, and from there into her heart or her lungs.... It's rare. Incredibly rare. But it happens."

"I'm sorry," Leanne said. "I shouldn't have made you go through that with me."

"No, it's okay. It helps to remind me that she was happy at the end, that she believed she had the best of everything. How many people can say that about their lives?" Mitch was finding it easier all the time to remember the good moments, to let go of the bad.

"You still talk to her, don't you?"

"Yes," he admitted.

"I heard your voice when I walked over here. That's what you were doing?"

Mitch nodded. "Do you think I'm crazy?"

"No. I talk to her, too."

Mitch was surprised at that, though he supposed he shouldn't be. Leanne had loved Kelly, also.

"Does she answer you?" Leanne asked.

"Not in so many words. But she does answer." Mitch waited for her to scoff, but she didn't. "You don't think that makes me a little crazy? That I believe Kelly listens to me and helps me?"

"I'd like to believe that she could still help us, that she exists somewhere and that she's okay." Leanne looked at him through eyes heavy with tears. "Mitch, do you believe she's okay? Do you believe she's happy where she is? Is that possible, when she can't be with you and the boys?"

Mitch reached for Leanne's hand and held it. "Kelly's just fine. I know it."

"How do you know?"

"Because I can still feel her presence sometimes, and I

can tell that she's just fine. If she's worried about anything, it's me and the boys. And you," he added. "I'll bet she worries about you, too. I know she wanted you to be happy."

Leanne squeezed his hand tight. "Ginny told me that she spoke to Kelly a few months before the boys were born. Kelly talked about how much she wanted to see our family come together again. For us to put the past behind and make peace with one another."

"She did," Mitch said. "We talked about it, too."

Leanne looked utterly lost. "I don't know how to do that, Mitch. I keep thinking, if only she were here, maybe she could show me, because I don't know if I can do that on my own."

"I'll help you," he offered.

"You will?" She was surprised.

Mitch nodded.

Leanne stood absolutely still and wondered just what she was seeing in those beautiful eyes of his, wondered why she felt so much better just because he was holding her hand.

Mitch was different in some way she couldn't begin to explain. He seemed so calm, so sure of himself, whereas this afternoon he'd been as shaken up as she had been at the prospect of Rena's trying to take the boys. And then Leanne thought she might have figured it out.

"You talked to the lawyer?" she asked.

"Yes."

"Good news?"

"No guarantees," Mitch hedged. "But I think I found a way out, a way to keep the boys. And that's the most important thing to me."

"I know."

"It's important to you, too, isn't it?"

"Yes. I don't know if I can explain to you how much that means to me. But ever since you told me about the lawsuit, I've been reminded so clearly of how I felt when

I lost Kelly and Alex and Amy. I couldn't stand to see Rena do to you and the boys what she did to me and my family."

"I won't let her," Mitch said. "But I need your help."

"Of course," she replied. "I'll do anything I can."

"You mean that?"

"Yes."

"Good. Leanne, this is going to sound crazy. At least, it will at first. But hear me out, okay?"

She nodded, and then she started to get scared. Mitch looked so intense, and there was so very much at stake.

"My lawyer said there are no guarantees, that there never are in court. She said one of the biggest strikes against me is the fact that the boys have been bounced around so much from sitter to sitter."

"But you're going to find someone. I won't leave until you do."

"The second problem," he continued, "is that there's still a bias in this country against fathers having sole custody, especially of very young children. Lots of people still believe the little ones need a mother more than anything else."

"You can't let Rena be their mother," she said.

"No, I can't. But *you* can be their mother."

"Me?" She didn't understand any of this.

"You love the boys?" he asked.

"Yes."

"And you said you'd do anything for them. You said that before you'd let me give them to Rena, you'd take them yourself."

"I would," she confirmed. "But...you're not going to give them up, are you?"

"No. I was hoping we could share them for a while."

Share? "As in joint custody?"

"No, as in a family. You, me and the boys. Temporarily, of course," he added. "You understand that we'd have to be married."

"Married?"

"It's extreme, I know. But effective. My lawyer said this is the closest thing to a guarantee that she could give me, that in this case, she can't imagine a judge taking two little boys away from their biological father and his wife."

"I don't know what to say," she responded, dumb-founded. "You want me to be your wife? Until the custody issue is settled?"

"Probably a little longer than that. I wouldn't want to get dragged right back into court when Rena found out this marriage wasn't real. Maybe for a year? You'd have to be here in Chicago, and I don't know what that would do to your career...."

"We don't need to worry about my career right now." She knew now that whatever satisfaction she'd gotten out of traipsing all over the world was long gone. She simply didn't want to do it anymore. Instead, she was thinking about the boys, about how she would feel if they were hers and if Mitch truly was her husband.

She was thinking about stepping into her sister's life and having everything her sister had ever had, everything her sister had lost.

It seemed a terrible thing to want, a selfish thing to do.

But she wanted the boys. She wanted this life. And Mitch? Well, they certainly weren't talking about a real marriage here. But still...to live with him for an entire year. To wake up in the same house, to see him half-naked as he wrestled with the boys on his rumpled bed every morning. To share a late supper with him or sit quietly on the sunporch with him in the mornings if they ever managed to get up before the boys. To watch the boys grow and change and to see them happy and secure in the home she and Mitch could provide.

These were dangerous dreams for a woman to have, particularly one who'd seen firsthand how very much Mitch McCarthy had loved his wife.

To him, Kelly would always be his wife. Leanne would

be the woman who had agreed to help him for the sake of the boys.

She could get her heart broken all over again, this time even worse than before. The first time, when she'd lost her family, she hadn't known how vulnerable she was, how dangerous a position she was in.

This time she knew. This time it might well kill her to give up the boys when this was over. Still, for herself, she wasn't sure she could resist. And for the boys, she didn't see how she could refuse.

"I don't know what to say, Mitch."

"Say you'll think about it."

"Can you do this?" she asked, glancing back at her sister's grave. It seemed so odd to her that they were talking about becoming man and wife here at her sister's grave. "I know how much you loved Kelly," she added. How much he loved her still.

"I would do anything to make sure the boys stay with me, and I know Kelly would understand that."

"You're right. She would. But...oh, God, what would everyone else think? They'd be shocked." And outraged, she suspected, remembering Alex's face when he'd walked into the house this afternoon and found Leanne in Mitch's arms. "If they ever thought there was anything between us..."

It was too odd even to think about. There could never be anything between her and Mitch. She was fooling herself imagining such a thing.

"I don't know what we'll tell them. Or what we can allow ourselves to tell them," Mitch said. "I don't know who's on Rena's side and who's on mine. And I don't think we can afford to trust anyone here with the truth. At least not right away."

"So we would try to convince everyone that this marriage is real?"

"I suppose we'd have to."

"Oh, Mitch. We could never make anyone believe

that.'' It was ludicrous even to think that they could. ''Everyone would feel we were dishonoring Kelly's memory for even considering marrying each other.''

''It would make things more difficult for you with Amy and Alex. I hadn't thought about that.''

Leanne shrugged helplessly, wondering if she'd ever really had a chance where her siblings were concerned. ''I don't know if we can let that play a great part in our decision. After all, it's not as though I'm on the verge of a breakthrough with either one of them.''

''Still, I'd hate to add to the tension between you.''

She brushed off his concern. ''Really, it's not—''

Mitch turned to her, stopping only when they were practically nose to nose. ''Don't say it's not important to you, because I know it is.''

She stepped back to give herself time to breathe. ''It's not my main concern right now. It can't be. Alex and Amy and I have been living like this for years. We can go on this way for a while longer.'' She searched her heart for her bottom line. ''I want to help you. I made a promise to Kelly and to you that I would do anything I could to help with the boys, and I meant it.''

Of course, she'd never thought helping with the boys would extend to anything like this.

''So,'' he said, ''you'll do it? You'll marry me?''

Leanne looked over at the headstone, with the pretty vines carved into it and her sister's name in a fancy script. She ached for her sister right then and for Mitch and the boys.

There were so few things she could do for her sister now.

''Yes. I'll do it,'' she said, turning her face into the warm, springlike breeze that seemed to come out of nowhere.

Chapter 9

Still drowsy, her head aching, her lids heavy, Leanne awoke to the feeling that someone was watching her. Opening her eyes, she saw not one, but two someones. Two miniature someones grinning mischievously at her and giggling.

"Up," Teddy said.

He was holding out his arms to her, and she rolled over to the side of the bed and lifted him up.

Timmy, who was more industrious, got a handhold on her covers, a foothold on the edge of the box springs and managed to hoist himself up.

"Up!" he said, delighted with his climbing ability.

Teddy, still warm and limp from sleep himself, crawled under the covers and huddled against her, while Timmy went to the headboard, hung on to it and started bouncing and babbling.

Looking at the clock, Leanne saw that it was after seven—amazingly late for the McCarthy household to be rising. "What's the matter, guys?" she teased. "Getting lazy in your old age?"

"Wayzee?" Teddy said, grinning and giving Leanne a big, wet, sloppy kiss.

She laughed because he was so cute and she was so in love with him and his wild man of a brother. Giving Teddy a quick kiss, then pushing her hair back from her face, she glanced toward the doorway and found Mitch there, watching as the three of them eased into the day.

"Your alarm clock didn't go off, either?" he asked, referring to the twins.

She managed a smile—barely. He was dressed, shaved, his hair smoothed down but still wet, and she was in her pajamas. They would have a lot of mornings like this if they were going to be married, and Leanne was looking forward to them, even if she was scared by all that lay ahead.

"I brought you coffee." Mitch set a steaming mug down on the nightstand, then grabbed a bouncing Timmy off the bed and hauled the boy against his chest.

"Coffee in bed?" Leanne grabbed it and took a long drink, not caring how hot it was. She needed something to jolt her awake this morning. "What service."

"Only for wives-to-be."

That woke her up. Instantly. "I guess that whole conversation was real."

Mitch nodded. "Second thoughts already?"

"I guess that means you haven't changed your mind," she said warily.

"Not a chance. You?"

She shook her head. "Just nervous. Mitch, how are we going to pull this off? How are we going to tell people? How will we explain?"

"They're going to be surprised, no matter how we break it to them. And I'm hoping we get away without offering a lot of explanations. We're both adults. We're free to do anything we want, and we don't have to justify our actions to anybody.''

''You honestly think we're going to brazen our way through this?''

He took a breath, then let it out slowly. ''I don't think many people will be rude enough to ask why we're getting married. And the ones who do ask can't make us tell them anything. It's not as if they're going to lock us in a room and interrogate us until we confess.''

''People are going to be angry.'' Alex and Amy for sure, Leanne thought as she hugged Teddy to her.

''They'll calm down eventually. This custody thing can't last forever. And when it's over, we'll explain. Alex and Amy will understand.''

''I want to believe that.''

''And you'll have a year here. Amy drops by to see the boys all the time, and Alex gets home five or six weekends a year. You'll have a lot of time to patch things up with your brother and sister.''

''I hope so,'' Leanne said, then thought of the hardest part of this whole thing—telling her stepmother. ''Rena's going to be furious. You know she'll see right through this.''

''What can she do? She can't stop us, and she can't prove this isn't a real marriage.''

Mitch sat down on the bed and ruffled Teddy's hair. Leanne's breath caught in her throat as he pushed a stray curl of hers to the side of her face and tucked it behind her ear, his hand lingering there.

''You need to understand something,'' he said. ''I take care of my family. And you're family now.''

Emotions swelled inside her, crowding in somewhere at the base of her throat and making speech nearly impossible.

''What is it?'' Mitch asked, his hand at her chin, tilting her face up to his.

Leanne twisted her face away and blinked back her tears.

I take care of my family.

Mitch had no idea how sweet those words were to her. Certainly, he had no idea what he was giving her by asking her to be his wife, even if it was only for a year.

She intended to make the most of the time she had here.

"Leanne?"

He sounded concerned.

"Tell me what I said to upset you."

"It's been a long time since I felt I belonged anywhere," she answered, her voice strained even to her own ears.

One of his hands covered hers, his touch warm and soothing.

"All of that's about to change," he promised.

And she wanted to believe him so badly she ached with the desire.

"Now, you need to get moving if you're going to grab a shower before I leave." Mitch held out a hand for Teddy, and Leanne lifted him into Mitch's arms. With a boy under each arm, he turned to go, then faced her again as he stood in the doorway. "Everything's going to be all right."

Leanne scrambled to find her clothes, showered, dressed hastily, then was about to make her way downstairs, when she walked past Mitch's bedroom. Next thing she knew, she was standing in the doorway, looking inside.

She was scared, she realized. There were other emotions, as well, but fear was the dominant one. Everywhere she turned, her gaze landed on her sister's face. There was a snapshot tucked into the side of the mirror on the dresser of Kelly and the boys in the hospital, a small ceramic frame on the desk in the corner with a shot of Kelly pregnant, Kelly and Mitch's wedding picture hanging on the wall.

Unable to help herself, Leanne walked into the room and picked up the photograph of Kelly in the silver frame that sat on the bedside table and started babbling to her sister. She told Kelly the boys were fine—that they were wonderful, in fact—that she would love them with all her heart and do whatever was necessary to protect them.

And then it came time to tell Kelly about Mitch.

Leanne couldn't get the words out—she couldn't articulate her feelings for her sister's husband. Going weak at the knees, she sat down on the bed—Kelly's bed—and waited, feeling miserable and torn as she'd never been before.

She had feelings for Mitch. There had always been that attraction, based on nothing more than the fact that Leanne loved the way he looked. And as she'd seen him together with Kelly, as she'd seen the way he mourned her and the way he now took care of the boys, Leanne had come to admire him, too.

He'd been so kind to her lately and concerned about her, and she was afraid her feelings were going to grow into something else, something hopelessly complicated and guilt ridden.

Yet she couldn't walk away. Mitch and the boys needed her.

So Leanne sat on the bed, staring at her sister's picture, waiting for something. A vision? A voice coming out of nowhere? A mere feeling that she wasn't alone in that room?

Honestly, she had no idea. She just needed to know that marrying Mitch was the right thing to do. And she got nothing. The longer she sat there, the more alone she felt.

Frustrated and uncertain what to do next, she looked down at the bed, then looked away. And that's when she saw Mitch standing there, watching her.

"I'm sorry." She jumped up off the bed and nearly dropped the picture. Mitch took it out of her hands and placed it safely on the nightstand. "I know I shouldn't be in here."

"It's all right," he said, looking around himself. "I

guess I'll have to make some changes in this room. In case anyone's in here, I can't have them seeing three photographs of Kelly in this bedroom after you and I are married.''

The thought of taking down Kelly's photographs made Leanne incredibly sad. Sitting back down on the bed, she said, ''I was talking to her.''

''And?''

Mitch put a hand on her shoulder, and he was close enough that Leanne found herself leaning against him, her face buried in his side. He was so warm and solid. His hand settled in her hair, holding her face to him.

To be this close to him felt as good as she remembered. And that hit at the heart of the problem that had sent her into the bedroom.

''How do you know this is the right thing to do?'' she asked. ''How do you know Kelly would understand?''

Mitch's hand was still in her hair, which was wet from her shower. He stroked it slowly, soothingly, and she leaned into his touch, wishing this moment would never end. If she could just stay there for a while, feel his hand in her hair and hear that strong, deep voice of his calming her, she would be all right. Maybe everything would.

''Leanne, I was so scared yesterday. I thought Rena really might take the boys away from me, and I begged Kelly to help me, to show me the right thing to do. And when I turned around you were there.''

Leanne pulled away far enough that she could see him. ''At the cemetery yesterday?''

''She sent you to me,'' he said. ''It's the clearest answer to a prayer I've ever been given.''

Leanne gave him a little smile. ''I don't think I've ever been the answer to anyone's prayers.''

Mitch sat down on the bed beside her, his face so close she could see the little lines at the corners of his eyes, the ones that wrinkled when he smiled.

"It's the right thing to do," he said. "Will you trust me to know that?"

"I suppose I'll have to, because I'm not sure of anything right now."

"Then trust me. And try to stop worrying so much." He took her hand. "We're in this together now."

Before Leanne could say another word, there was a great commotion in the hallway. Then the boys came flying into the room. Chattering excitedly, they raised their hands to Mitch, each twin wanting to be held and probably to get up on the bed and play.

"Oh, God. You climbed the steps?" He was asking them to tell him it wasn't true, when it obviously was. Turning to Leanne, he said, "I forgot to put the gate up."

The boys just giggled, plainly proud of themselves.

"Monkeys!" Mitch said.

He grabbed them both and threw them onto the bed, making them shriek with delight. The boys bounced back quickly, attacking Mitch in what disintegrated into an all-out tickling war, and before Leanne could get away, Mitch snagged her, too.

"What do you say, boys?" he asked once he had her pinned to the bed. "Should we let her get away?"

In answer, Timmy took a flying leap at her, but Mitch saved Leanne from the worst of the blow. Timmy giggled and wriggled around until he got away from his father and could get to Leanne. Sitting on her stomach, he tickled her sides and howled like a wild man. Teddy did his part, as well, and by the time she escaped, Leanne was laughing, too. Pulling back, she watched the three of them play for a few minutes, and for the first time, she felt a part of the family, as if she belonged.

And she found that she wanted desperately to belong.

Leanne was just thinking about starting dinner around six o'clock, when the doorbell rang. Mitch was still at work, and the boys were so full of energy they were practically bouncing off the walls. Like a pack of wild dogs, they charged the door and stood there, yelping and dancing around until Leanne came to open it.

"Shh," she said. "You'll scare our company away."

She pulled open the door and found Ginny there. "Hi."

"Hi. I've come to kidnap your children. Mitch's orders."

"What? Is anything wrong?"

"Not a thing. We're having a party, and Mitch asked if I could give you some peace and quiet so you could get ready."

"Party?"

"Okay, a cookout. That's about as fancy as entertaining gets at our house these days."

"You're going to get ready to throw a party, plus watch your two kids and the boys?"

"I am ready for the party, and I want you to have some time to get dressed. I think it's going to be a very special night."

"What's the occasion?"

"I'm not sure. Marc wouldn't tell me, and it's killing me. But I guess I can last another hour until I find out what's going on. I had instructions to thaw some steaks, toss a salad and get the twins. Marc is bringing home some beer and some champagne. Now, why would we need champagne?"

Leanne felt the blood draining from her head, leaving her a little dizzy. He wouldn't! She closed her eyes and reassured herself that surely Mitch wouldn't tell anyone they were getting married without talking to her about it first.

"You know something." Ginny smiled as if she might have a secret herself. "And so does Marc, that rat. Tell me."

Leanne paled. "I have to talk to Mitch."

"And then you talk to me," Ginny said, taking the boys by the hands. "Come on, guys. Hannah and Will are in the backyard with their cousins, and they've found a worm. Maybe if you're lucky, it's still alive and you can watch it wiggle across the rock.''

Turning back to Leanne, she said, ''Forty-five minutes, okay?''

In a panic, Leanne thought about confiding everything to Ginny. But before she got the words out, Ginny and the boys were headed across the street.

Mitch wouldn't do it this way, Leanne told herself again. But just as Ginny and the boys reached the other side of the street, Ginny turned and shouted, ''I forgot. Amy and Alex are coming. See you soon.''

''Oh, no.'' Leanne clung to the door and watched them go.

This was it. She would have to face her brother and sister as they heard the news that she was marrying Mitch.

Walking into Ginny and Marc's house that night was one of the hardest things she'd ever done.

''Perfect timing,'' Ginny said as she pulled Leanne inside. ''They were just getting ready to tell me what's going on.''

She motioned toward the two men huddled together in the living room. Mitch was standing with his back to the fireplace; Marc Dalton was in front of him.

Marc, a tall, dark-haired man with the shoulders of a football player, walked over to Leanne and kissed her on the cheek. ''Hi,'' he said.

She took that to mean Marc understood what she and Mitch were about to do, that he was offering his support. ''Hi, Marc.''

Then he slipped his arm around his wife's waist and turned her toward the kitchen. ''Sweetheart, I think these two need a moment alone. Let's find the rug rats, and I'll tell you what's going on.''

Leanne stood frozen to her spot by the door, not sure if she was going to tell Mitch how angry she was at him for springing this on her or if she was going to go straight to the important part—begging him to put off the announcement a little longer.

"I'm sorry," he said, coming to her and taking her hands in his. "I know I should have talked with you about this first, but I thought if you knew, you'd just be nervous all day about it."

"You're telling me you were trying to be considerate by springing this on me with no warning?"

"I don't know. Could I get away with that?"

Leanne couldn't be angry with him, because he was devastating when he smiled. She was so glad to see him looking happy again, amazed to find him teasing her. So she smiled herself and put her faith in him.

"God, Mitch, I'm so scared I'm shaking."

He put his arm around her waist and pulled her against him for a moment, the movement as easy and as natural as if it were something he did all the time. Leanne realized that he seemed to think nothing of touching her this way.

"Okay, I'll confess," he said. "I was afraid if I told you, you'd try to talk me out of it."

"I would have."

"Leanne, this is the hardest part. It's all downhill from here."

"There is this one little detail. The wedding ceremony."

He shrugged that off. "Piece of cake. I know a judge who'll marry us in his chambers. How does next Friday sound?"

"Oh, God. Mitch!"

"Waiting isn't going to make it any easier."

"I know," she cried, sagging against him, because it did help to have someone so big and so solid to lean against.

Mitch put a hand into the pocket of his suit jacket and took out a ring box. Snapping it open, he said, "I almost forgot the props."

Leanne saw a small circle of light. Diamonds, she realized. He'd gotten her a gold band encrusted with diamonds all the way around it.

"I hope this is all right," he said, taking her hand in his and slipping the ring on her finger. "I didn't think you'd want anything big or flashy."

Leanne thought it was just about perfect, but she couldn't seem to speak.

"It fits," he announced as the ring slid into place.

Nodding, feeling incredibly stupid and all too emotional, Leanne just stood there for the longest time. Finally, she managed to say, "Mitch, would you just hold me for a minute?"

"Of course I will."

He turned her into his arms, and Leanne slid into his embrace. She'd discovered, much to her dismay, that they seemed to fit together as though meant for each other. Her head fell to his shoulder, which was the perfect height, and then she felt his chin settle on the top of her head.

She craved the warmth of his body, the reassurance of his touch, the safety of his arms. How was she ever going to leave him and the boys when this was over? Already, it seemed nearly impossible, and the charade had barely begun.

"You're shaking," Mitch said, tightening his hold.

"I can't help it."

"What can I do to make this easier for you?"

She wanted to weep. As if it could be that simple. She would tell him what she wanted, what she needed, and he would give it to her? The world didn't work that way. Leanne had learned that early.

Fighting against what seemed an all-consuming need to be close to him, she eased away.

"I wanted to make this as painless for you as possible," he said. "Did I blow it? Are you just not ready to commit to this by telling everyone?"

"No," she said miserably. "I mean, I'm not ready, but I don't think I'll ever be ready."

"You hate the ring," he suggested with a smile.

"No. It's a beautiful ring." Definitely, a perfect one, for a most imperfect situation. This was totally unlike any scenario she'd ever concocted when imagining the day a man proposed to her and slipped a ring on her finger. She felt Mitch's hands at her shoulders then, rubbing at the tension there.

"Just hang on to me and let me do the talking. And try not to look as though you're facing a firing squad, okay?"

She nodded, and he put an arm around her and pulled her with him as he headed for the kitchen.

"Wait a minute," Leanne protested. "What are you going to tell them?"

"I told Marc that Rena's trying to take my kids away, that you and I are getting married and that if I said anything else to him, he might have to repeat it in court someday. He's a smart man. He didn't ask any questions. He's going to tell Ginny the same thing."

"She will ask questions."

"Probably, but she'll be on our side in this."

"And Amy and Alex?"

"I'll tell them to congratulate us because we're getting married."

Leanne's heart sank at the thought of how that announcement would go over. Before she could protest any further, she heard a shriek from the other room.

"Ginny knows," Mitch said. "She'll be here to congratulate us."

Sure enough, within seconds Ginny appeared. She came to stand in front of the two of them. With tears in her eyes and a smile on her face, she reached out for them, first Mitch, then Leanne.

"It's going to be fine," she said, hugging them both.

Then the doorbell rang.

Later that evening, after Alex and Amy had arrived, along with a few neighbors and some of Mitch and Marc's friends from work, Leanne and Mitch finally had a moment alone in the kitchen.

"You all right?" Mitch asked softly.

"I think I'm going to be sick," she said.

Mitch laughed and had the nerve to smile, and she marveled at the change she'd seen in this man in the past twenty-four hours. From the time she'd agreed to be his wife, he'd been like a new man. Calm, cool, confident. Happy, even. It was as if he didn't have a care in the world. Mitch was certain this would work; to hear him explain it, he had no qualms about making another woman his wife under the circumstances.

Leanne herself was close to panic. And Mitch wasn't helping matters by standing so near to her.

"We could still run away," she said.

"Cowardly," he said, dismissing the notion immediately.

"And that's relevant in a situation like this?"

Mitch's smile told her it wouldn't do any good to argue anymore, but she had to try.

"We'd still be married, whether anyone knew beforehand or after," she stated. "And once it's done, no one can stop us."

"Leanne, no one can stop us, period," he said.

From where he was standing, he had her trapped between the kitchen cabinet, the wall and himself. She had her back to the cabinet. He leaned one hip against it, his hand in front of her, resting against the wall. She was sure that to anyone else the scene must look quite intimate, which no doubt was what Mitch hoped. But Leanne was finding it felt intimate, as well.

"Leanne?"

Her name rolled softly off his lips, sounding unlike it ever had to her own ears. And his tone set off this feeling of anxiety low in her stomach. How was she ever going to pull this off?

''What?'' she asked, dreading what was to come, wishing so much that this night were over.

''I think I'm going to have to kiss you.''

''Now?'' Her heart kicked into high gear. Earlier, standing in the backyard, they'd discussed this like perfectly rational adults. Done right, one kiss, tonight, in front of her sister and brother, should be enough to set them all to wondering if this marriage was real, particularly since they were so quick to believe the worst of Leanne, anyway.

One kiss, she thought. It sounded so simple, and yet, with Mitch this close to her, nothing seemed simple at all.

''Amy's coming in the back door,'' he said, leaning ever closer, tilting his head to the side to match his lips to hers.

Leanne watched as he did so. She gave a whimper as he got within a breath of her mouth. Her heart was racing.

Mitch must have seen the panic in her eyes. ''Shh,'' he coaxed in that same tone he used to soothe the boys.

She remembered the way he touched them, the gentleness that was so surprising, so incredibly appealing, in such a big, strong man. He would never hurt them. Leanne didn't think he'd ever harm anyone intentionally.

But it wasn't his intentions she feared. It was her own treacherous heart, her traitorous longings. For him.

''Hang on to me,'' he whispered, as his mouth finally settled over hers.

Her hands came up to clutch at his arms, because she didn't want to fall down, and she wasn't sure if he knew how unsteady she was. His lips were every bit as soft as she'd imagined. And warm to the touch. And as smooth as silk.

Unwittingly, her lips parted ever so slightly, and she sighed, a sound Mitch absorbed into his mouth, as his lips parted, too. His grip on her arms tightened yet again as he adjusted the fit of his lips over hers, drawing her bottom lip into his mouth and sucking gently on it.

His taste was sweet and sinful and absolutely forbidden. Quite easily, she could become addicted to it. He pushed forward until her back was firmly against the cabinets, and then held her there with his body pressed intimately to hers. Desire surged through her and him. There was no mistaking the feel of it.

He wanted her. Terribly, it seemed. All from just a kiss.

His mouth opened more fully over hers, his kiss bordering on desperation now. And for a moment, the world seemed just about perfect.

"Oh, my God! It's true!"

Amy's outraged voice cut cleanly through everything else.

Mitch broke off the kiss instantly. Leanne turned just for a second to look at her sister, then buried her face in Mitch's chest. Shaking even harder than before, she leaned into him, grateful when his hands gathered her close and held her against him.

His chest was heaving; he was breathing just as hard as she was. Leanne took some comfort in knowing he'd been every bit as lost in that kiss as she had been.

"We didn't want you to find out like this," Mitch said.

"Alex was right," Amy cried. "He said he saw you in each other's arms at the house the other night. And I told him he was crazy, but I guess he's not."

Leanne winced at her sister's anger, and had to force herself to face Amy. Her cheeks burning, she lifted her head, her gaze colliding with Mitch's stormy one, then her sister's outraged look.

"Amy," Mitch began, "Leanne and I are going to be married."

"What?" Amy's gaze caught on the flash of light coming from Leanne's hand, which was hanging on to Mitch's right arm. Then she looked at Leanne. "How could you do this? She was your sister."

To that, Leanne could say nothing.

"And you?" Amy fixed her attention on Mitch. "I thought you loved her."

"I did," he said, steel in his unyielding tone. "But Kelly's gone. And she's never coming back."

"I can't believe this," Amy said. "I thought nothing Leanne ever did could surprise me, but this... Alex!" She whirled around and walked out the door, calling to her brother as she went.

Leanne felt the fragile hold she had on her emotions crumbling rapidly as reaction set in, and she turned to the man still holding her loosely in his arms.

"The expression on her face... it was so much worse than I'd ever imagined. She hates me, Mitch."

He took her face in his hands and made her look at him. "Amy's upset right now, but she'll calm down."

Leanne shook her head. "No. She hates me. My own sister hates me."

Mitch pushed her head down to his chest once again and locked his arms around her. "I'm sorry," he said. "I'm so sorry."

Leanne was sorry, too. She also wasn't far from hating herself. Because she knew exactly what Amy had seen when she'd walked in on that kiss.

There'd been nothing phony about it. No playacting. No pretenses. Somehow, Mitch McCarthy wanted Leanne every bit as much as she wanted him. And by this time next week, she would be his wife.

Day and night for the next year they would live in the same house, sleep in beds that weren't twenty feet apart. Wanting each other like this? Leanne wondered.

She'd never last a year.

Chapter 10

They were married the following Friday in the judge's chambers at the main courthouse downtown. What was to have been a simple, private ceremony had somehow ballooned into a crowd of more than thirty people gathered in one of the domed lobbies of the building. Mitch's friends and co-workers, his brother and sister-in-law, who lived about forty-five minutes away, his parents, who drove in from Ohio and had been quite kind and supportive, and Marc and Ginny all attended.

So far, there was no sign of Alex or Amy, although Mitch had invited them. Thankfully, there was no sign of Rena, either, who hadn't been invited but would have had the nerve to show up regardless. She'd expressed her outrage to Mitch over this scam of a marriage, but found herself unable to stop it.

Five minutes before the ceremony was scheduled to begin, Leanne was a mass of nerves. Though Ginny knew exactly what this marriage was, she insisted it look real. And Mitch had agreed that it should. So he'd ordered a small bouquet for Leanne—lilies and yellow roses—the scent and the gesture so sweet she wanted to cry.

With Ginny at her side, Leanne had gone shopping. She'd finally selected a soft, flowing dress in white silk with a skirt that nearly swept the floor. Though it was quite casual, the dress was more romantic than anything she had a right to wear.

The boys had new suits in navy blue, to match the one their father had chosen to wear. And they had tiny carnations in the buttonholes of their jackets. At every opportunity, they picked at the petals of the little flowers, altogether puzzled over their purpose and, it seemed, insulted at the idea of wearing such things. They also had matching satin ring bearer's pillows, which they kept throwing at each other as they giggled and dodged each other's blows.

And because Leanne knew it would delight Hannah so much, the little girl had a brand-new princess dress, a halo of flowers in her hair and a basket of rose petals to scatter when she preceded Leanne to the point where Mitch and the judge would be waiting.

Hiding in a room off the lobby, Leanne felt Ginny's hand close over her forearm. "Steady. It's almost time."

"The judge still isn't here, is he?" she asked nervously, grateful to the man for giving her this extra time.

"Court never runs on time," Ginny reassured her. "But don't worry. The judge will arrive."

Leanne stopped to breathe. "Mitch is so certain this is the right thing to do," she said, wondering if Ginny agreed.

"And you trust Mitch."

"Yes."

"And you love the boys."

"I do. But…" Leanne didn't mean to say it. The words just slipped out. "I think I love Mitch, too."

Ginny froze for an instant, understanding dawning. "Oh," she said softly.

"I'm not just doing this for the boys," Leanne confessed. This was what she wanted with all her heart, what she simply couldn't have. "What am I going to do?"

Ginny took a breath, then let it out. "You're going to marry Mitch. You're going to be a wonderful mother to the boys. And I think you're going to find out that Mitch's heart may be bruised and battered, but it isn't broken."

"He could never love me," Leanne said desperately.

"Why not?"

"You saw him with Kelly. You saw him when he lost her. Ginny, he loved her."

"That doesn't mean he can't love you now."

"But she was my sister," Leanne said.

Ginny took a handkerchief from her pocket and started dabbing at the tears in Leanne's eyes. "It's not as if you're taking anything away from Kelly by loving the boys or Mitch," she said.

"It feels that I am."

"Then you're just going to have to examine those feelings when you're not feeling so guilty and you're done mourning your sister. Because I don't think she'd rest any easier knowing Mitch was alone and the boys didn't have a mother. I think Kelly would want her family to be taken care of, and that includes having someone like you to love them."

"I want to believe that," Leanne cried.

"Then believe it."

Ginny looked out from the door of the office where they'd hidden themselves away, to see what all the commotion was about.

"Get ready," she warned. "The judge is here."

For Leanne, the ceremony was like looking at a bad videotape, one in which someone kept changing the recording speeds. Things moved dizzyingly fast, then slowed to a crawl, only to speed up once again.

She saw a crowd of smiling faces waiting for her, a clump of people that parted in the middle to make an aisle for her to walk down. Mitch stood at the end, the boys dancing around him. He tried to quiet them, and finally managed to draw them to his side. Teddy smiled shyly at Leanne, then wedged himself between her right leg and Mitch's left one. That and Mitch's hand steadied her when she feared nothing could.

The judge, still in his solemn black robes, opened his book and started to speak. Leanne worked hard to follow the words of the sacred ceremony. Feeling like a fraud, she looked into Mitch's eyes. Whatever he saw in hers must have worried him, because his arm slid around her waist, and his face came down toward hers.

"You can't back out on me now," he said, his lips dangerously close to her ear. "Five more minutes, and we've got it made."

Swallowing hard, she leaned into him and waited for her cue. Mitch spoke his vows with no hesitation, using that same deep, sexy voice that always had her heart tripping over itself. Her vows, when they came, were uttered so softly she doubted anyone but Mitch heard her. Her fingers shook so much she nearly made Mitch drop her ring.

And then there was nothing left but the kiss.

"Oh," she said, realizing it was time. The last time he'd kissed her was before that disastrous scene with Amy in Ginny and Marc's kitchen, and Leanne had forgotten she had to get through one more of his kisses while put on for public display.

Feeling the heat flooding into her cheeks because she'd hesitated so long that people had to notice, she wished she could just sink into the floor. Of course, that wasn't an option.

Mitch winked at her and muttered, "You're making me look bad, Leanne. These people are going to think I'm a dreadful kisser."

"Mitch," she warned, knowing he was going to prove them all wrong, that this wasn't going to be any polite peck on the cheek.

But it was too late. When she opened her mouth to beg him to go easy on her, he settled his lips against hers, his tongue teasing at the opening of her mouth, then thrusting inside.

It was the most blatantly sexy kiss she'd been given in years. Clinging to him, she felt that blast of heat that always came when she was this close to him, felt the steely grip of his arms, the hard wall of his chest and thighs.

Not until the applause sounded behind them did Leanne remember that no less than three dozen people were witnessing this. Teddy was squirming around their legs and tugging on Leanne's dress. Mitch, appearing a little sheepish but still entirely too sexy, picked Teddy up. Timmy scooted in front of them, and together they went to accept congratulations from the friends of Mitch who'd gathered there.

Leanne wasn't sure what she expected next. To go home and pretend this was any other ordinary day, she supposed. And then Marc announced that the reception would begin in fifteen minutes at a hotel three blocks away.

"Reception?" Leanne repeated. "We're not having a reception."

"Surprise," Ginny said as she came up behind them. She kissed Mitch on the cheek and gave Leanne a hug. "I'm so happy—for both of you."

Leanne waited for Mitch to say something, but all he did was kiss Ginny and tell her, "Thank you," before someone on the other side of the room called out to him. To Leanne, as he headed across the room, he merely reminded her, "The hard part's over."

As she watched him go, Ginny leaned close to Leanne's side. "That was some kiss," she said.

There was indeed a reception, in a pretty suite atop one of the hotels bordering Lake Michigan. Finger food, a small cake and lots of champagne had people lingering and laughing and talking.

Mitch tried his best to stay at Leanne's side, but he kept getting pulled away. She found herself missing him when he was gone, nervous when he was so close his hand was at her back or his arm around her waist.

The memory of that kiss kept replaying in her head, just as the first one had kept her awake at night for much of the past week. And now she'd confessed her deepest, darkest secret to Ginny.

She'd fallen in love with Mitch, and she honestly couldn't explain to herself her primary motivation in marrying him today. For the boys, of course. For Kelly, because she knew her sister wouldn't want Rena to have the boys. For Mitch, because Leanne didn't think he would survive without Timmy and Teddy.

But she'd done it for herself, as well. For all the foolish dreams she'd once had of a handsome, grinning boy named Mitch McCarthy who'd barely known her name. For the man he'd grown into, the love he'd shown her sister and the joy and the love he lavished upon his children. She'd done it for the future she wanted to have with this man.

As she turned around, she felt a hand slide around her waist once more, felt a man's body brush against hers.

"You look awfully pale, even for a bride," Mitch said.

And when Leanne turned toward him, he was right there, so near she felt his breath rush past her lips. Once again, everything seemed to slow down, to fade away, everything except his face.

She wanted him, in every way a woman wants a man. And she wanted this to last.

"Leanne?" he said, obviously worried now and coming even closer than before.

She watched the tightening of his jaw, the narrowing of his eyes, the erratic thumping of blood in one of the pulse points at the side of his neck. Swallowing hard, telling herself to back away, Leanne inched forward, instead.

It was the first time she'd ever taken the initiative with him, the first time she'd ever shown him so clearly that she wanted him to touch her, and she wondered what price she'd pay for revealing so much of herself. But that was for later. For now, she knew the deep satisfaction of hearing Mitch groan and feeling his hands tighten on her arms as his mouth slid seductively over hers.

"I swear you've cast some sort of spell over me," he said a moment later when he'd backed off just enough to catch a breath.

And then he was kissing her again, tasting her, teasing her, until her breasts felt swollen and heavy, aching for his touch. She loved the taste of him, the strength and the solidity of him, the firm pressure of his mouth on hers as she offered herself to him.

Leanne wasn't sure where that kiss would have led them if someone behind them hadn't called out, "Would you two like us to leave you alone?"

There was good-natured laughter and a few other teasing comments from the crowd. Leanne's face was flaming, she knew, and Mitch was staring at her in a way that left her totally unsettled.

She'd cast a spell over him?

Exactly how did a woman go about casting a spell over a man? She was certain she'd never done anything like that in her life. Men simply didn't go crazy over Leanne Hathaway. She doubted anyone was going to start now when she was thirty-two.

But it had been wonderful to hear that from him.

She would never have his heart, Leanne knew, but maybe she could have everything else.

Could she live like that? As a second mother to his children? As his lover, but without his love?

"What are you thinking?" Mitch asked once the noise of the crowd settled down and people's attention drifted away from the two of them.

Feeling uncharacteristically bold and in the mood to talk—probably because she'd had two glasses of champagne on an empty stomach—Leanne said, "I'm thinking this isn't going to be as simple as we believed."

Mitch's chest rose and fell as he took a long, slow breath. "And I'd say you're right."

"What are we going to do?" she wanted to know, scared now.

He must have known she was afraid, because, as he always did when he came to understand her fear, he took her hand in his and held on tight. "I don't know."

But he stayed by her side, kept right on holding her hand, and soon she wasn't so scared anymore. Soon she came to realize that whatever happened, Mitch was going to be by her side. Considering the life she'd led, there was no greater gift he could have given her.

Finally, people started drifting toward the door. There was more handshaking, more kisses on the cheek, more congratulations that sounded sincere.

Mitch's parents were among the last to leave. They said some things to Mitch that Leanne couldn't hear. Then Mitch's mother gave Leanne a hug.

"Take good care of him for me," she whispered.

"I will," Leanne said cautiously, wondering just how much her feelings for Mitch showed on her face.

"I worried for a while that he would be alone for the rest of his life."

"So did I."

Her new mother-in-law smiled. "I'm glad he won't be."

And then Mitch's parents slipped away. Leanne and Mitch were alone with Ginny and Marc. The boys had left earlier with Ginny's sister-in-law, who'd come to take Hannah home after the ceremony.

Marc had his arm around Ginny, who was smiling broadly as she told them, "The suite's paid for until Monday morning, and we're not giving the boys back until then. So you might as well stay."

"Ginny!" Leanne protested.

"How would it look if you two didn't have a honeymoon?"

Beside her Mitch stiffened, but said nothing.

"I packed you a bag," Ginny continued. "It's in the bedroom. You—" she turned to Mitch "—are on your own, although I'm sure the concierge can help with some of the basics. And there's a department store next door. Don't worry about the boys. They'll be fine."

Marc looked a little contrite, but merely shrugged and stuck out a hand to Mitch. "What can I say? I have no control over my wife."

Ginny laughed, kissed Mitch goodbye and murmured "Good luck" to Leanne.

And then the two of them were alone.

Leanne shook her head and looked around the room in something of a daze. Darkness had fallen in the time they'd been inside, and someone had opened the blinds to show off a stunning view of the city skyline and the river.

She was so tired she wasn't sure how she could still be on her feet. And she was more nervous than she'd been the night she'd finally surrendered her virginity to a fellow photography major she'd met during her freshman year in college.

Of course, nothing was going to happen tonight, Leanne reasoned.

Just because she and Mitch were staying, it didn't mean anything would happen. Just because they'd kissed like people who were ready to absolutely devour each other, it didn't mean that anything would ever happen between the two of them.

Still, Leanne was nervous. Looking around, she saw the bar that had been set up in the corner, chairs all around, a sofa pushed back against the wall and, behind that, a door to the right that must lead to the bedroom.

One she was expected to share with Mitch?

"I—I" she stammered, then had to start over. "I think I need to sit down."

Mitch turned with her toward the sofa, but a knock at the door had them both turning back that way instead. A unformed waiter pushing a service cart asked if they were ready for him to clear the room.

"Of course," Mitch said.

"Congratulations." The man smiled. "I'll be out of your way in no time at all."

And then they had no choice but to head through the connecting door to the bedroom. Leanne saw her bag on the luggage stand in the corner, flowers on the bedside table, a bottle of champagne on ice on the vanity.

"I can't believe they did this," Leanne said. And she had to wonder—had Ginny done this before or after Leanne had confessed her feelings for Mitch? Surely she'd done it before. It had taken some planning, after all.

So, had Leanne given herself away even before this? Was it obvious for anyone to see? Even Mitch? The thought was so embarrassing she wished she could just disappear.

If that wasn't an option, she'd probably have to face Mitch. Soon. She heard his footsteps. As he stopped behind her and settled his hands lightly on her shoulders, Leanne tensed. Those big, warm hands of his started kneading the knots of tension in her neck and arms.

"I have no idea what to say to you right now. Or what to do," he admitted.

He was so close she felt his breath stirring the hairs at her nape, could imagine his mouth following the path of his hands in a soft, sensual trail.

"This is a good start," she told him, willing herself to relax.

"You look beautiful today."

The words seemed to have been wrenched from him, sincere, but not easily shared. Leanne hadn't realized how much she longed to please him, even in the smallest of ways.

"Thank you," she said, wondering what she'd do if he

eased her back against him and started kissing his way down her shoulder. She shivered at the thought.

"Cold?" he asked.

"No." She'd answered too quickly.

"Tired?"

Leanne shook her head, because she simply couldn't say any more. One of his thumbs was making a slow circle on the part of her neck left bare by the dress.

"I never anticipated this," he confessed.

His words, his voice, his touch set her whole body on fire. What had he not anticipated? she wondered. Wanting her? Wanting anyone? Or doing anything about the wanting?

Was he going to do anything? Was he waiting for some sign from her? Hoping she would give him one? Hoping she'd push him away? What?

She felt his face pressed against her hair, which she'd worn in a loose topknot today, felt her hair fall as he removed the pins one by one. His arms slid around her waist as he fit his body to hers. Leaning back against him, she knew instantly that he was painfully aroused. She gasped as she felt him pressed hard against her back. Then her legs turned to mush. The only reason she stayed on her feet was that he wouldn't let her go.

Glancing over at the big bed, she thought it would be so easy. A few steps, and they'd be on that bed. The way they'd responded to each other the three times they'd kissed, the whole thing would be over in seconds.

And it had been so long since Leanne had let any man touch her, so long since she'd felt this way, if she ever really had.

"You're going to have to help me here, Leanne," he whispered into her ear. "Tell me what you're thinking."

She went with her gut reaction, her deepest fear. "I don't want you to hate yourself for this in the morning. Or me. I really couldn't stand it, Mitch, if you hated me again."

She felt him take a long, shuddering breath, then step away from her, which she took to mean that he might well hate one of them by morning if he spent this night with her.

She bit down hard on her bottom lip and tried with everything in her not to cry. The last thing she wanted was for Mitch to see her cry.

Finally, he said, "Leanne, will you look at me?"

Closing her eyes, praying for strength, she turned around. Tilting up her chin, she made herself look at him, still dressed in his wedding suit. Warily, she met his gaze, hoping that he couldn't read anything more in hers than she saw in his.

Life just wasn't fair, she decided with more certainty than ever. How could he look this good to her? Feel this wonderful? How could she find herself married to this man, unable to have him, yet unable to leave?

He took her chin in his hand, and she cursed the new-found ease and frequency with which he touched her. Willing herself to show no reaction, to give nothing away, she waited.

"I honestly don't know how I'd feel in the morning," he said. "But one thing is certain. I don't want to hurt you, and I think it's probably far too easy for me or for anyone to hurt you."

And then he closed his eyes and kissed her softly on the lips, his touch exquisitely gentle, with none of the heat of his previous kisses.

Leanne found this one just as devastating and decided she loved him even more at that moment than she had this afternoon when he'd made her his wife.

"You know, it's a gorgeous night," he said, still holding her chin in his hand. "How would you like to take a walk on the lake?"

And get out of this room and away from this bed?

"Let's go," she said.

* * *

Although it was unseasonably warm for September in Chicago, the wind off the lake was still cold. Mitch took off his jacket and bundled Leanne into it a few moments after they got to the walkway along the lake.

There seemed to be a million stars out that night, a million lights from the city behind them.

"I'd forgotten how beautiful this place is," she said, quite content just to walk arm in arm with him.

They hadn't said much on their way downstairs, and Leanne would have given anything to know just what Mitch was thinking. Did he regret already what had almost happened? Was he relieved that she'd stopped him?

Would she ever get that same chance with him again?

Her doubts plagued her. Still, she was Mitch McCarthy's wife; his diamond was on her finger, his suit jacket wrapped around her, his arm encircling her waist as they walked side by side beneath the million stars.

It was a moment to savor, to treasure, and she was happier than she'd been in ages, regardless of how precariously her entire life was balanced at this moment.

"Did you really miss Chicago?" he asked.

"I ached for it," she said, the heartfelt reply reminding her of just how far she'd come from her ordinary life.

Or maybe this was her ordinary life; maybe all those years away were the aberration. Maybe she was meant to be right here.

"You're not missing your work?" Mitch asked. "Or the travel?"

"I miss having a camera in my hand and taking pictures, but I'm sick to death of the travel. All those planes, the airports, the suitcases, the cramped hotel rooms and the strange food. Some of the places were interesting. A lot of the people were, too. But I've seen all I need to see of the world."

Because he waited, because he seemed to sense there was more, she found herself wanting to tell him, wanting to make him understand. "It was something I did because

I couldn't be here. I thought if I kept myself busy enough, I wouldn't miss my home and my family."

"But it didn't work?"

She shook her head sadly. "I should have come back a long time ago."

Mitch stopped walking, and she stopped, too, and turned to him. He slid his hand along the side of her neck and then into her hair. His other hand captured a strand of hair fluttering across her face and pushed it back into place. Then he held her face in his hands.

"I'm glad you came back when you did. I don't know what I would have done without you," he said.

Lowering his mouth to hers, he kissed her softly, then let his lips linger against hers.

"I don't want you to be sad anymore," he whispered.

The next kiss was just as soft, just as leisurely. But there was something utterly seductive about it. It was a tasting and a testing, an exploration of her mouth that started a slow fire simmering inside her, one that burned hotter and higher with each kiss.

It was as if he wanted to know her mouth completely, to commit the shape of it to memory. And he acted as if they had all the time in the world, when she knew there was a limit on everything they did together.

A year, he'd said. A year was what she'd promised. And then she was supposed to walk away.

Leanne let go of his jacket and it slid down her back as her arms wound around his neck. She tried hard to keep her hold light, when she desperately longed never to let him go. She tried to temper her response to his kiss, to hide how very much she wanted him. But she probably failed miserably.

When they finally broke apart, she was gasping for breath. She was grateful to notice that he was, as well. Looking through the darkness at him, she couldn't be sure what she saw. Wariness? Surprise? A flicker of anger?

"You can't stand the fact that you want me, can you?"

she asked because she believed it and because it hurt her so much to think that.

"No. It's not that." He put a finger to her lips to silence her when she might have called him a liar on that point. Taking in a deep breath, he said, "I'm...surprised."

"Surprised?"

"Okay, more than surprised. I didn't think I was going to be celibate for the rest of my life, but I didn't expect to want anyone quite this much. Of course, it's been a long time, and..."

"I know. Maybe you just need to be with someone. Maybe it doesn't matter that it's me, just that I'm the one who's here with you right now." And the one who was going to share his life and his home for the next year. Maybe she was simply a convenience to him.

"I don't think it's that," he said, then swore softly. "It would be so much easier if it was that."

Leanne froze. It was more than she expected from him—that he would want her for herself, that he would admit it. Yet she knew where this was headed. "You feel guilty?"

"Don't you?"

"Yes."

With his hand at her chin, he made her look at him. "Funny thing about this guilt of mine—it hasn't managed to stop me from wanting you. Neither has feeling that I'm taking advantage of the fact that you're doing me and the boys a tremendous favor by spending the next year here. Nothing yet has managed to make me want you any less."

Her heart tripping over itself, hope springing to life inside her, Leanne decided it just wasn't fair that a man could be this gorgeous, this seductive. She'd fallen for him without his ever having shown the least bit of interest in her. And now that he had, he was simply devastating and breathtaking, mind-numbingly sexy. How was she supposed to resist this?

Drawing up her courage, she asked, "So, what do we do now?"

"You tell me," he said.

He was close enough that she could easily reach up and take his mouth with hers. She could seduce him, she thought headily. He wouldn't stop her, although he might be sorry in the morning.

Of course, she wanted the impossible. She wanted him with no regrets, and she wanted his love. Leanne wondered if Mitch McCarthy would ever love another woman. She wondered if she could be that woman.

"Look, we don't have to settle this tonight," he said, rubbing his hands up and down her upper arms. "Especially not while you're freezing out here."

Mitch bent over and picked up his jacket, settled it around her once again, then pulled her close as they walked back to their hotel.

She shut her eyes and let herself enjoy the experience of simply being with him, of feeling safe and protected and cared for. She realized it had been weeks since she'd felt the first twinge of loneliness—that he and the boys had taken that away.

Looking down, she saw his ring on her hand, saw the diamonds sparkling in the glow from one of the overhead lights along the path by the lake.

She decided it was the most beautiful ring she'd ever seen, and the man who'd put it on her finger wanted her in that wonderful way a man wants a woman.

For the moment, that was enough.

Chapter 11

Because he felt like torturing himself, Mitch gave her one more steamy kiss at the door to the bedroom before he told her good-night.

Then he walked into the suite's living room and pulled out the convertible sofa. As he lay in bed, he absolutely ached. For her.

At some point when he closed his eyes, he expected to find Kelly's face superimposed over Leanne's, some wretched guilt-induced image. But it didn't happen.

In fact, he had trouble bringing Kelly's image to mind at all.

It frightened him a little, angered him, as well, because he seemed to find himself forced along the whole grieving process by powers that were simply out of his control. At each step along the way, he always seemed to be shoved forward, whether he wanted to be or not.

Well, this was one step that was proving more difficult than most. Honestly, he'd never anticipated this when he'd asked Leanne to marry him. Oh, he liked having her close, liked holding her in his arms, but he'd thought he was simply lonely.

Once he'd kissed her that first time, he'd realized he was starving. It was too easy to be with her. It felt too good. He couldn't seem to keep his hands off her.

Today, during the ceremony, he hadn't cared that three dozen people were looking on. He knew only that he'd waited a long time to kiss her again, and that once he had, he could barely bring himself to stop.

And now he was supposed to share his house with her for the next year?

It sounded like an eternity, if he was supposed to keep his hands off her.

Mitch had no idea what to do. Punching his pillow, then rolling over and burying his face in it, he tried to find some peace in sleep.

He awoke to the sound of someone knocking on his door. Wincing as the sunlight hit him square in the face, he remembered where he was and who was sleeping right next door.

The knock sounded again and a voice called out.

"Room service."

Mitch grabbed his pants and pulled them on, zipping them and fumbling with the catch. He slid his arms through the sleeves of his shirt but didn't take the time to button it. Grabbing his watch for a second, he saw that it was almost ten o'clock in the morning. He hadn't slept this late in years.

When he opened the door, he found a white-coated waiter with a cart full of food, compliments of Mrs. Dalton, the man said. Mitch signed the check as the waiter set up the food. Then, bracing himself, he headed next door to find Leanne.

If she was still in bed, he was going to be in trouble, because he wanted to climb into bed with her. And as crazy as it sounded, he didn't think she'd offer any objections.

She responded to him like something out of a dream, as if she was as hungry for him as he was for her. And that wasn't helping his resolve to stay away from her.

Mitch ran through the list of reasons he should stay away. She was Kelly's sister. She'd done him a tremendous favor by agreeing to this marriage, by giving him this time to get his life together and hopefully foiling any attempts Rena might make to take the boys away from him.

Sex was not part of their bargain.

But it could be.

Mitch came to a halt just inside the room. The bed was empty, the covers mussed, a pillow thrown on the floor. He suspected she hadn't slept any better than he had.

Then he heard a sound coming from the bathroom. No, he realized, the cessation of a sound. She must be getting out of the shower.

Instantly, Mitch had a picture of her, dripping wet, her hair piled onto her head, wrapped in nothing but a towel.

It was going to be a long day, he decided, crossing the room to the bathroom door and raising a hand to knock.

Before he could do that, the door swung open.

Leanne, dripping wet, her hair indeed pulled into a loose knot on her head, her skin dewy soft, her cheeks all pink from the heat, stood before him. Not in a towel. Mitch thought for a second he should be grateful for that. Then he got a look at this whisper-thin robe. White, nearly transparent when it came in contact with a drop of water on her body, it clung to her every curve and indentation like a second skin.

Mitch heard a roaring sound in his ears—his own pulse pounding, he realized a moment later. And he was instantly, viciously, painfully aroused.

"I thought I heard a knock," Leanne said.

"Breakfast," he explained, watching in utter fascination as a drop of water fell from a lock of her hair onto her collarbone, then rolled down her neck and onto the swell of her breast, before it was soaked up by her robe.

Before he could stop himself, his hand was there, one finger tracing the same path as that drop of water.

Leanne gasped and shuddered. He watched her lips part, her eyes widen in surprise, then turn all smoky with desire.

His finger was at the edge of her robe, and then he traced that, as well, down to that enticing V where the two sides of the robe crossed, held together by a little knot in a sash at her waist.

"You don't have a thing on under this, do you?"

"No," she whispered.

She sounded as if she ached for him every bit as much as he ached for her.

He studied the wet marks in the thin silk where it clung to her skin. She hadn't taken the time to dry off when she'd climbed out of the shower, and he found the thought of her skin, warm and wet, incredibly erotic.

His hand hovered above her breast, his finger still toying with the neckline of her robe. Her breath caught in her throat, and he could see the blood pounding past one of the veins in that delicious-looking neck of hers.

He wanted a taste of her neck, of her ear, her shoulder, of all that wet skin of hers. But he settled for trailing his thumb along the underside of her breast and watching the look on her face when he did so. Her muscles tensed, and she squeezed her eyes shut. Her lips parted—an invitation he barely managed to resist.

Before his eyes, he saw her nipples harden and push against the silk of her robe, their outline clear. He took his thumb and flicked it across her right nipple. Smiling, he heard that catch in her breath, heard her breathy moaning of his name.

Because he was still a little afraid of touching her the way he wanted, he opened his hand until it was flat and then rubbed at her nipple with his palm, all the while imagining the weight of that breast once he held it in his hand. And took it into his mouth.

She was an amazingly responsive woman. Her whole body was quivering now, her hands clenching the rim of the marble vanity behind her.

Because she wanted to touch him, too?

He smiled, liking the fact that she couldn't help but want him, no matter how hard she fought the feeling.

Coming closer, he put his hands on her hips and pulled her to him, nudging his arousal against the softness of her stomach because he wanted to make sure she knew just how near to the edge he was. If she was going to stop him, it had to be now. But as he felt his body settle hard against hers, he knew he was lost.

He shut his eyes, savoring the feeling, unable to stop a gasp of pleasure.

Leanne made a little sound of surprise, a sinfully sexy sound. When her hand fell to his chest, pushing his shirt open, he felt the trembling in her fingers. She let her palm brush across his chest, moving slowly and taking her time, as if she absolutely loved touching him. Her simple touch, the look of pure pleasure on her face, threatened to bring him to his knees.

Tightening his hold on her hips, he thrust gently against her.

Leaning his head down to hers, he whispered urgently, "I'm trying very hard not to let myself think about how easy it would be to move your robe out of the way. To unzip my pants. To slide your thighs apart. And then slip inside you. It would be so easy."

"Do it," she said, her hands trailing down his chest and finding the catch to his pants, then the zipper. "Do it now, before you remember all the reasons we shouldn't."

And then there was nothing but heat and a sensual haze that settled around his head, blocking out his ability to judge and his will to resist.

It was indeed just that easy to get inside her. He parted

her robe. She unzipped his pants and pushed them aside. Mitch lifted her until her hips were against the side of the marble vanity. Then he grabbed her hips and pulled her to him.

Effortlessly, he slid inside, finding her warm and wet and welcoming.

The heat enveloped him then, the pressure building before he'd so much as kissed that luscious mouth of hers.

"I am never going to be able to make this last," he confessed.

"Next time," she said, wrapping her legs around his.

Mitch moaned, sensation piling on top of sensation. He was like a starving man. A greedy, starving man. He wanted her stark naked, stretched out on his bed in broad daylight, wanted all the time in the world to explore every inch of her, but he ended up taking her right there, standing up in the bathroom.

One kiss. One deep, delicious kiss. His hands digging into her hips, his body straining ever closer, those deep, inner muscles of hers gripping him as though she'd never let go.

He didn't want to ever let go, didn't want to let this end, but didn't have one ounce of self-control left. She'd robbed him of it.

He felt the pressure building, felt his body simply explode, as he poured himself inside her. She called out his name, sank her nails into his back, and then he felt that deep, rhythmic pulsing of her body around his, before she simply collapsed in his arms.

Leanne couldn't move, could barely breathe. All she could do was cling to him and squeeze her eyes shut, not wanting to let go of that sensual haze that enveloped them. She nearly cried out in protest when she felt him loosen his arms, then ease away from her. Steeling herself for whatever happened next, she was surprised and pleased when he lifted her into his arms and carried her to the bed.

She felt the mattress give beneath her weight, and she reached for the sides of her robe to cover herself. But Mitch grabbed her hands in his and stopped her.

Lifting her arms above her head, he placed her hands against the edge of the headboard and held them there. Smiling down at her, he asked, "We're not done, are we?"

Leanne let out a shaky breath as she felt something give way inside her. A knot of tension, maybe a sense of impending doom that had eased. If he'd turned away from her now, something inside her would have shriveled up and died on the spot.

Instead, she smiled up at him and left her hands where he'd placed them. "No," she said, joy flooding through her. "We're not."

In that moment, he was the most beautiful man she'd ever seen, even more handsome now than he had been in the courthouse yesterday as he'd made his vows to her. Even more devastating than he had been a few minutes ago when he'd walked into the bathroom with his bare feet, his unsnapped slacks, his white shirt left hanging open, showing a wonderful strip of gloriously bare skin.

She would have done anything to have him then. To have taken her so quickly, with such heat and driving impatience, he must have felt the same way.

Now he stood at the side of the bed. She got to watch as he stripped off his shirt, kicked off his pants and stood before her without a hint of embarrassment or a stitch of clothing.

Greedy now, she reached for him.

"No," he said, putting her hands back into place above her head, then sitting on the side of the bed. "This time is for you."

And then he set out to please her as no man had ever done before.

First, he undid the sash of her robe, then pulled it open. She shivered, just thinking of what he was going to do next. He started near her ear, nibbling and tasting and sucking in a way that had her squirming and alternately begging him to stop and begging him not to. He worked his way down the side of her neck, to the curve of her shoulder, where she'd imagined him kissing her last night when they'd walked into this room.

He continued on to her chest, until he was nibbling on the inside curve of one breast and rubbing his nose against her skin, taking in the scent of her. His jaw was a little rough, scratching and scraping along her skin. She'd never understood just how erotic razor stubble could be.

Her nipples absolutely ached as she waited for him to get to them. She was surprised when he didn't bother to push her robe aside further, instead taking her nipple into his mouth and sucking on it through her robe, leaving the cloth wet and clingy where his mouth had been.

Then he kissed his way down to her stomach, spreading fire as he went. She knew what he was going to do, and she wasn't sure if she could stand that much more pleasure. But he positioned his lips farther down, turning his attention, instead, to the inside of her ankle.

"Mitch?" Her voice sounded weak and thready.

"Hmm?"

He didn't stop, didn't even lift his mouth from her leg.

She was squirming on the bed, never having imagined it could feel this good to have a man kiss her shin. When he got to the underside of her knee, she was shuddering. When he started nibbling on her thighs, she couldn't keep her hands off him any longer. They wound their way into his hair, pulling him to her.

Reluctantly, he lifted himself, keeping his weight on his hands, his head coming up so he could look at her. "I'm not done yet," he told her.

He said the words with a stamp of what she could only describe as satisfaction on his face.

Then he was working with his tongue on her thigh again.

"Mitch!"

But he didn't listen. Leanne didn't think she'd ever been so conscious of her body or of a man's. He settled himself onto her, his arms around her thighs as he parted them, and buried his face between her legs.

She very nearly screamed the pleasure was so intense. Instead, she just said his name again and again. "Mitch, please. Mitch... Mitch."

She knew very soon that she would simply shatter. He must have known it, too, because one minute he was pleasuring her with his mouth and the next minute he was pushing his way inside her. His mouth at that tender spot on her neck, he whispered to her, "Hang on to me."

"I will."

And she did. After all, she would have done anything for him. So the next time he surged into her body, she let go of everything inside her that said that they shouldn't be together, they had no right to find such happiness in each other's arms. She just held on to him and came apart in his embrace.

It was like having an explosion go off inside her body, she decided later when she could think. They had never bothered to take off her robe, so she was still wrapped up in it, her head pillowed on Mitch's bare chest, his arms wound tightly around her.

Even in sleep he would not let her go.

After their second encounter he'd drifted off, and Leanne couldn't bring herself to leave him.

He *would* have to be the best lover she'd ever had, she thought, wondering if they would ever feel free to be together like this again.

They had to be, she decided. Now that she knew what it was to be with him this way, she couldn't go back to how things had been. He'd ruined her for other men.

She was curious what he would say if she told him that no one had ever brought her such pleasure or drawn such a response from her. Would he think she was naive? Or sadly lacking in experience?

She certainly wasn't a prude. Still, she'd never felt quite like this.

Shutting her eyes, she snuggled closer to him as he started to stir. Their time together like this was coming to an end. With tears threatening, she pondered what in the world she would tell him when he did wake up.

Did she try not to make a big deal out of the whole thing? As if she were perfectly willing to sleep with him, as well as mother his children and pretend to be his wife for the next year, before simply walking away? Would they just add sleeping together to the bargain they'd already made?

He shifted again, and she felt a rumbling in his chest when he spoke.

"You're worrying," he said.

It sounded like an accusation. Afraid to lift her head and look into his face, she didn't even move.

"And I know you're not asleep," Mitch said, rolling her over until she was on her back and he was leaning over her. "This is what you wanted," he said, as though not quite sure.

"Yes."

And then he kissed her, so softly and so sweetly she wanted to weep. His hand brushed her hair aside, then caressed the side of her face, soothing her and reassuring her all at once.

"Why don't you tell me what's wrong?"

Through tear-filled eyes she looked at him, trying to figure out what was going on inside his head, seeing nothing she could distinguish in his expression, except perhaps concern for her.

"I was afraid you'd regret this," she said, bringing her fear right out into the open.

He nodded. Maybe he tensed a little. She couldn't be sure, because she wasn't that good at reading him yet.

"You do," she said, her heart aching even as she went to pull herself out of his arms.

"Leanne, wait." He wouldn't let her go. Rolling onto his back again, he pushed her face down to his chest. "This is so awkward."

"I'll say it for you so you don't have to. You're sorry we did this. Maybe you hate yourself a little for doing it, and you don't ever want it to happen again, although you're probably too much of a gentleman ever to tell me."

"No," he said, speaking more forcefully. "That's not how I feel."

"Then tell me how you do feel," she said, not ready to believe him.

"I feel about a million different things right now. And yes, guilt's a part of it." He laughed a bit, then added, "I probably wouldn't feel so guilty if I hadn't enjoyed myself so much."

Leanne lifted her head from his chest and gazed at him, not believing he'd said that.

"This is not some tragedy," he insisted. "Don't make it out to be one. And don't twist my words around to where you think I'm saying this didn't mean anything to me, either. Because it did."

Cautiously optimistic, she asked, "So, you're saying...what?"

"I don't know, Leanne. Honest to God, I don't." He sighed. "Are you going to kick me out of your bed now?"

Leanne went still, so surprised that he'd make a joke. And then she thought she understood. He was a man, after all.

"You don't want to talk about this, do you?"

Mitch looked her right in the eye and said, "It would be easier to talk about it if I had some idea of what I wanted to say."

She couldn't fault him for that. And maybe they needed some time to sort out their feelings for each other. "I'm sorry. I'm acting as if I'm entitled to some explanation here, and I know I'm not.''

"Wait a minute. You are the woman who's in this bed with me," he said with a smile. "In my book, that means you're entitled to an explanation. I'm just not sure I have one for you. I do know that I'm starving and that I'd probably have an easier time putting my thoughts together into some coherent form if I wasn't naked in bed with you.''

"Oh.''

"Why don't we take a shower, get dressed and find some food?''

"Okay.''

And then he kissed her one more time, his lips lingering over hers in a touch she found as reassuring as it had once been arousing.

"Remember what I told you the other night. I take care of what's mine, and you're mine now." He pulled away slowly, hesitated, then said, "I'm going to get in the shower, all right?''

She nodded, then turned away as, stark naked, he climbed out of the bed and padded across the floor. Only after he'd shut the bathroom door behind him and after she'd heard the shower come on did she let the first tear fall.

She was shaking and cold and her bed was empty now. Curling into the spot he'd just vacated, finding a warmth lingering there from his body, she pulled the covers over her and closed her eyes, to see if she could still feel his arms around her.

But that just made her tears fall faster.

She cried because of everything he'd said to her, everything about his manner—kind, concerned. He'd worked to put her at ease and to reassure her, had told her how good it felt to be with her, that it meant something to him, and, she thought, he'd been honest with her about his own jumble of feelings where she was concerned.

That was the kind of man he was—kind and considerate,

honest and loving. Handsome, she added. So very handsome. And sexy.

She was his now, he'd said. And he took care of his own.

Oh, God, she wanted to be his. In every sense of the word. She wanted her marriage to be real, wanted the boys to be hers, wanted Mitch—

"Leanne?"

Sure that there had to be some mistake, that she'd conjured up his voice somehow, she turned and found him standing beside the bed. His hair dripping wet, his feet bare, he had on nothing but a white towel wrapped around his waist.

He was watching her, and it was too late to hide the tears on her face. Feeling utterly foolish, and having no idea how she was going to explain, she went to move away.

Mitch wouldn't let her. He sat down on the bed and pulled her into his arms. With her face pressed against his chest, his heart thudding beneath her ear, she felt her emotions coming on so strong she was sure they would choke her.

She felt one of Mitch's hands stroking her hair, felt his lips place a kiss on the top of her head, felt surrounded by a strong, sexy and utterly solicitous man.

He brought his lips down to her ear, his breath brushing past her cheek as he whispered to her.

"I told you, I take care of what's mine. That means you're not alone anymore. It means that if you're upset, you come to me. No more crying alone, Leanne. All right?"

She tried to nod, but what he'd said only made her cry harder, which had him holding her tighter against him.

"I'm not very good at that," she said, the words muffled against his chest.

"What?" He drew away enough that he could see her face.

"Letting myself depend on someone."

Something in his expression seemed to soften, making him even more attractive than before.

"That's all right. I'll teach you."

Chapter 12

By the time they made it out of their room, it was almost three o'clock. They decided to have a late lunch, so Mitch took Leanne to an Italian place down the block from the hotel.

Sitting across the table from her, he couldn't help but be amazed at how very much his life had changed in a few short weeks. And he was curious how much more it was about to change because of her.

A week ago, he'd asked her to marry him with an absolutely clear conscience, with no reservations, thinking he was simply ensuring that the boys remained with him.

The marriage wasn't supposed to mean anything to him. Or to her.

He wondered now just what it meant to Leanne, wondered just how unfair he'd been to her by bringing her into this situation, then finding himself unable to keep his hands off her. He hadn't lasted twelve hours alone with her in that hotel room before he'd ended up in bed with her.

She absolutely took his breath away. Even now he couldn't take his eyes off her. She was a woman who was very much at ease with herself and her body. Tall, with those incredibly long legs, the hair that fell several inches past her shoulders, she dressed casually, in loose-fitting things that shouldn't be sexy but somehow were.

She looked touchable, he decided. Leanne was the kind of woman a man could take into his arms and touch and kiss and hold without ever worrying that she'd complain about his messing up her hair or her lipstick or anything else.

The thing that slayed him now was knowing that bit of reserve in her, which he'd mistaken for coldheartedness, was just a ruse to cover up how vulnerable she really was.

That damned vulnerability of hers was threatening to break what was left of his heart.

And still, somewhere in the back of his head, was an awful feeling that by being with Leanne, he'd somehow betrayed his wife.

Except Kelly wasn't his wife anymore, he reminded himself. The woman sitting across from him was.

He watched as Leanne toyed with the stem of her wineglass, watched the elegant movement of her hands around the goblet, noticed the way the diamonds he'd put on her finger caught the light from time to time.

His ring. His wife.

"You're staring," she said, looking at her own hand now. "The ring?"

He nodded.

"Do you regret marrying me?"

"No. I just can't believe I was foolish enough to think something like a marriage could be simple."

"It doesn't have to be that complicated just because..."

"We're sleeping together?" He finished the sentence for her, then had to ask, "We aren't going back to the way things were before, when we didn't sleep together, are we?"

She took her time about answering. "Do you want to?"

"No," he shot back, latching onto her hand, the one that held his ring. "Do you?"

"No."

"Good. You want to talk about Kelly, don't you?" He felt her try to tug her hand away, but he wouldn't let her. And he figured he might as well get this conversation over with, because there was no way to avoid it altogether. "I can say her name without becoming upset."

"But you can't sleep with another woman without feeling you've done something you shouldn't have."

Mitch had the perfect comeback—Leanne couldn't sleep with her sister's husband without feeling guilt, either. But he wouldn't say that to her, because it would hurt her. And he'd promised himself he wasn't going to hurt her.

"I think it was an inescapable fact that I would feel guilty the first time I was with another woman, no matter how long I waited or who I was with."

"But it's worse because that woman is me."

"It's...surprising. And more than a little unsettling. It's awkward," he admitted.

She nodded her agreement, then asked, "Can you handle this?"

"This?"

"Us."

"I don't see that we have a lot of options here." Mitch considered for a minute, and then he got scared thinking of one other option. "Unless this is just too much for you and you want to leave."

He had a very bad moment imagining that she might, though he couldn't blame her if she did. Instead, her face took on that lost-little-girl look, the one that had him realizing she'd been hurt too often and was expecting to get hurt again now.

"I loved Kelly, too," she said.

"I know." Mitch squeezed her hand and wished he

could hold her. Gently, he asked, "Do you feel what we did somehow negates that?"

She shook her head. "I don't know. But I never wanted to hurt her."

"Leanne, I don't think anything has the power to hurt her anymore. Right now, you're the one I'm worried about."

"Me? What about you? I know it's bothering you, too."

"It is, but I've done a lot more to come to terms with Kelly's death than you have. You've been trying to run away from it, rather than face it. And I blame myself for that."

"You? Why?"

"Because I laid into you at the cemetery the day of her funeral and made you feel you weren't welcome."

"Oh, Mitch. I've been running away from things all my adult life. It didn't start with you the day of Kelly's funeral."

"Still, I hated the entire world that day, and I took it out on you. I'm sorry about that."

"I just couldn't get there in time," she said. "The letter took so long to reach me, and by the time it did, it was too late."

"Hey, I know that now."

"I keep telling myself, if only I hadn't been so far away, or if I'd been in any other place at the time. If I'd called her and asked if I could come when the boys were born, instead of waiting for her to invite me, then I—"

Mitch slid his seat over until he was beside her, then silenced her with a hand against her lips. "No. You can't do that to yourself. Leanne, if I've learned one thing from losing Kelly, it's that 'what ifs' don't mean a damned thing. We don't have the luxury of knowing what's going to happen and basing our decisions on that."

"I should have been here long before she died," she insisted.

"And Rena should never have treated you the way she

did. Your father shouldn't have let her. Your mother shouldn't have died when she had four little kids to take care of. Do you blame all of them for this?'' He watched, wondering if he was getting through to her. Then he had to add, ''Do you blame me?''

''You?''

''I could have encouraged Kelly to reach out to you long ago, rather than being so stubborn about it and blaming you for the whole mess.''

''I don't blame you,'' she said.

''And you shouldn't blame yourself. Leanne, you couldn't have saved her, even if you had been here. No one could have known what was going to happen. No one could have stopped it.'' He squeezed her hand, then slipped his arm around her and pulled her to him until her head fell to his shoulder. ''It took me a long time to accept that. I spent months blaming myself for getting her pregnant.''

''You did?''

He nodded, dropping a light kiss on her forehead. Then he remembered something. This morning... Mitch swore softly. ''Leanne?''

''Hmm.''

''Last night. I didn't... We didn't...''

She lifted her head from his shoulder. ''It's all right. I've had a problem with migraines in the past year or so, and my doctor put me on the pill. I don't know how or why, but it seems to help control them. And I had a complete physical after Kelly died. I don't have anything you need to worry about. And I haven't...been with anyone since then.''

''I had myself checked out from head to toe, too, after Kelly died.'' Mitch let out a long, slow breath, his heart just now starting to settle into a normal rhythm after he'd realized the crazy chances they'd taken. ''I'm so sorry,'' he said. ''I can't believe I was that irresponsible.''

"It's been a long time since you've had to think of anything like that, Mitch."

"Yes, it has." He was starting to relax now, and he hoped she was, as well. "So, are we okay with all of this?"

Leanne hesitated, then nodded.

Mitch sighed. He knew she had a long way to go before she felt comfortable with him and their attraction for each other.

They spent one more glorious night and day in that hotel suite, barely making it out of the bed, then decided to go home Sunday evening. Mitch wanted some time with the boys before he had to go to work Monday morning. Leanne found that she missed them a great deal herself, and she wondered if they missed her.

Driving home, Mitch slipped his hand over hers and asked, "Nervous?"

"About being in the house?"

"Yes."

She nodded. She and Mitch both had accepted the fact that they were going to feel guilty, that there was no escaping it. But they weren't going back to the way things had been before, either.

"Give it some time," Mitch said. "And try not to worry so much."

"But I'm so good at worrying," she said, hoping she could make him smile.

He did. "We'll work on finding you a new hobby. Did you ever think about taking pictures?"

"I'm going to buy a camera tomorrow if mine don't arrive by then. And your children are going to be the most photographed toddlers in the whole state. I've missed them," she said.

"I bet they've missed you, too."

And then they were pulling into the driveway. There were no lights on in the house, so she and Mitch walked

across the street to Marc and Ginny's place. The boys must
have been waiting and watching, because sheer pande-
monium erupted when Marc opened the door and the boys
charged past him to Mitch.

They shrieked and giggled and climbed all over him.
Will toddled out onto the porch and jumped into the middle of the pile, until Marc pulled him off. And Hannah put
her hands on her hips and shook her finger at everyone for
making so much noise.

Ginny was the last one to arrive on the scene. She said
something to her husband, then took Leanne by the hand
and pulled her inside, closing the door behind her.

"To the kitchen, quick. And maybe they won't find us
for a few minutes."

Doing as she was told, Leanne followed her. Once the
two of them were safely alone, Ginny turned to her.

"Well? You look like married life agrees with you."

Leanne blushed in a way she hadn't in years.

"Oh, that good?" Ginny teased. "I just needed to make
sure I did the right thing."

"You did," Leanne said, feeling incredibly lucky right
then and feeling the need to explain why. "Ginny, I don't
know how to thank you. For everything."

Ginny gave her a big, warm hug. "Be happy," she said.
"Make Mitch happy. And the boys. And yourself."

"I want to," she said. "I want so much to believe that
everything's going to work out."

Before they could say anything more, the door to the
kitchen burst open and Teddy stood there grinning and
holding out his arms. "Weeann!"

Leanne recognized that mangled pronunciation of her
name and felt sheer joy flooding through her at the look
on his sweet little face.

"Come 'ere, Teddy bear." She leaned over and picked
him up. "I missed you."

"Mizz ooh." He grinned, giving her a wet, sloppy kiss
on the nose.

Mitch showed up a moment later with Timmy sitting on his shoulders. He smiled seeing her and Teddy together that way, then asked if Leanne was ready to go home.

Home, she thought. What a wonderful word. What a wonderful feeling—to be home with this man and these children.

They went home, played with the boys, bathed them and put them to bed. Leanne stood outside the twins' room while Mitch tucked them in. Watching him with them, seeing the tenderness, the gentleness he showed them, always got to her.

He'd been every bit as tender and as gentle with her in their bed in the suite where they'd hidden away for a day and a half. Now that they were in this house he'd shared with Kelly, she wondered what was going to happen.

Mitch came to the door. ''I think they're really out this time.''

The boys had been so wound up Leanne didn't think they'd ever sleep tonight. Glancing at her watch, she saw that it was nine-thirty.

''Are you hungry?'' she asked, because neither one of them had had dinner, although they had eaten a late lunch.

''No. You?''

She shook her head, worried about what would take place next. And then she couldn't hold back a yawn.

Mitch came closer still, smiling easily. ''Bedtime?''

''I think so,'' she said, her heart nearly tripping over itself. Please, she said to herself, don't let him turn away now.

''Let me check the locks and the lights downstairs, and I'll be up,'' he told her.

Leanne dashed into the bathroom, brushing her teeth, scrubbing her face, taking down her hair, then finding herself unable to decide what to put on. The white silk nightgown Ginny had bought for her? Mitch had certainly liked the matching robe. But if she wore that and he didn't want to be with her...it would be so awkward. Her only other choice was her pajamas, and there was nothing sexy about them.

She went with the white silk, opened the bathroom door and found herself face-to-face with Mitch. As she watched, his gaze fell from her face, to her neck, her breasts, then lower. One of his hands came up to her shoulder, toying with the thin strap of the gown, tracing its path down her shoulder, then across the neckline.

Leanne couldn't hold back a tiny sound of pleasure. Nor could she stop the way her breasts swelled in response, her nipples jutting out against the cool silk, begging for his caress.

She felt the warmth of his skin before he ever touched her there, felt him teasing her as he had that first time the other morning.

"Mitch," she moaned.

"Hmm?"

"Please." She never would have found the courage to ask if he hadn't put his hands on her first. "Touch me."

"I intend to," he said, still teasing, trailing one finger along her collarbone now.

With a devastating smile, he took her hand and led her into her room, to the bed. He tugged back the covers, and she climbed in. Then she watched as he started unbuttoning his shirt, her mouth going dry at the sight of all that wonderful skin and the muscles in his chest and his arms. He discarded the shirt, then unbuttoned and unzipped his pants. Her hands were aching to take over the job for him, but she couldn't seem to move. So she watched him, instead, as he stripped down to nothing, then climbed into bed beside her.

His hand at her throat, he let a finger rest along the pulse point there, smiling at what he found. Her heart was thundering.

"Did you really think everything would change once we left that hotel room?" he asked softly, his hand caressing her throat.

"I wasn't sure."

Mitch nodded. "This is where I want to be." And then, finally, he kissed her and drew her into his arms. He made love to her, tenderly, gently, until he couldn't anymore, until there was no place for restraint between them. Leanne nearly screamed when the climax hit her. Mitch covered his mouth with hers just in time, and when he pulled away, he was laughing deep in his throat and reminding her that the boys were right next door.

And then Leanne was laughing, too. Until she had tears running down her cheeks, tears Mitch found and fussed over as he wiped them dry.

"Leanne?"

"Yes?"

He settled her against his side, her head pillowed on his shoulder. "You thought I was going to walk away from you tonight. That I would walk into that bedroom across the hall and leave you here all alone. I don't think I could do that even if I wanted to."

She opened her mouth to say something to him, but he brought his head down to hers and kissed her softly on the lips.

"Go to sleep," he said, tightening his hold on her, anchoring her to his side.

The bed was tiny, but it didn't matter that much because they slept in each other's arms.

Early the next morning, Mitch woke her with a slow, sexy kiss. She wound her arms around his neck and turned her body into his. Just as his hand settled over her breast, she heard a giggle.

Mitch lifted his head and looked at her. "I didn't realize I was so amusing."

"Wasn't me," she said.

They looked up together and found Timmy standing beside the bed, gesturing animatedly and chattering about something to do with his brother. Then they heard Teddy cry, "Out!"

"Oh, you didn't help him out of the crib this morning?" Mitch asked.

Timmy grinned and pointed. "Tee, out!"

"I'll get him." He turned back to Leanne, who was clutching the sheet to her because she wasn't wearing anything else, and he gave her a slow, sexy smile. "Back to the real world?"

She let her hand rest on his arm for a second. "I happen to like my real world. I like it a lot."

The following days were like magic, like a gift out of time, Leanne thought. She was absolutely in love with the boys, and just as in love with Mitch.

As a man fiercely intent on protecting her sister, he'd been incredibly attractive. But as an utterly fabulous and loving father, a kind and supportive ally, a generous, enthusiastic lover, he was positively irresistible.

Leanne could have sworn he was happy, too.

Still, she kept waiting for the guilt to overwhelm him and her and ruin what they'd found together. But so far it hadn't happened.

One morning in early October, when she and Mitch had been married for two weeks, Ginny convinced Leanne it was time to try Mothers' Morning Out at Ginny's church. It was a wondrous thing, she claimed, three entire hours to themselves while the children played in the nursery at church. They could shop all alone, which was good, because Ginny was redoing her bedroom and she wanted a new bed.

"Marc would sooner gnaw off his right arm than go shopping," she said. "So you can help me pick it out."

"Okay," Leanne agreed once they were in the car on their way to the church. "What's the catch?"

"Catch?"

"To this Mothers' Morning Out thing?"

Ginny sighed. "The kids will probably pitch a fit and make us feel like terrible mothers for leaving them. And once every six weeks or so, you and I have to watch eighteen crying toddlers who've been abandoned by their own cruel, heartless mothers."

Leanne grinned. "I take it this means it won't do any good to tell you I'm not sure if I can leave the boys with total strangers."

"These aren't strangers. They're perfectly wonderful women who go to my church."

Leanne still wasn't sure. "The boys will really cry if I leave them?"

"Of course. They've gotten attached to you. Besides, they're toddlers, and toddlers are the greatest manipulators in the world. They sense that guilt inside you, and they attack you right where they know they have their best chance of getting to you and getting what they want."

"Which is?"

"To stop their cruel, heartless mother from leaving them with a couple of strangers," Ginny quipped. "You have to promise me you won't cry when they start to cry. Otherwise we'll never get out of here. Just tell yourself that motherhood is a wonderful and precious gift, just not one that anyone should be forced to enjoy twenty-four hours a day, seven days a week. We're allowed to get away from them every now and then."

"Okay. I can do this." Leanne took a breath to steady herself and would not let herself look into the back of the van, where the boys were sitting in their car seats, chatting away, with no idea of what was in store for them.

They pulled into the church parking lot, and Will seemed a little uneasy. He'd been here before, after all. He knew what was coming. He was crying by the time they walked into the nursery, a bright, shining room filled with toys, with a dozen or so children playing happily. One little girl in the corner was clinging to her mother, as another woman tried to coax her into coming to play. And in the rocking chair, a child was sucking his thumb and sobbing with his head on the shoulder of a woman Leanne was sure was not related to him.

Teddy appeared a little uneasy, and Leanne started to worry.

"We're going to do this fast," Ginny said. "Trust me. It doesn't get any easier, no matter how long the goodbyes are. And don't panic. If you do, the boys will pick up on it, and they'll panic, too."

Teddy pressed against her leg, his arms going around her knee. And Timmy looked suspicious. Will was howling, and Hannah was reassuring both Ginny and Leanne that she would take perfectly good care of all the babies. Hannah didn't consider herself one of them. After all, she was big.

Leanne put Teddy into the arms of a woman Ginny introduced as Laurie, gave Timmy a toy tractor, which he loved, and told them both goodbye. They gazed at her with sad, puppy-dog eyes filled with big tears. Teddy held out his arms to her and sobbed. Timmy looked defiant once he stopped looking scared.

All of a sudden, Leanne could imagine herself a year from now, her time with them over. And she was supposed to just walk away?

Feeling as though she'd been kicked in the stomach, she turned to the boys. Quickly, she told them she would be back very soon, that they were going to have lots of fun playing with all those toys and with Hannah and Will. Then she turned and fled. Timmy was calling her name as she left.

"Okay," Ginny said once they were in the van again. "That was awful."

Leanne nodded. "Teddy was crying."

"He'll stop. We've got the car phone. We'll call in ten minutes to check on all of them, and I swear, they'll be fine." Ginny glanced over at her, then said, "Come on. We're leaving them for three hours, not three months."

"No," Leanne said. "It's not that."

"What?"

"I'm not their mother. And I can't let myself forget that. As wonderful as the past weeks with them have been, it's not real. It's not my life."

"You love them." Ginny said.

Leanne nodded.

"How can you believe that's not real?" Ginny argued.

"I'm lying to myself," she insisted. "It's as if I'm playing house with Mitch, pretending this marriage is real and the boys are mine, and I can't let myself do that. Because I don't know how in the world I'm going to let them go when this is over."

"Leanne, how can you be so sure you'll have to let them go?"

"Because Mitch and I have a deal. A year. That's it. Then I'm supposed to leave."

"Mitch is not going to ask you to leave. If you could see the way he looks at you sometimes, you'd know that. Leanne, he's like a new man. He's happier than I've seen him in...months."

"Seventeen and a half months, to be exact?" Leanne knew precisely how long it had been. "Since before Kelly died?"

"Yes."

"Kelly's the one he loved."

"That doesn't mean Mitch can't love you," Ginny persisted.

"No. He's been kind to me because I'm helping him with the boys and because he's a kind man. And I think he's come to care for me, but I could never take Kelly's place in his heart."

"You don't have to. You'll make your own place in his heart."

"Oh, Ginny, I wish I could."

"You can."

"No." Leanne shook her head. "You don't understand."

"Oh, yes, I do." The van came to a stop in a parking lot at a little café, and Ginny said, "Come on. Shopping's going to have to wait. I think it's time I told you about a man named Joe Reed."

"Joe Reed?" Leanne climbed out of the van and followed Ginny into the restaurant. "Who's Joe Reed?"

"A man I loved very much," she said cryptically. "One I married. And had a child with."

The hostess came to seat them, lingered at the table, telling them about the breakfast specials. Leanne didn't think the woman would ever leave. Finally, she had a chance to ask, "You have another child somewhere?"

"No." Ginny laughed. "It's Hannah."

Leanne didn't understand. "Hannah's not—"

"Careful," Ginny interrupted. "Marc doesn't take it well when anyone tries to say he's not Hannah's father. He is, in every way that matters to her and to him. We say she has two fathers—Marc and Joe."

Stunned, Leanne leaned back into the big booth in which they were seated. "I can't believe this. I mean, I've seen Marc with her and..."

"I know. I think Marc fell in love with her as quickly as I did."

"So you and Marc haven't been together that long."

"Three years," Ginny said. "Hannah was six months old when we got married, although I'd known Marc since I was a little girl. Leanne, it's not a secret, just not something you bring up in casual conversation. I wanted to tell you. But I wasn't sure you were ready to hear it. And I wasn't sure how you really felt about Mitch until the day of the wedding. Otherwise I would have told you already. It's strange how many similarities there are in our situations."

"Similarities?"

"Joe and Marc were the best of friends," she explained. "Marc was practically part of the family, as far as the Reeds were concerned. So you can imagine how they reacted to the news that Marc and I were involved. And that wasn't nearly as difficult as the way Marc and I felt about getting involved with each other.''

Leanne didn't say anything at first. She was too surprised. Marc and Ginny looked like the perfect couple to her. In fact, Leanne had envied her new friend's happiness as much as her sister's.

She would never have guessed Ginny ever had her heart broken, or that Hannah had ever lost a father.

''And you loved Joe?'' Leanne asked.

''Very much. We were married for ten years. I never imagined I'd so much as kiss another man. I didn't until Marc came along.''

Leanne hated to ask the next question, but she desperately wanted to know the answer. ''Do you love Marc as much as you loved Joe?'' She winced just hearing the words. ''I'm sorry. That was awful, I know. But...''

''How do you measure love?'' Ginny asked. ''Love is an absolute. It doesn't come in varying degrees. I loved Joe. I was happy with him. And now I love Marc.''

The waitress interrupted them again, serving their coffee this time. Leanne took it black, but Ginny doctored hers with cream and sugar. When she was satisfied with the taste, she put her cup down and turned to Leanne.

''It's possible to love more than one man. To honestly and truly love two. And to be happy with them both.''

''So what happened to you and Joe?''

''He was killed before Hannah was even born. And I was just like Mitch. Devastated. I think the only reason I got through it was that I had to pull myself together enough to take care of Hannah.''

''That's amazing. Mitch told me you and Marc were so helpful to him after Kelly died, but he never mentioned what you'd been through.''

''He's a wonderful man,'' Ginny said. ''And I want him to be happy. I want you to be happy, too. You've got to believe that can happen for the two of you.''

"I want to believe it," Leanne said.

"After Joe died, I wasn't looking for anyone else to love. And I certainly never imagined that I could ever be this happy again. But I am. I swear to you, I couldn't love Marc any more than I do. And I don't see how my feelings for him in any way diminish what I felt for Joe. Now, I'll admit I didn't always feel that way. Marc and I have battled our share of guilt, and Joe's family had a hard time accepting that Marc and I were going to be together. But we worked through all that. You and Mitch can, too."

"I want that, Ginny. I want to be Mitch's wife, not because he needs me or the boys need me, but because he loves me."

"You are his wife, and he and the boys do need you. You're living in his house, and you're sleeping in his bed every night. I think he's half in love with you already. You couldn't be in a better position to get what you want."

"So what do I do?" Leanne asked.

"When you find every bit of happiness you've ever imagined right in front of you?"

Leanne nodded.

"Happiness is a gift. A rare and wondrous gift. You get down on your knees and thank God for it, and then you reach out and take it."

"I wish it could be that simple."

"Leanne, I don't think anything happens by accident. I believe you're here for a reason, that Mitch and the boys desperately needed someone—that you did, too. And now the four of you are together, and it's working. How can you think it wasn't meant to be?"

"I don't know. I never viewed it that way. I have this bad habit of expecting the worst of everything, at least when it comes to my personal life. And I'm usually not disappointed." Leanne thought about how much she'd just admitted, how sad it was, how true. "I've been so sure I wouldn't get what I wanted that I never imagined Mitch and I were meant to be together.''

Leanne sighed and leaned her head back against the booth. "I do love him."

Ginny put her hand over Leanne's. "And he's going to love you. Wait and see."

Chapter 13

Something was wrong with Leanne. Mitch knew from the minute he came home that evening. But she didn't want to tell him about it.

He played with the boys for a while, and she went out for a run. He didn't like that, because it was getting dark when she left, and even though the neighborhood was safe, a woman alone couldn't be too careful.

When he'd said he didn't like her running alone after dark she'd looked surprised at first, then had told him she could take care of herself. So he'd held his temper and watched her walk out the door.

Mitch felt the tension seeping into his body as she disappeared into the darkness. He was angry at himself for letting her go, angry at her for so blatantly ignoring her own safety this way.

And he was scared, scared she wouldn't come back.

How would he feel if she didn't?

The boys demanded his attention right then, and he worked quickly to get them ready for bed, then to convince them to stay in their crib long enough to actually fall asleep. Now that they could climb out, bedtime had turned into a big game.

All the while, Mitch kept glancing at his watch and waiting for the sound of the front door opening so he would know Leanne was back. Nearly an hour had passed. Normally, she was back in forty-five minutes.

Mitch closed the door to the boys' room for what he hoped was the last time, then went downstairs. Hastily searching the house, he saw she wasn't there. He swore softly, then headed for the front door. Looking down the block to the right, then the left, he realized he'd never even asked her what path she took.

How could he have been so careless with her safety not to find out?

In something close to a panic, he called Marc and Ginny's house. Ginny answered the phone. Quickly, he told her what happened, then asked if she or Marc could come over and sit with the boys while he went out to look for Leanne. Ginny agreed to send Marc over, and then Mitch asked if anything had happened that day to upset Leanne.

"Well, I told her about Joe."

"She didn't know?" Mitch was surprised. Leanne and Ginny had gotten very close.

"Well, it just never came up."

Mitch thought there must be more to it than that. "Why would hearing about you and Joe upset her?"

Ginny hesitated. "Mitch, I think you should ask her about that."

"All right. When I find her, I will," he said.

He heard a knock on the door, hoped it was Leanne and she'd forgotten her key. But it was Marc.

"Ginny, Marc's here and I'm going to go now." He hung up the phone.

Marc stood there for a minute, staring at his friend, then asked, "What's wrong?"

"Leanne went out for a run, and she should have been back twenty minutes ago."

"That's it? You look like you could chew nails right now."

"It's dark, she's alone and she's late. That's not reason enough to be worried?"

"I didn't say you shouldn't be worried. I just thought something else was going on."

"I want her back safe." He grabbed his jacket, his keys, his cell phone. "Call me if she shows up."

"Sure."

"And if the boys get out of that crib, throw them right back in it and threaten them with some dire consequences if they climb out before morning."

"Threaten little children? I can do that," Marc said, closing the door behind Mitch.

Mitch thought about driving because he could cover more ground faster, but rejected the idea, since in the car he couldn't take the footpath to the park nearby. Surely she'd gone to the park. It was well lit and there were almost always people around at this time of night.

Once again, he asked himself why the hell he'd ever let her go out without finding out the path she intended to take, or why he'd ever let her go when it had been so dark by the time she left.

Marc was right. There was more going on here than he'd admitted.

For just a second, he imagined what it would be like if he lost Leanne, too. And in a rush, all the emotions he'd experienced the day he'd lost Kelly came back to him. It had been like taking a hit from a live wire, and it had left him reeling.

He couldn't breathe at first, and he could barely think. All he could do was feel.

He wasn't supposed to care this much for Leanne, he told himself. He wasn't supposed to care for anyone, really, except the boys. Mitch had made a promise to himself after Kelly had died that he wouldn't ever put himself in a position to be hurt like that again.

It had been too late to stop himself from loving the boys, but he honestly thought he could guard his heart against falling for anyone else. And he hadn't worried at all about falling for Leanne, even after he had decided to marry her.

After that weekend together in the hotel suite, he told himself there was simply no understanding or explaining the mysteries of what attracted a man to a woman. They were adults, and they wanted to be together. There was certainly no crime in that.

Of course, he'd reached the point where he could hardly wait to get home at night, not just because he was anxious to get into bed with her, but because he liked being home now. Because the boys were happy, and home was a pleasant place to be. Because he wasn't alone anymore. Because…he was happy, Mitch realized.

When he'd least expected it, he'd found happiness again.

With Leanne.

Mitch walked faster as he turned onto the footpath that led between the backyards of the houses around the perimeter of the park.

It was because of Leanne that he felt this way; he couldn't deny that anymore.

Did he love her? Was that possible? Was he really that stupid as to allow himself to love another woman, after what had happened the first time?

Scanning the edges of the park, his fear growing with every step he took, he saw nothing, nothing but trees and grass and an empty jogging path.

He couldn't love Leanne, he told himself. He was grateful to her for what she was doing for him and the boys. He felt guilty about the way he'd treated her in the past and wished he could make that up to her by helping her find her way back to her family. He wished she weren't so damned vulnerable or that she didn't hold so much inside herself, not sharing it with anyone, even him.

And when he took her to bed, every other thought flew right out of his head, except for the possibility that he might never get enough of her.

At the moment he was about to take off running to cover the ground a little faster, because there was an image in his head of her lying on the ground somewhere, bruised and bleeding and needing him. It haunted him with his every step.

But none of that added up to love, he told himself, trying very hard not to panic.

Then his cell phone rang.

For a second he was afraid to answer it. When he dug it out of his pocket, he realized his hand was trembling. Dear God, where was she? And what had happened to her? He flicked the button that activated the phone and said, "Hello."

"She's back," Marc said.

"And?" He waited for the bad news.

"She's fine."

Mitch sagged against a tree trunk as the tension left him.

"Look," Marc continued, "I don't know what's going on with you tonight, but I thought I should warn you. Your wife doesn't seem too happy about you searching for her, and I don't think you're going to make things any better if you come charging home to give her a piece of your mind."

"Well, that is just too damned bad, because that's what she's going to get."

Marc laughed. "Did you figure out why you were so worried about her?"

"You think this is funny?" Mitch inquired, unable to believe his partner was actually laughing.

"No. Really, I don't. I've just been wanting to ask how the two of you are getting along, and I don't think I have to ask anymore."

"What the hell does that mean?"

"That things must be going well for you to get this bent out of shape because she's a few minutes late coming home."

Mitch said something vile.

Marc only laughed harder. "Try to calm down a little before you get back home, okay?"

Mitch tried, because he supposed Marc was right. He wouldn't get very far with Leanne by jumping her the minute he walked in the door. Women did not respond well to orders, he'd discovered, even when something like their safety was involved. And he normally managed to control his impulses to give orders to anyone outside of the job. But he was finding it very hard to do that right now.

He forced himself to take his time walking back home. Marc was gone. Mitch managed not to slam the front door behind him when he got inside. As he shrugged out of his jacket he could hear the upstairs shower running.

He climbed the steps, walked across the hall and looked in on the boys. They were out cold. Then he walked to the bathroom door, checked the knob and found it was unlocked. And the shower had stopped.

He was still more upset than he had a right to be and more angry, and he didn't think there was any way he was going to be able to hide that from Leanne tonight.

Turning the knob, he opened the door and found her standing in that damned white robe, with her hair still dripping wet. But she was safe. He hadn't quite believed it until he'd seen her with his own eyes.

Judging from the look on her face, she was angry, too, he noted, wondering where he could find some bit of diplomacy and patience inside him to help him deal with this.

It might help if he could keep from staring at her in that robe, especially if he could keep from remembering she'd looked just like this that first morning at the hotel, when he'd taken her so quickly and a little roughly, without a bit of patience or finesse.

And he wanted very much to do that again.

"Dammit," he muttered, feeling like a quarterback who'd just fumbled the ball in the stupidest way possible.

"You burst in here to curse at me?" she wanted to know.

"No, but I'm reevaluating my options right now."

Leanne leaned back against the cabinet and crossed her arms in front of her, the motion pulling the material taut across her breasts. "Oh, really? And why is that?"

"Because right now, you look so much like you did the morning after our wedding, and I can't seem to think of anything else but that."

Leanne was ready to yell at him, to ask him what he thought he was doing, tearing off after her like that, when all she'd done was take a couple of extra laps around the park. And while she was at it, she was going to ask what he thought gave him the right to tell her not to go out after dark, and whether he was mistaken about exactly what century this was.

And then he started undoing the buttons on his shirt, and she forgot exactly how she intended to launch into the whole conversation.

Next he reached for the zipper on his jeans, then for her.

"Mitch," she protested, knowing they needed to settle this.

"Later," he said.

He drew her hard against him, his mouth opening over hers. She found herself flush up against him as he pulled at her robe, then groaned in satisfaction when bare skin met bare skin. She clutched at the muscles in his arm as he lifted her onto the vanity and settled himself against her.

Leanne felt the heat instantly in him and in her. And the memories of that first incredible time they'd been together heightened all her senses. She'd been crazy to have him inside her then, and he'd trembled with a vain effort to hold back. Not that he needed to, or that she'd wanted him to. She'd been his for the taking from the instant he'd walked inside that door.

And she'd gone into his arms more than a dozen times since, just as eager as she was now, just as needy and as greedy. When nothing but a look or the sound of his voice could turn her into some kind of maniac.

He was kissing her deeply now, his tongue thrusting into her mouth. She was hungry for every bit of him, not wanting to let herself think of how very much she needed him.

Urging him closer, she opened herself to him, and he slid inside her. Clinging to him, she rocked her body against his, wanting him to take her quickly, powerfully, wanting him as out of control as she was.

And he was. She smiled against his lips as he groaned out her name. She felt him pulsing hotly deep inside her body, felt an answering shuddering inside herself as she called out his name.

His arms were crushing her to him, so that she could barely breathe, and every muscle in her body seemed to have worked itself beyond exhaustion, to the point where she wasn't even certain she could stand, much less walk.

She felt a bone-deep satisfaction at being with him this way, a happiness so intense it frightened her.

But she wouldn't give in to the fear now, she told herself, hugging him tightly against her and pressing her face to his shoulder. She couldn't lose a moment like this to her fears, not when she and Mitch were as close as two people could possibly be, not when he was still deep inside her, connected to her body and soul.

Leanne very nearly told him that she loved him.

But in that instant, he drew away from her, just enough that he could see her face, kiss her with his wonderfully soft, full lips, then lift her into his arms and carry her to her bed. She leaned against him, let him tuck her under the covers, then pull her into his arms.

"Do you always argue and make up like this?" she asked, drowsy and satiated and so comfortable lying next to him.

"Whenever I can get away with it," he said.

Leanne laughed, loving the humor that had been reborn in him of late. The grimness of the past year and a half were fading. She wondered how much of that Mitch was aware of, wondered whether he was really as happy as Ginny had claimed.

She was just getting comfortable, when she opened her eyes and noticed something out of place in her room. It was the window—in the wrong place. Confused, she glanced down at the bed and found that it was too big. The pattern on the sheets was one she didn't recognize.

"Surprise," Mitch said, leaning past her to snap on the lamp on the bedside table.

A new bedside table, she realized. A new lamp. New drapes. New comforter. New bed. New *room.*

Leanne went still, trying to understand what he'd done and why. This room was no longer his and Kelly's. She barely recognized it, in fact, because it was so different now.

The wedding picture, the one in which Mitch and Kelly had looked so young, was gone, as was the one in the silver frame that had graced the nightstand.

The new bed was whitewashed iron that scrolled at the top of the headboard and the footboard; the chest and dresser were stained a dark green that matched the scrolling vines of the sheets, the comforter and the shades. They were all things she'd admired on her shopping trip with Ginny this morning.

Would a man do this for a woman who was staying only a year? Leanne wondered.

"You don't like it," Mitch said.

"No, it's...just what I helped Ginny pick out for her bedroom this morning."

"Ginny's not getting a new bedroom."

"I figured that out." She turned on her side, facing him, trying for something neutral to say. "I guess I know why Ginny didn't want to come home this afternoon. You must have worked fast."

"I want you to be comfortable here," he said earnestly.

"Thank you."

He reached around her again and snapped off the light. Leaning back onto his pillow, with one hand up behind his head, he said carefully, "About running in the dark... Leanne, let me win this one. Think of it as having a get-out-of-jail-free card. You can play it anytime you want with me. But don't ask me to give on this."

Leanne was surprised—more than anything by the sincerity of his plea. Still, she needed to get away sometimes, and he needed to understand. She could take care of herself.

"Mitch, I've been in some of the worst hellholes in the world, usually by myself or with one local person as a guide. I'm not stupid or careless or helpless when it comes to defending myself. Would you like to see my certificates from self-defense class? Or should I just throw you flat on your back on the rug?"

"I didn't say you were helpless," he said carefully. "What I meant to say was that I was worried about you."

"Oh." How could she argue against that? The idea of having him worry over her and want to protect her, even if she was perfectly capable of protecting herself, was a wonderfully appealing one. Still, running time was sacred time. "It's going to get dark earlier and earlier now. And I need to get out and run to clear my head and to think."

"How would you feel about a treadmill?" he wanted to know.

"Bored."

"We'll get you a Walkman. Or a running partner, for when it's dark. I could live with that."

Feeling mischievous and just wanting to give him hell,

she added, "And maybe someone to hold my hand while I cross the street?"

But Mitch didn't smile. He didn't look the least bit amused. Leaning toward her, he put his hand along the side of her face, his fingers sliding into her hair. "Leanne, I've lost one wife already. I don't want to lose another."

She stared into his dark-green eyes, so deep she thought she could drown in them. He looked tired and somehow vulnerable tonight, she decided.

And he didn't want anything bad to happen to her.

It was the closest he'd ever come to saying he needed her, that she was important to him, and not just because of the threat to take the boys away.

Leaning closer, Leanne brushed her lips to his, and when she would have drawn away, he held her there and kissed her deeply, urgently, sweetly.

When she finally pulled her lips from his, she agreed to what he wanted.

Two days later, Mitch still hadn't figured out what had been eating her that night before she'd gone out running. It hadn't all been about her wanting to run in the dark by herself and him trying to tell her not to.

She'd given in on running alone. Fortunately, Marc liked to run, too, and they had agreed to get out three or four nights a week together. Mitch was incredibly relieved knowing Leanne wouldn't be out alone.

And she seemed pleased with the changes he'd made to their bedroom.

But something was still bothering her.

Mitch wondered if maybe he was just more in tune with her moods now, or maybe he was concerned about whether she was happy with the boys and him.

More and more often, he forgot that all this had come with a time limit, that a year from now she was supposed to pack her things and walk away, and he wasn't supposed to care that she left.

The thought nagged at him—Leanne walking out the door.

When his hands were on her, even in the smallest of ways, he felt immensely better. Touching drove the panic away, and it lit a little fire inside him. Not necessarily a sexual one, but a different kind of need. To be close to someone. To be a part of someone. To forget how it had been to be so alone.

At the moment, he wanted to know what was eating away at her.

It was a Sunday afternoon. Will Dalton's first birthday had been ten days earlier, but various family obligations had kept the entire clan from gathering to celebrate until today. Marc and Ginny's backyard was crowded with friends and relatives.

Leanne's cameras had finally arrived from New York, and she'd been as happy as a kid on Christmas morning. He was amazed at how quickly she'd gone through film, how she seemed to have stashed cameras all over the house and was forever snapping shots of the boys.

He'd watched her work and was pleased that it made her happy. But he'd watched her take casual shots haphazardly on many evenings. Now he saw her work the party like a professional photo shoot. She was concentrating hard, focusing on the kids. He heard the click of the shutter and the whirl of the film advancing automatically as she fired off shot after shot.

She worked with an intensity that amazed him, and she looked…satisfied, in a way he'd never seen her before.

Mitch felt the first flutterings of dread.

This was what she used to do, and from what Kelly had told him, she did it very, very well. She must have; after all, people had sent her all over the world to photograph places and things.

Even that morning after their wedding day, when she'd told him how sick she was of all the travel, she'd admitted she still loved taking pictures. Well, there were only so many pictures she could take in the backyard of the boys and the neighbors' kids.

What if she missed taking her pictures more than she would miss him and the boys if she left?

He watched her work until she was tired and she sat down in a corner of the backyard, staring at something with a wistful expression on her face. Mitch couldn't tell what she saw until he went and sat down beside her.

Because his ever present compulsion to touch her was even stronger than usual now and because he didn't see any reason to fight it any longer, he let his hand close over one of hers.

"What are you looking at?" he asked.

"Marc and Hannah. They're amazing together."

"They're very happy," he said, feeling as if he were dancing around the edges of some emotional wound. "Why would that make you sad?"

Leanne turned her head to him, blinked once, then again, then stumbled over her words when she said, "It just surprises me...now that I know. He's not her father. I mean...I know he is. But he's not. I'm not explaining myself very well."

"No, I understand what you're saying."

"They're so happy together. I saw it when I was looking through the camera lens. I'm so used to viewing the world that way, I swear I see more through that lens than I do with my own eyes."

Either that, or she was more comfortable with the lens between her and other people, maybe between her and other people's emotions, Mitch decided. She'd just told him something very important about her, he thought. She'd rather look at the world through a camera lens. To hold herself apart from everyone and everything? He suspected that was the reason.

"What do you see through the lens?" he said, thinking about all the times in the past when he'd plowed right over her tender emotions.

"You can see magic sometimes," she explained. "You can tell when something's genuine and you've captured a bit of it forever on film. Marc loves Hannah, and she loves him. It's going to come through on the print. I'll show you."

"I'd rather you tell me why that's such a surprise to you. Even better, you could tell me why it worries you." That part absolutely baffled Mitch.

"Worries me?"

He nodded, watching her withdraw from him and cursing himself for confronting her this way. He should know better than to come right out and ask Leanne about something that frightened her.

"I don't..." she began, then let the words trail off.

"It's all right," he insisted, when it really wasn't. But he could see in her eyes that she was practically begging him to let her off the hook.

He'd only asked for a year, Mitch reminded himself. She'd agreed to nothing more than that. And he hadn't bothered to renegotiate the deal, even after he'd taken her into his bed.

What would it take, he wondered, to make Leanne happy enough to stay? Because suddenly, he couldn't imagine living the rest of his life without her.

Chapter 14

Five days later, after Leanne had put the boys down for their nap, she heard the doorbell ring. Praying that the noise hadn't woken up the boys, she pulled open the door to find her little brother standing on the porch.

"Alex." She hadn't seen him since the night of her engagement party, when Amy had found her and Mitch kissing in the kitchen. "Hi."

"Hi."

He looked a little uneasy, and incredibly grownup.

"Can I come in?"

"Of course." She stepped back and held the door open for him. "Have a seat. Is something wrong?"

"No. Nothing. I was just...heading back to school, and I thought I'd stop by."

"Oh." Leanne was too surprised to say anything for a minute.

"Rena's really going off the deep end about this... marriage of yours and Mitch's," he began.

"I know." And it frightened her. It hadn't occurred to

Leanne that for Rena to lose the boys to Mitch would be difficult, but to lose them to Mitch and Leanne was something entirely worse.

Leanne feared the whole thing would turn into a vendetta as far as Rena was concerned, that Leanne might somehow make the whole custody fight even worse by making herself a part of it. After all, Rena hated Leanne. She would also hate the idea of Leanne having the boys.

Trying with everything in her to smile, when all she felt like doing was crying, Leanne said, "To hear Rena tell it, I tried to take you and Amy and Kelly away from her all those years ago. Not the other way around."

It was, she realized, the first time she'd ever tried to talk directly about this with Alex. He looked surprised and skeptical, maybe even hopeful.

"Was that the way it was, Leanne?"

"Yes."

"Because I don't remember anything except being scared. I was scared because you were going away. I don't remember our mother at all. I don't remember when she died. But I remember the day you walked away from us."

"Alex, I was eighteen," she said, thinking about saying goodbye to a beautiful, sad-eyed little boy. Why was it she always ended up having to say goodbye to the people she loved?

"I was eight," he said. "And you were the only mother I'd ever known."

"Alex, I wish I had been your mother, because then I might have stood a chance against Rena. But I wasn't. I was a scared, lonely teenage girl. Think about it," she begged. "I was four years younger than you are now, and Rena scared me to death. She scares me now."

"Are you doing this to get back at her?" he asked.

"Doing what?"

"Did you marry Mitch just to spite her?"

"No."

"To keep her from getting the boys?"

"No," she said. She had reasons too numerous to count for marrying Mitch.

"I don't know what's worse," Alex said. "Your marrying Mitch to keep Rena from getting the boys or your marrying him because you wanted him for yourself. Leanne, he's Kelly's husband."

To that, Leanne didn't think she could say anything. She let her gaze drop to the floor and turned away. All the while, she wanted to scream and to shout and to somehow make him understand.

Any other time, she would have simply left. She would have been on one of those incredibly uncomfortable, but brief, visits home, wishing things would be different this time, but sure that they wouldn't.

And it wouldn't take long for her expectations to be proven correct. At the first real sign of trouble, she would have packed her bag and left. Months later, maybe even years, she would have tried again. The results were always the same.

Except this time she couldn't leave. She'd promised Mitch a year, and she couldn't go back on that promise to him, no matter how painful it was to be there.

She wondered now how different things might have been if she'd stood up for herself, no matter how ugly the scene became, and honestly tried to patch things up with her sister years ago.

And if she'd learned anything from her sister's death, it was that she couldn't let Alex go like this, because she couldn't be sure she'd ever have another chance with him.

He was almost to the door, when Leanne stopped him. "I love the boys," she said. "I love Mitch, too, although I haven't found a way to tell him that yet. I loved Kelly. And I loved you, Alex. From the minute you were born. And if you could remember anything about the night our mother died, you'd remember that I was the one who held you tight and tried to explain. When you called out her name late at night, I was the one who came and got you out of your crib and dried your tears. I was the one you hung on to when you were scared. I was the one who made sure you got fed and dressed and bathed. I played silly games with you and made faces, even stood on my head, all because it made you laugh just for a minute.

"I would have done anything for you," she vowed. "I still would."

Alex looked at her as if he couldn't quite believe her. And he was still perilously close to the front door.

"It's true," she said, telling herself that she had to be the one to make the first move, to ask for what she so desperately wanted. "Please don't go. Please don't push me away."

He didn't say he believed her. But he didn't leave, either.

It was a beginning, Leanne decided.

As always, Mitch was eager to get home. He wanted the boys exploding with excitement just because he walked through the door. They'd break into a run to get to him and then practically dance in circles around him until he picked them up. And then they'd babble on about whatever was inside their little heads at the moment.

And he wanted to see what sort of mood his wife was in. He wanted to pull her aside, out of the chaos, and kiss her sweet lips, maybe put a smile on her pretty face.

He wanted her to stay and to be happy with him.

She'd been quiet since Will's party five days before, and he'd made love to her every night so he could hold her close, feel her arms around him, feel for a while that he was a part of her and that she could not deny the connection between them.

She slept with her head on his chest, her hair falling across his shoulder, and he would lie awake, stroking her hair, holding her hand and listening to her breathe.

Her silence and her sad little smiles were eating away

at him. Something was desperately wrong, and he had to get her to tell him.

He saw the minute he walked in the door that she'd been crying. Her eyes were tinged red, and she tried to hide her face from him, but he saw anyway.

Mitch played with the boys for a little while, let them burn off the worst of that burst of energy they got when he walked in the door, then went to find Leanne.

She was in the kitchen, beside an old desk stashed away in the corner where she'd been keeping some of her photographic equipment and some business papers that he didn't understand, ones he'd been afraid to ask about.

He walked up behind her, slid his arms around her waist and relaxed a little as she leaned back against him, her head falling against his shoulder. He kissed her cheek, then found her mouth, thinking to soothe her with his touch.

Make her happy.

Make her stay...

"I spoke with Alex this morning," he said, though he hadn't been sure he should even mention that to her, because he didn't know if anything would come of it. "He's still mad, but I think he may stop by sometime. Maybe the two of you could talk."

"You did that?" She turned in his arms so that she was facing him. And she was smiling, a genuinely happy smile.

"Yes."

"He came by this afternoon. It was some sort of school holiday."

"And?"

"And...I thought for a minute it was going to be like every lousy half argument we ever had over the years, the kind that ended with me walking away and not coming back for another year or so to try it again. And then I thought about Kelly and everything I wish I'd said to her. And I thought, what if I don't get another chance to say any of this to Alex, either? So I told him. I told him I loved him, and that I would do anything in the world for him.''

Mitch used the pad of his fingers to wipe away her tears.

''He didn't say much to me. Mostly that he was so angry when I left and so hurt.''

''That's okay,'' Mitch said, trying to reassure her. ''He needs to get that out on the table, and it's always easier to tell someone how mad you are than to tell her you really care.''

She nodded. ''I told him I was angry and hurt and lonely, too, that for the longest time I just couldn't seem to say that to him. But I did today, and I think it's going to make a difference. I think Alex and I might be able to work through this.''

Mitch dried a few more of her tears, and she leaned over and kissed him softly on the lips.

''I should have known it was you who talked him into coming to see me. Thank you.'' She took him into her arms and squeezed him to her. ''You're so good to me, Mitch.''

''I want you to be happy here,'' he said, needing so much to hear that she was.

He'd never asked her straight out, never come as close to asking as he had just now. And she'd never told him how she felt, except to say that she loved the boys and loved being with them.

But that had been weeks ago, before he'd made her his wife, before a whole myriad of emotions had sprung up between them.

Mitch held on to her when she went to pull away, because she hadn't said what he wanted to hear yet. He thought about what she'd told him about never having a chance to tell Kelly how she felt, about deciding to talk to Alex today because she didn't know when or if she'd get another chance.

Maybe Mitch should do the same thing. Maybe it was

time he told Leanne that he cared about her, that he needed her, that he didn't want her to leave.

He was about to do so, when the doorbell rang. "Damn," he muttered, hearing the boys take off running for the door. They loved to see who was on the other side.

Leanne slid out of his arms. "I think I'd better save whoever's there from the wild ones. And keep them from escaping."

Mitch let her go.

Tonight, he told himself. He could tell her how he felt tonight.

Following her into the living room, he watched her take an overnight letter into her hand and sign the delivery-man's clipboard. Walking to her, Mitch asked, "What is it?"

This wasn't the first special delivery letter she'd received. She'd always brushed them off, as if they were nothing. But Mitch was starting to wonder how significant they were, as the envelopes piled up on the desk.

Leanne ripped open the oversize cardboard envelope and pulled out a letter. Mitch saw the New York City address on the letterhead and his stomach began to turn.

"It's more of the same." She shrugged the letter off, sliding the papers back into the envelope. "From my agent. He's having trouble accepting the fact that I've turned down all the job offers he's found for me lately."

"He has job offers for you?" Mitch asked.

Leanne sighed. "Yes. I may have to go and talk to him face-to-face."

"He's in New York," Mitch said stupidly.

"I could fly up for the weekend. I still have a lot of things to settle there. I have to do something about my apartment. Move my bank accounts. Either ship the rest of my photography equipment or store it. It might be easier just to go there and get it all done."

And come back to him, Mitch told himself. She was only

going for a few days, and then she was going to come back to him and the boys.

Except, what if she got there and the visit reminded her of all she was missing by staying in Chicago and mothering two little boys all day?

Looking after the boys was exhausting work, Mitch knew. As frustrating and as tiring, even monotonous, as it was rewarding and wonderful to watch them grow and change every day.

And she was a woman who'd been all over the world, who'd seen things he could only imagine. How could what he had to offer her compete?

"Mitch? Are you all right?"

"Sure," he said, knowing he couldn't tell her how he felt now. He would wait and see whether she would come back to them. "When are you leaving," he asked carefully.

"I don't know. Maybe next weekend? If I could get out of here Friday afternoon, I could be back Sunday night."

Seven days, he thought.

Nine until she came back.

"I'll make arrangements to get away early Friday." He would take her to the airport, watch her leave and try not to panic.

While he was at work the following Wednesday, Mitch got a message to call his attorney. When he returned the call, Jane was in court. All her secretary could tell him was that she'd likely be there all day, but that she'd try to call him back.

They played phone tag all day. He finally took a chance by showing up at her office shortly after six, and found her there.

Mitch settled himself in the chair in front of her desk and told himself to be prepared for just about anything. But Jane still managed to surprise him.

"Good news," she said. "Social services is finally done

with their investigation. They're satisfied that the boys are fine right where they are. I'm sorry it took so long, but it was just as I suspected—they're drowning in paperwork over there, and yours isn't the kind of case they're going to give priority to, because your boys are fine, according to the agency.''

"Good," Mitch said, thinking that was it.

"And—even better—your mother-in-law has lost her attorney.''

"What do you mean *lost* her attorney?"

"I mean he's not handling her case anymore. I told you we had to file our official answer to the charges they made in their custody suit. I did so and mailed a copy to Mr. Richardson's office. It was returned with a letter saying he no longer represented your mother-in-law.''

"Which means?"

"Well, I'm speculating, but I know Ted Richardson, and he doesn't take on a case he's certain barely has a prayer of winning, particularly something as nasty as a custody case. I'd say he talked to someone at social services, found out that you were married now and told his client she was probably wasting her time and her money with her suit.''

"But Rena could just find someone else to represent her, couldn't she?" Mitch asked.

"She could. So don't go thinking this is over just yet. But it's very good news, Mitch. I don't think there's a reputable attorney in this town who'd be eager to handle this case and be optimistic about the chances of winning. Maybe that will be enough to discourage your mother-in-law from taking this any further.''

Jane stared at him for a moment, then said, "You don't look very happy about this.''

"I'm surprised," Mitch announced carefully. He leaned back in his chair, feeling as if someone had knocked the breath out of him. He'd expected relief at the news that the custody mess was over, and he was relieved. But Leanne had married him to keep Rena from getting the boys. And if Rena was done trying to take the boys away from him, he didn't need to be married to Leanne anymore.

Of course, he did need her, very much. And she had a whole other life calling to her. She was leaving for New York Friday. He was going to watch her leave.

How could he tell her Rena might be giving up? What would Leanne say?

Mitch turned back to his attorney. "Is that all?"

"Yes. You sure you're okay?"

"I'll be fine," he said—one of those polite little lies. He would not be fine without Leanne.

"Well, I'll call you if I hear anything else."

Mitch got to his feet. "Thank you."

"And, Mitch? Congratulations."

"What?"

"On your marriage. I hope the four of you will be very happy together."

"We are," he said, praying that it was true.

Marc and Leanne planned to run in the park that night. Leanne stood just inside the doorway, chatting with Ginny while she waited for Marc to find his running shoes.

"Did Mitch get in touch with his lawyer?" Ginny inquired.

"What?"

"The lawyer. About the custody suit. Marc said Mitch had a message to call her, but he hadn't managed to connect with her by the time Marc left work today."

Ginny's husband walked into the room then, catching the end of their conversation. Both of them were looking expectantly at Leanne.

"I don't know. He didn't say anything to me about it." Surely he would have, she thought. He wouldn't keep bad news from her. "But you know how it is. The kids go crazy when he walks in the door, and I was rushing to get over here before it got too late."

"He must not have been able to reach his lawyer,"

Marc said, kissing his wife. "She was in court all day. That's why they didn't talk earlier."

"I'm sure that's it," Leanne said, then thought—what if he didn't want to talk about it in front of the boys?

When Leanne returned from her run, she took a quick shower. She didn't bother to dry her hair, just dressed in the nightgown and robe he liked so much.

She walked into the kitchen and found him stirring some rice she'd left on the stove. Chicken in a cream sauce was simmering in another pot. It had become a tradition to eat later in the evening so they could eat alone.

The little table in the corner of the kitchen was set, a glass of wine at her place, and Mitch was pulling a salad she'd made earlier out of the refrigerator.

"You're so handy to have around," she said, thinking that might win her a little smile.

He turned, caught sight of her in that robe and gave her much more than a little smile. His look heated her whole body.

Mitch put the salad on the table and came to her. Letting himself do nothing more than place his hands on her arms, he asked, "Handy? That's what you think of me? That I'm a convenience?"

Leanne laughed huskily, because she knew they weren't going to be eating dinner anytime soon, and she didn't mind. Some nights they crept back downstairs around midnight, ravenous. Some nights Mitch brought her dinner in bed. She'd learned to prepare something that would keep on the stove.

"You *are* convenient to have around," she teased.

Mitch glared at her, as if she'd insulted him.

"Well, look at this kitchen," she said. "You made the rice, set the table, poured me a glass of wine. And those wild boys of yours are asleep. All I have to do is eat my dinner and go to bed. This is first-class service," she said, thinking it was incredibly easy to live with him.

Already, she was dreading being away from him this weekend, which seemed so silly to her, a woman who'd lived her life on the go. She hadn't been more than a few blocks from this house in weeks, and she loved New York, though she'd seldom given herself time to enjoy it properly. Yet here she was thinking about nothing but missing the boys and spending two nights without Mitch.

God, she needed him so much already. And their year had just begun.

"You know," he whispered into her ear as he eased himself against her, "there's just something about you wet from the shower that drives me absolutely insane."

He slid his palm across the front of her robe, pushing it against her skin, catching a drop of moisture here and there as he went. "Either that, or it's the way this robe clings to your wet skin."

Mitch lowered his mouth to her neck and let it hover there, his breath fanning her throat.

"Or maybe it's knowing how the skin beneath it tastes and smells."

He nibbled lightly on her skin, sending her collapsing against him as she struggled to stand on legs that had turned weak and shaky.

"Come to bed with me," he said.

Leanne clutched at his shoulders, her body heavy and swollen with desire, her skin so sensitive, one touch from him and she might scream.

"I don't know if I can make it that far," she said, a catch in her voice as he cupped her breasts in his hands.

Mitch lifted her into his arms and carried her to the sofa, where he sat down and pulled her on top of him.

Her pulse hadn't even slowed to a normal rhythm. He hadn't even loosened his arms from around her. They held her so fiercely tonight, and he'd taken her so powerfully, with such an intensity.

She was still sitting on his lap, her thighs spread wide

to either side of his. He was still inside her. Leanne was kissing him softly, trying to soothe him, because she sensed he needed that from her now.

His jaw was rough, as it always was this time of day, and she enjoyed the sensation of having his skin pressed against hers. She'd have marks on her body by morning, little red patches from his mouth and his chin and his cheek. It turned her on just to see the patches in the mirror.

"Mitch?" she whispered, wishing she had the courage to tell him that she loved him.

"Hmm?"

And then the doorbell rang. They just looked at each other at first, sure they hadn't heard it, then sprang apart. Leanne started laughing as she adjusted her robe and he went to work on his pants.

"I can't believe we got caught like this," she said. It was almost nine, and nobody came to the door this late.

Mitch stood up, snapped his pants and then turned to her, as she tried to smooth out the robe.

"Forget it," he said, grinning at their predicament. "It's hopeless. You look exactly like a woman who just got caught making out on the couch. Why don't you go upstairs, and I'll get rid of whoever's at the door, then join you?"

"Fine with me." Leanne gave him one quick kiss on the lips and headed out of the room.

"If this is Marc, I'm going to strangle him," Mitch said as he walked over to the door.

Leanne figured it must be Marc. Or Ginny.

She paused near the top of the stairs and turned toward the door.

It wasn't Marc or Ginny.

It was the last person she ever expected to see there, the last person she wanted to see—Rena.

Chapter 15

From her position at the top of the stairs, Leanne heard Mitch ask Rena, "What do you want?"

The woman looked taken aback, as she stared at him.

Leanne knew what Rena saw. Mitch's shirt was unbuttoned, his hair mussed from where Leanne's hands had gotten ahold of it. And Leanne knew she was a mess. Her lips felt swollen from Mitch's kisses, her face and her neck rough from the sweep of his jaw, her nipples pushing against the thin fabric of her robe.

"Well?" Mitch asked, when Rena was left speechless. "As you can see, we're busy."

Leanne, who had started down the stairs, determined to stand by her husband, felt an embarrassed flush flooding her cheeks, and Rena appeared furious.

"Busy?"

She practically spit the word at Mitch, then her powers of speech seemed to fail her again.

"Well?" Mitch repeated.

"I know this marriage isn't real," she shrieked, turning

to Leanne. "You may have fooled those people at social services, but you're not fooling me. I know you're doing this just to keep those little boys from me."

"Rena, what do you think we were doing when you came to the door? Take a good look at my *wife*, if you have any doubts left. This marriage is very real."

She sputtered and swore, in a rage the way Leanne had never seen her.

"You little witch," she snarled at Leanne.

Mitch stepped between them so Leanne didn't have to see her stepmother's face. "Get out of my house," he barked at Rena. "Now."

And then he practically pushed her out the door and slammed it in her face.

The sound reverberated around the room, and Leanne listened carefully, amazed and grateful that all the commotion hadn't woken up the boys. Turning around, Mitch stood against the door with his arms folded across his chest and fury still evident in his face. When he came to stand beside her on the steps, some of the shock of what had just happened faded. When he put his arms around her and held her close, she felt a little better, though she was still trembling badly.

"Oh, Mitch. She scares me to death."

"I know, but she's gone now. And you're with me. I'm not going to let her hurt you. Not ever again."

It was a promise, an incredibly sweet-sounding promise. Tightening her arms around her husband, Leanne decided she'd never loved him more. She'd never trusted anyone this much, never leaned on anyone this way, never had her happiness tied so closely to a man's.

Leanne leaned heavily on Mitch, drawing strength from him, wishing she never had to leave his side. He stood there with her for a while, and she felt his tension start to ebb, thought that she'd managed to help take away the worst of his anger, as he'd absorbed the worst of her fear.

"Better?" he asked, dropping a light kiss on her cheek.

She nodded.

"I'm going to check on the boys," he said.

"All right. We left dinner on the stove, didn't we? Are you hungry?"

"No. Let's go to bed."

"All right." There was no place she'd rather be than curled up next to him in their bed.

Leanne turned off the burners on the stove, stored the hot food, checked the locks and turned out the lights. When she went upstairs, the door to the boys' room was open and Mitch was standing beside their crib.

It was Teddy, she saw, once he lifted his head from his father's shoulder. Big tears rolled down his face as he sobbed.

"What's the matter, Teddy bear?" she asked, surprised and happy when he held out his arms to her.

She took him from Mitch and cradled him close. Stubby little arms tightened around her, and he tucked his wet face against her neck.

"Poor baby. Did you have a bad dream?" she inquired, her gaze meeting Mitch's as he leaned toward her and Teddy. Mitch moved to stand behind her, both his arms coming around her, his face next to hers as they watched his son.

Mitch's hand rubbed the boy's hair, and Leanne kissed Teddy's head, but he still cried.

"It's all right, baby," Leanne crooned to him. "Everything's going to be all right."

She felt Mitch's arms tighten around both of them, and she felt the bond between the three of them. Her love for both of them grew stronger with every passing day.

This was the way it was meant to be. This was her place now, her family. She couldn't lose them.

Teddy snuggled against her and stuck his thumb in his mouth, sucking furiously as he fell asleep again. She and Mitch stood there quietly in the dark for a few more minutes. Mitch kissed her on the cheek, on her temple, her forehead, each touch infinitely sweet and kind and gentle. She imagined that he was telling her with his touch what he wasn't ready to put into words, and she imagined that one day he would give her the words, as well.

Life would be so full and so precious. She could see it in her mind when she closed her eyes.

"I think he's asleep," Mitch said, his lips against her ear.

She went to put Teddy down, but Mitch took him from her, instead, and he tenderly lowered his son into the crib, then rubbed a hand against Timmy's back.

Leanne couldn't help but remember watching him with Timmy that first evening in the hospital. She'd fallen in love with him a little that first night, she decided.

Crossing the hall with him to go into their bedroom, she thought about how very far they'd come in a few short weeks. Just a few days ago, she'd been afraid to hope that Mitch would ever love her the way she needed to be loved. But something had happened to her when she'd heard Ginny's story.

Ginny had lost her husband, a husband she'd loved very much, and yet she'd found love again with Marc. It was possible. At first, the notion had scared Leanne badly. She'd steeled herself against believing Mitch would ever love anyone again, and in a way that had helped her protect herself from him. He could simply never love her the way he'd loved Kelly.

But seeing Ginny and Marc together proved that it was indeed possible to love that way again. And letting herself believe that seemed even more dangerous than telling herself it could never happen.

Eventually, she couldn't help it. Hope won out. Leanne thought of what Ginny had said that day in the coffee shop—that happiness was a rare and wondrous gift, that she should reach out and take whatever happiness was offered to her.

Lifting her arms, Leanne reached for Mitch. He pulled

her down to the bed with him, then drew the covers around them.

"Just let me hold you for a minute," he said.

She closed her eyes, feeling his warmth seep into her. Utterly content, she was nearly asleep when she remembered. "Mitch?"

"Hmm?"

She lifted her head from his chest. "What did Rena mean about us fooling social services?"

He went still, looking worried, then put his palm to her cheek. "I talked to Jane today. It's good news."

Strange, she thought. He didn't look as though he'd had good news. And if the news was good, why had he waited so long to tell her?

"Social services is done with its investigation. And there's nothing in the agency's report that Rena can use against us."

Leanne watched him, wishing it weren't so dark in their bedroom, wishing she knew him better and was more adept at reading his moods.

"You don't seem happy," she said carefully.

He started to say something, then stopped. Appearing almost flustered, he said simply, "I just want everything to be squared away."

"It will be," she told him, still not understanding. "I thought you were convinced that all we had to do to stop Rena was to be married. I thought that was what your lawyer said."

"I don't think Rena's going to take the boys away from us," he said.

So why was he so tense? Was it that scene downstairs with Rena? Maybe. But if he was sure she wouldn't be able to take the boys away...

Leanne felt his arms tighten around her, felt him push her head back down to his chest, and she shivered, though she wasn't that cold.

* * *

Leanne was running on sheer nerves the next day. The boys were tense, especially when she explained to them again that she had to go away for a few days, then cried over them because she would miss them so much.

She packed a small carry-on bag while the two of them watched. Timmy was again defiant, pulling the things out of her bag as quickly as she put them in. And Teddy looked heartbroken.

"Just two days. Promise," she told them, wondering how they could be this upset, when she doubted they even knew what she was telling them.

Downstairs, the doorbell rang. Leanne tensed, hoping it wasn't Rena. Then she scooped up a child in each arm and carried the boys downstairs with her.

When she pulled open the door and saw her father standing there, she couldn't have been more surprised.

"Can I come in? Please?" he asked. When she hesitated still, he added, "Rena's not with me."

The boys smiled at him and welcomed him. Leanne folded her arms in front of her chest and steeled herself against what was coming. It was hard for her to be in the same room with him, her feelings for him were so jumbled.

He shouldn't have expected so much from her after her mother had died, Leanne knew. No matter how upset and how lost he'd been, she'd been nothing but a child. A twelve-year-old. And she'd lost her mother, as well.

Once he'd met Rena, nothing had been as important to him as his new wife's happiness.

Her father had actually told her he thought Leanne would be happier with Rena there, that Leanne wouldn't have to do so much anymore, that Rena would be their mother now. Her father swore that things would get better, if only Leanne would give it a little time.

She'd suspected he meant his own life was going to get easier. After all, Rena had some money of her own. She was young and energetic—she could keep up with three children much easier than Leanne's father could. He was relieved to pass on his parenting duties to his new wife, happy that she was so interested in raising his children.

Leanne had felt betrayed by the only grown-up in the world who was supposed to love her and protect her. And now she was alone, standing face-to-face, with him for the first time in years.

Taking the boys into the kitchen, she gave them the grape Popsicles they loved so much. Then she told them to stay in the kitchen because the Popsicles always dripped onto the floor long before they were done. One day last week, after cleaning grape-colored sugar water out of the carpet, she'd convinced the boys that the drips looked prettiest on the kitchen floor, and now they agreed. They walked around dripping in circles just for fun.

Leanne didn't care. It should buy her a couple of minutes alone with her father, and she didn't want the boys to hear what they had to say.

"What are you doing here?" she asked.

"I wanted to talk to you and Mitch."

"Mitch is at work," she said quickly, wishing her father would leave. She wasn't up to any more scenes, especially not so soon after Rena's visit.

"Well, I suppose you could tell him for me. Rena and I talked last night, and I wanted you to know the custody suit is finished."

"What?"

"She promised," he said, decidedly uncomfortable.

"Are you telling me you asked Rena to drop the suit?" Leanne couldn't believe it. After all these years, he was finally going to stand up to Rena?

"I told her I wouldn't be a part of it. And as much as she cared for Kelly, there are no blood ties between the two of them, none between Rena and the boys. Her lawyer has told her all along that she needed me to be a part of the suit in order for her to win."

"Why are you doing this?" Leanne wanted to know. "Why would you want to help me and Mitch?"

"Rena's not an easy woman to live with," he began, "but she's my wife—"

"You're going to defend her to me?" Leanne asked incredulously, and her father fell silent.

Finally, he said, "I don't suppose I could."

Leanne shook her head, hating him a bit but still wanting him to love her so much that she ached inside.

"I won't help her try to take the boys away from you and Mitch, and she won't take this any further on her own," he said, then headed toward the door. Opening it, he turned back to her. "I do hope you and Mitch will at least let us see the boys from time to time."

Leanne stood there trembling, filled with a combination of hurt and anger. He hadn't asked for her forgiveness, and she hadn't offered it. Not yet.

"Please believe me when I say that I hope the four of you will be happy together."

Leanne had no idea how to reply.

"I thought about the boys and what they needed, what was right. But mostly, I thought of what I might do for you," he said haltingly. "And I hoped this would make you happy. I hoped that someday you and I..."

Amazed, Leanne watched as he dipped his head and said nothing for the longest time. She tried to find the words.

He'd done this for her? To make her happy?

After all these years, he was worried about *her* happiness?

She was still so very angry at him, had been for so long. And a part of her wanted to tell him, wanted him to know how very much he'd hurt her. But not today. Not now that he'd taken this first step.

First steps were so very hard. Second chances were so rare. She couldn't blow it by letting nothing but her anger show.

Her father was halfway down the porch steps, when she called out to him. "Dad?"

He turned back, looking every bit as reserved and as

unyielding as she imagined she looked herself when she was scared and trying not to show it.

She thought about what she could do for him, thought about healing and about family ties. "I'll ask Mitch to let you see the boys," she said.

Her father very nearly smiled then, before he turned again to go.

Leanne watched him leave. It was so incredible, so hard to believe.

Then she heard the boys calling her name from the kitchen. In there, she found them grinning and covered with a grape-colored, sticky mess. Their mouths, their chins, their noses, their hands, their clothes. They gave her sticky, grape smiles, handed her their empty Popsicle sticks and pointed toward the freezer.

"More?" they chimed hopefully.

She gave them more, putting new Popsicles into tiny, sticky hands, accepting a wet, sticky kiss of gratitude from Teddy, a genuine smile from Timmy.

They sat on the floor and started to eat once more, happy with the simplest of things.

Leanne couldn't look at them, because if she did, she'd start to cry. Turning her back to the boys, she lifted a trembling hand to the phone and called Mitch.

Mitch was sitting at his desk in the middle of a loud, crowded room full of cops. His head ached, and a knot of tension festered in his stomach, feeding on the five cups of coffee he'd drunk because he'd barely managed to sleep last night. He'd been too worried about what was going to happen with him and Leanne, with Rena and the boys.

His phone rang, and he wondered what little treasures of information awaited him. Business or personal, he doubted the news was good. Mitch picked up the receiver and said, "McCarthy."

"Mitch?"

At the tone of her voice, that knot of tension made it to

his throat in two seconds flat, and it was so big he could hardly speak. "Leanne? What's wrong?"

"My father was here."

"What happened? Are the boys all right?"

"They're fine."

"And you?" Mitch would knock the man to the ground if he hurt Leanne. He didn't care if Richard Hathaway was twenty-five years older than him. "What did he do to you, Leanne?"

"He told me he refused to be a part of Rena's custody suit any longer. Mitch, he says the whole thing is over, that Rena can't go on with the lawsuit without his cooperation."

Mitch couldn't say anything. *Over.* The word reverberated inside his head, not making any sense at first.

It was over. The boys weren't going anywhere. He should be deliriously happy, but all he could think about was Leanne leaving. After all, there was nothing to keep her now.

"Leanne," he said, because he could tell how upset she was. "Are you all right?"

"Yes, I just..."

"What? Anything you want. Tell me, and I'll get it for you."

"You," she said shakily. "I just wish you were here, that you could hold me for a minute."

"I'll be there," he promised. "Fifteen minutes. I'll be there."

"Thank you," she said.

He broke the connection, then dialed his lawyer's number.

Leanne felt so foolish when she hung up the phone. She was dragging him away from his work just so he could come home and take her into his arms.

But he was coming, she reminded herself. Surely that meant something.

She sat on the kitchen floor, next to the boys, who were watching their Popsicles drip and drip and drip. They were one big purple mess, but she didn't care.

"I love you guys," she said to them.

"Wub?" Teddy said, while Timmy ignored her in favor of licking his fingers.

"Yes," Leanne said, smiling. "Love. You." She pointed to Teddy, poking him in the belly and making him laugh. "And you." She turned to Timmy and did the same thing.

They gave her grape kisses and grape hugs, got the stuff all over her, and she laughed until she nearly cried. The boys looked perplexed by her reaction, then lost interest and returned to watch their dripping treats.

After a while, she stood and cleaned herself up. She was thinking of throwing the boys in the tub, when she heard the front door open. Trying to pull herself together and feeling foolish that she had asked Mitch to dash over here, Leanne took a minute before she turned around.

But before she had a chance to move herself, Mitch had his hands on her shoulders and was turning her around. He held her at arm's length, looked her over from head to toe, then hauled her up against him.

It was like coming home, she decided.

"What did he say to you?" Mitch asked fiercely.

"I told you. He's going to make Rena back down. He promised."

"No. Not about the boys. You. I'm worried about you, Leanne. What did your father say to upset you so much?"

"Mitch, I can't breathe. You're holding me so tight I can't breathe."

He backed off instantly. "I'm sorry."

"It's okay. It felt good." She forced a smile. "Until I got dizzy."

"Being here is tearing you up inside, isn't it?"

He looked as if it pained him, as well, to know that about her.

"It hurts. But it's never going to be easy. And I can't kid myself about that anymore."

"I'm sorry," he said, taking her into his arms gently this time, his hand smoothing the fabric of her blouse against her back, his lips somewhere near her ear. "I'm so sorry."

Leanne sighed and made herself pull away. Working to make her tone light, she said, "Hey, this is...silly. Rena's done. She's not going to take the boys away from you. We should be happy."

She made the mistake of looking down to avoid his gaze, and caught sight of the beautiful circle of diamonds he'd put on her finger, when he made her his wife.

She remembered then. *He didn't need a wife anymore.*

She'd never expected it to end quite this soon. She thought she'd have more time to love him and to make him love her, if that was possible.

Leanne took two steps away from him so she wouldn't be so tempted to touch him. "I'm sorry," she said again. "I don't know what came over me...falling apart like that and begging you to come home. It's the middle of the day, and I know you're busy. I'm sorry."

"Leanne, if you need me, I'll be here for you."

Then he would simply never leave her, she thought, because she would always need him, always love him as much as she did right now.

"Leanne?"

Composing herself as best she could, she said quietly, "Thank you," as if he'd given her some sort of trinket and not a beautiful promise always to be with her in times of need.

It was gratitude, she told herself. He would do that much out of gratitude. He loved the boys that much.

"I guess you need to get back to work," she said. "I'm going to throw these messy boys into the tub, and then I need to pack."

"Pack?"

She didn't look at him, couldn't bear to think about leaving him, even for just two nights and days. "New York, remember? Tomorrow?" She picked up Timmy, let Mitch put Teddy in her other arm and turned to go up the stairs.

"Wait a minute," he said, forcing her to face him. He gave Teddy a kiss and rubbed Timmy's hair. He didn't try to touch Leanne again. "I'll be home early," he said, then forced himself to walk out the door.

Chapter 16

"How did you find out about Joe being killed?" Mitch asked Ginny later that afternoon. He'd just shown up at her house. She'd taken one look at his face and brought him inside to her kitchen. "Do you remember the words? Do you remember the first thing that actually sank in after the shock?"

"Marc came to tell me," she said, "looking a lot like you did today when I found you outside."

"I'm sorry about showing up and scaring you."

"No, it's okay. Nothing's going to happen to Marc. He's always telling me I have a better chance of winning the lottery than losing two husbands in the line of duty, and I know he's right. But you want to hear about Joe." She put her hand on Mitch's for a minute. "I don't think Marc said anything. He didn't have to. He came to my door looking as though he'd just watched his best friend die, which he had. And he had Joe's blood on his shirt. And I knew instantly. All I really remember after that was

Marc just hanging on to me and telling me over and over again how sorry he was.

"What do you remember?" she asked gently.

"I was in the room when her heart stopped. So they had to kick me out. Or pull me out. It took three huge orderlies. They led me to the waiting room down the hall, and it's a wonder I didn't wreck the place." He laughed a little—it was that or cry. "And finally the doctor came, and I wouldn't look at him. I heard his footsteps. I heard him stop in front of me. But I just wouldn't look at him. Because I knew I'd be able to tell from his face that she was gone."

Mitch stood and started walking across the room. "But when he told me, I ended up on my knees. I just fell to my knees. I was ready to swear and to beg and to do…anything, except…I couldn't even stand."

"And somebody had you on your knees again today?" Ginny asked quietly.

Mitch just nodded. That was exactly how it had felt—as though he'd been knocked to his knees by the thought of losing Leanne. He was too scared even to talk about it, he realized.

Turning to Ginny, he said, "You're a very intelligent woman. And a kind one. Thanks for listening to me rant and rave."

"Anytime," she said.

"I'm sorry for scaring you and for making you tell me about the worst day of your life."

"Mitch, what happened with you and Leanne?"

He supposed he owed her an explanation, at least, after she'd rescued him off the street and listened to him babble.

"Rena's dropping the custody suit," he said. "And Leanne's leaving."

"Leaving you? No way."

"She's going to New York tomorrow."

"To close her apartment and to get her agent off her back."

"Okay, maybe she's not going to leave me for good tomorrow. But she will leave. There's no reason for her to stay anymore. The custody thing is over."

"So give her a reason to stay," Ginny said. "I'll give you a hint. 'I love you' is a good starting point."

Mitch told himself not to panic.

Leanne was going away for two lousy days, after all. She would be back. Even if she wanted to leave him, now that the custody thing was settled, she wouldn't do it right away.

So he had some time, and there was no need to panic. He probably had weeks to make her love him so much she would endure being in Chicago with people who were supposed to love her but instead were constantly hurting her feelings and pushing her out of their lives. He could make her want to give up the small fortune in salary that she earned traveling all over the world, photographing places he'd never see in a lifetime. He could make her want to spend her days with two little boys who gave her sticky, grape-flavored kisses and were months away from being potty-trained. He could teach her to ignore the guilt he worried that she still felt because he used to be married to her sister, the doubts he was certain she had that he would ever love her the way he had loved Kelly.

That one still surprised him and amazed him and had him thanking God for giving him this second chance, because he saw now that he did love Leanne.

Mitch thought the hardest task he faced was somehow making sure she never felt like second best or second choice in his life, because it certainly didn't feel that way inside his heart.

Sure, he could convince her of all those things.

All he had to do was get over his sheer panic at having to let her walk away from him today.

It was turning into one of the hardest things he'd ever done.

They arrived at the airport in what had to be record time, and he never even took the car over the speed limit to get them there. He found a prime parking spot, right down front, and the damned flight was on schedule.

Leanne stood at the gate, saying goodbye to the boys. Mitch could tell the minute they comprehended the fact that she was leaving them. Panic set in. They clung to her and cried, begging her not to go.

Dammit, he thought, if he'd been almost eighteen months old and could have gotten away with it, he would have done the same thing.

"Two days," she said, holding up two fingers for them to count. "See? Just two."

Teddy held up four fingers, and Leanne got down on her knees in front of him and gently adjusted his little hand until he held up two fingers, too.

"Doo?"

He said it so sadly Mitch had to look away for a second.

"Yes." She tried to smile through her tears. "I'll see you in two days, and I'll miss you."

"Miz ooh?" Timmy nudged his way in beside her now.

"Of course." Leanne turned to Timmy. "I'll miss you, too, my little man."

Mitch knew her flight was already boarding. Any minute, they were going to give a last-call for passengers. And the boys weren't any more ready to let her go than Mitch was.

"I love you," Leanne said to them, still on her knees in front of the twins.

"Wub ooh," Teddy echoed. He was simply inconsolable now.

"Come here, Teddy." Mitch took his son in his arms and told himself he had to be strong, because he was the dad.

Leanne picked up Timmy and squeezed him one more time, then asked Mitch, "You want this big guy, too?"

Reluctantly, Timmy let go of her and went to Mitch.

"Doo?" Teddy asked hopefully, holding up four fingers again.

"How can this be so hard?" Leanne wanted to know, wiping away her tears. "I thought they'd barely notice if I left."

Mitch, a little boy on each arm, leaned toward her so he could kiss her hard and fast, on her mouth, then pressed his cheek to hers for a minute and whispered to her, "Have a safe trip."

When he went to pull away, he realized the boys had gotten hold of her again. They held on for dear life now. The gate attendant was on her way over, and Mitch hadn't said nearly all he wanted to say.

"Ma'am?" the attendant began, "the plane's leaving. You have to board now."

For a second, Leanne looked as scared as Mitch felt, though she covered her fear quickly, using skills she'd no doubt perfected ages ago.

Surely that's what she was doing, Mitch decided. She could love him more than anything in this world and hide it better than any woman he'd ever met.

He was going to have to get used to that, to make a home for her in his house and in his heart where she felt safe and secure and wasn't afraid to tell him or to show him how she felt.

Mitch knew he could do that. It was one of the things he could give back to her, because she'd given so much to him.

He kissed her one more time. "We'll be right here when you get back," he said, feeling reassured by the notion. Hell, he and the boys might just camp out here and wait for her.

He tightened his grasp on his sons as he tore them away from her. Then he had to endure standing there with two heartbroken little boys in his arms as she turned and walked away from them.

There would be other times like this, Mitch knew, bracing himself in case he had to do this again and again. If she stayed but she decided she still wanted to work, he and the boys would stand here just like this, watching her get on a thousand other airplanes, jetting off away from them.

But he could endure that. He could handle anything if he got this one wish.

He closed his eyes and prayed as he hadn't in a long time. *Please, God. Bring her back to us.*

Leanne fell apart on the plane. She got to her window seat, slid into it and turned her head away, so the other passengers wouldn't see. But that was a mistake, because in the window of the terminal, she could see the outline of two tiny boys huddled against a man, the three of them watching solemnly as her plane pulled away from the gate.

Tiny hands came up to wave sadly, and that made her cry even harder.

It was all so ridiculous she simply couldn't understand it. She was leaving for two measly days, crossing nothing more than one time zone, yet they acted as if she were abandoning them forever. The situation totally baffled her, and it was tearing her up inside.

It was also incredibly sweet to see that they would miss her so much. She didn't remember anyone who cried over her at the airport before, and she'd been in a lot of airports, gotten on thousands of planes to take trips much longer than this.

She'd never left anyone behind who'd miss her as much as Teddy and Timmy would.

And Mitch? Would he miss her, too?

He'd slept on the downstairs sofa rather than coming to bed with her last night, something he hadn't explained and she hadn't let herself ask him. But she'd ached to have him hold her in his arms. Had he missed her last night? Would he miss her tonight, when he was alone in the bed they normally shared?

She supposed she would find out. In the past few days, she'd come to see this as a test of sorts. Could she do it? Could she walk away from him now? And if she could do it now, could she do it in two months? Or six months? Or that wretched year's time they'd agreed to before she'd come to love him more than life itself?

She had some decisions to make once she got to New York. Did she turn her back on her entire life there? Or did she simply try to put everything on hold for the remainder of the year?

Surely it would be easier to get over him once she immersed herself in her real life back in New York. Surely she wouldn't miss him as much as she did right now.

As it was, she had to keep reminding herself that she was going right back to Chicago, to him and the boys. They'd be there waiting for her the minute she stepped off the plane.

No one had ever done that for her before, either.

"I could drive you to the airport," Marc said.

"What?" Mitch was barely listening to his friend. He was too consumed by counting the hours he had left to endure until Sunday evening. Checking his watch, he swore. She'd been gone for only three hours.

"The airport," Marc said, making a little airplane with his hand that zoomed along in front of Mitch's face. "You know, where the planes take off? I think there's a flight that leaves practically every hour for New York."

"What are you talking about?"

"I'm talking about the fact that you look like hell, and I don't think you're going to be able to make it through the next two days without your wife. I don't understand why you let her go in the first place."

Mitch covered his face with both hands. He rubbed at his eyes because he couldn't quite see straight. And he was as jumpy as a cat. "She's coming back," he said.

"And when she comes back, we'll talk about some things."

"You could talk in New York," Marc said. "That way you wouldn't have to wait until Sunday to hear what she has to say."

Mitch thought about Sunday, still a grueling forty-eight hours away. He thought about the way he hadn't let himself come to bed with her the night before because he'd known that if he'd taken her into his arms, he wouldn't have been able to let her go this morning.

So he'd stayed downstairs, lying down on the sofa but not sleeping. He'd stayed there in the dark and thought about his house and how empty it was going to be without her, thought about those big holes inside his heart that she'd filled, the joy and the laughter she'd brought back into his life.

And he'd thought about losing her.

In the morning she hadn't said anything about his staying away from their bed. But he could tell she was hurt, though she hadn't asked him to explain.

She expected people to hurt her, especially the people she loved.

Oh, God, Mitch thought, seeing it all so clearly now. That was the problem. She had expected him to hurt her, too. That was the biggest reason she hadn't said anything, hadn't asked anything of him. She thought she already knew what his answer was going to be.

"I am so stupid," Mitch said.

"Hey, it happens to the best of us." Marc stood up. "Come on, pack your bag. I'll drive you."

"What about the boys?"

"Ginny's been upstairs for the past ten minutes packing a bag for them so we can take them home with us. But you owe us one for this. I'm going to need a long, long weekend alone with my wife once you get your life straightened out."

* * *

It was almost ten o'clock Friday night before Leanne got back to her apartment. Marty walked her to the door, still pleading his case, though he'd had all evening over drinks and dinner to do the same thing.

"I'm not going to stop asking," he said.

"Fine." Leanne shook her head, amused. His persistence was one of the things she valued most about him. "I'll just stop listening."

"I know you'll change your mind," he insisted. "You won't last six months there."

"Watch me." She fit her key into the door, dreading going into her dark, lonely apartment. She couldn't help but think of all the other times she'd arrived on her doorstep, bone tired, emotionally drained from the intensity of the work, aching for anything at all that was familiar to her.

The apartment was familiar, but it simply wasn't a home. It never would be.

Home was Mitch and the boys.

The door swung open. Marty stood in the doorstep, holding her back. "Leanne, we've been together for ten years," he said. "I know you. I know this is where you belong."

She gave up on convincing him that she knew exactly what she wanted and where she wanted to be. "Marty, I'm tired. Can we talk about this tomorrow?"

Let him call, she told herself. She'd take the phone off the hook and refuse to answer the door.

"Okay. Tomorrow." He put his arms around her and kissed her on the cheek. "It's great to have you back."

Leanne closed the door and locked it, then stood with her forehead pressed against the door, her heart aching. She had never missed Chicago more.

Jerking her head to the right, she suddenly sensed some movement behind her, and all her senses went on alert. Not giving herself time to think, because if she did she would have been too afraid to move, she whirled around, just as an angry voice behind her demanded, ''Who the hell was that?''

It was a man's voice, and she saw the distinct outline of a tall, imposing-looking male, standing in the dark, not two feet from her. Leanne opened her mouth to scream, but he grabbed her first.

She cocked her elbow forward and shoved it into his stomach, then brought her other hand up, heel first, hoping to connect solidly with his nose.

The man groaned in pain but recovered quickly, managing to avoid the hand headed for his nose, and then he grabbed her once more. Leanne spun around in his arms, thinking she could elbow him again, but he held her too tightly now.

And then there was something about the feel of his body that cut through her panic and told her she'd been here before. Something about him was achingly familiar.

The roaring in her ears receded, and she could finally hear what he'd been trying to tell her all along.

''It's me,'' he said, his mouth somewhere near her temple. ''Leanne, relax. I'm not going to hurt you.''

She slid around in his arms to face him, then didn't quite believe what her eyes were seeing. She put a hand to the side of his face, afraid that when she touched him he'd simply vanish into thin air.

But he didn't. He pressed his lips to her palm and kissed her sweetly.

''Mitch.'' She sighed, having trouble breathing at the moment. ''I thought for a minute I was hallucinating.''

''I'm very real,'' he said, letting his arms drop to his side. ''And I'm so sorry I frightened you like that. I flashed my badge and the building superintendent let me in.''

Leanne couldn't quite make sense of this herself, and she desperately needed to. ''Mitch, what are you doing here? What...is anything wrong? The boys?''

''They're fine, except they're missing you like crazy.''

She wanted to ask whether he had been missing her, as

well. She was stunned to find him here. And then she remembered how hard she'd hit him.

"Are you all right?" She went to him and pressed a hand against his right side, over the ribs she'd jammed her elbow into moments before. "Did I hurt you?"

"I think I'll live. Although I'm damned lucky my nose isn't broken. That was some swing you took." He smiled. "I guess I may have overreacted a little to your running alone after dark."

She nodded. "I told you I could take care of myself."

"I know," he said, almost regretfully. "But I'm wondering—when are you going to understand you don't have to do it all by yourself anymore?"

It sounded curiously like an invitation to let him take care of her. "Mitch, why are you here?"

"I realized there are a lot of things I should have said to you before you left, and then I got this crazy idea in my head that you might not come back to me."

"Sunday," she said, really scared now. She wasn't any good at this sort of thing. "I'm coming back on Sunday."

"But that's two days away." His tone was filled with impatience.

Two days? Could he possibly be trying to tell her that he simply couldn't live without her for two whole days?

"I think I need to sit down," she said. Her legs didn't feel that steady beneath her.

Mitch took her in his arms again. "Hold on to me, instead," he invited.

She did, closing her eyes and absorbing the feel of him, his warmth and his strength. This was the best place she'd ever been, she decided, this space he made for her in his arms.

Tears came to her eyes, tears she hadn't a prayer of stopping. And he still hadn't explained why he was here.

"You know after Kelly died, I told myself I would never love another woman."

"I know," she whispered, hiding her face against him.

"It seemed like too much of a risk to take, like too much to expect to be that happy for a second time in my life," Mitch said. "Maybe that's why it took me so long to understand and to tell you how I felt. I was so grateful to you for helping me keep the boys and for making them smile again."

She didn't want his gratitude. When she went to force herself away from him, Mitch only held her tighter.

"It was nice not to be so lonely anymore once you came," he said, speaking slowly, waiting for her to absorb the words.

"It wasn't long," he continued, "before I couldn't keep my hands off you, before I wanted you desperately."

Just as she wanted him.

"The night Jane told me that Rena's lawyer had withdrawn from the custody case, all I could think about was you deciding that you didn't need to stay with me anymore." He eased away from her and cupped her face in his hands. "Which is exactly what you did when your father came to see you and told you Rena was giving up. I saw you, Leanne. One minute, you were crying in my arms, and the next, it was like you'd put a wall between us. Like you were pulling yourself right out of my life. Do you have any idea how it felt to watch you force yourself away from me like that?"

"Like I was dying inside," she blurted out. "That's how it felt to do it—like I was dying inside."

"Me, too." Mitch searched her eyes, his gaze steady and direct. "I don't want to live without you. I suppose I could, because I have the boys and I love them. They're what got me through the first time. But, Leanne, I can't lose another woman I love."

"What?" Tears were streaming down her face by then, and she had to be mistaken about what he'd just said.

"I love you," Mitch repeated, his voice rough and raw. "Please don't leave me."

Leanne sucked in a desperately needed breath, and

thought of the time she'd photographed the divers in Acapulco, thought about the way they just launched themselves off the cliffs, hurtling past the face of the rock to the shallow water below.

As much as she loved Mitch, it felt as though he was asking her to do something every bit as dangerous.

"I'm scared," she admitted.

"I know, baby. You're going to have to trust me a little on this. I'll never let you down."

"Oh, Mitch."

"You can still be a photographer if you want. You can travel if you need to. I don't care as long as you come home to us."

"I've seen the whole world, Mitch. There's nothing left I need to see."

"And your work?"

"Chicago's full of people and interesting sights. I'm sure if I feel the need to pick up a camera, I can find something there to photograph." She brushed away a tear. "I was so scared when I left this afternoon."

"I never would have let you leave, except I was afraid if I pushed too hard, you'd get scared and try to convince yourself you didn't need me or want me or love me."

"No." She hung her head, looking off to the left because it hurt to look at him. She hadn't done that, but something just as wrong. "I just about convinced myself that *you* wouldn't want *me* anymore. Or that you couldn't. Or that you might want me for a while, but that you'd get over it."

"Wrong," he said. "On all counts."

"Oh, Mitch."

"I love you," he said again. "The boys love you, too. I don't think they'd take me back if I came without you."

"I love them so much. I just couldn't resist them."

"They're easy to love, Leanne. So am I. Come home with me and I'll show you."

"I know how easy you are to love," she admitted.

"Say it," he begged. "Please."

"I love you, Mitch."

She saw the bone-deep satisfaction light his eyes, saw him smile as he brought his lips to hers.

"Let's go home," he said again.

Home, she thought. What a beautiful word, a beautiful feeling. Home to her was with Mitch and the boys.

* * * * *